GRID DOWN 2

PERCEPTIONS OF REALITY

Volume 2, Part 1

Bruce "Buckshot" Hemming

Sara Freeman

ISBN-13: 978-1481856683
ISBN-10: 1481856685

This is a work of fiction. Names, characters, places, and incidents are products of the author's imagination or are used fictitiously and are not to be construed as real. Any resemblance to actual events, locales, organizations, or persons, living or dead, is entirely coincidental.

Every effort has been made to ensure that the information contained in this book is accurate and complete. The information contained in this book cannot replace good judgment and decision making. Nothing in this book is intended to express or imply any warranty of the suitability or fitness of any product or service. The reader should consult with a professional or a specialist to ensure the suitability and fitness of any product or service they intend to use. The author is not engaged in rendering professional advice or services to the individual reader. The ideas, descriptions and suggestions contained in this book are not intended as a substitute for consulting with a professional or a specialist. The author and/or publisher shall not be liable or accept any responsibility for any loss, damage, injury, prosecution or actions brought against any person or body as a result of the use or misuse of any information or techniques contained in this book.

Outdoor activities are, by their very nature potentially hazardous. Those participating in such activities assume all responsibility for their own actions and safety and should consult with a physician prior to engaging in such activities if they have any medical conditions or health issues.

Interior Layout by MrLasers.com.

Editor's Note

Grid Down 2 - Perceptions of Reality

In the first book, *Grid Down - Reality Bites*, we experienced a man-made disaster, an electromagnetic pulse or EMP, as it is commonly known. The explosion of a nuclear bomb, detonated three hundred miles above the center of America, caused this EMP. The EMP destroyed the electrical grid and caused the failure of our society as we knew it.

Without electricity, our water and sewage systems stopped working, along with anything else that required a pump or electricity to operate. Refineries could no long produce gasoline or other petroleum-based products, so that meant no gasoline at the gas pumps, no delivery trucks restocking the grocery shelves, nor any other types of deliveries.

The world as we knew it stopped existing. When people got to the point where they had to leave their jobs to protect themselves and their families, the entire system broke down and chaos ensued. There were no more firemen to put out fires, no more politicians to keep government going and, most importantly, no more military, police, or any types of law enforcement to stop violent crimes.

The world became a free-for-all with individuals and gangs taking what they wanted, not fearing retribution from a legal system. If they wanted something they just took it and, if anyone got in their way, they would simply kill them.

So, this was the world that our cast of characters had to deal with. Because the cast consisted of three separate groups of individuals with several different characters in each of those groups, it seemed beneficial to separate them and devote future books to just one group of characters at a time.

Book 2, *Grid Down 2 - Perceptions of Reality,* follows just Joe and his wife Jane, Preston and his soon to be wife Amy, and an orphaned twelve-year-old boy named Michael.

It is the authors' wish for you to have a pleasant reading experience as we follow our groups through each of the next series of books, and I hope you enjoy the story.

A special thank you to all the great people who made this book possible. Without your expert help it would not read so well or have the expert knowledge to make the book very believable.

Contents

Prologue

Grid Down 2 - Perceptions of Reality

The following book tells the plight of one group of individuals: Joe, Jane, Preston, Amy, and Michael after the Rainbow Warriors destroyed their farm in the first book *Grid Down - Reality Bites.*

After an EMP had destroyed the world as we knew it, a fanatical group called the Rainbow Warriors raised an army to travel the new world and "cleanse" it of anyone who didn't believe as they did: that eating meat was wrong and that we should all be vegetarians, worshiping Mother Earth, or Gaia, The Great Mother of All, as they called her.

In separate parts of the country, the Rainbow Warriors had recruited thousands of men, some voluntarily and some by force, to travel the countryside, making people join them or die. They would kill anyone who refused them, burning and destroying all buildings to prevent people from returning, and then they would continue marching on.

The army was well-armed and had 105mm anti-tank cannons, which they pulled along with them, raining destruction on anyone who stood in their way.

We left our characters injured and separated after their farm was destroyed, and members of their group were killed or injured.

We will now follow the survivors through additional ordeals and survival situations where they must fight for their lives to survive.

Chapter 1

Lost & Forgotten

"I put my heart and my soul into my work, and have lost my mind in the process."

~Vincent van Gogh

Jane slowly became aware of her surroundings. It was hot and she was covered in perspiration. That was what woke her up. She was very thirsty and her ears were ringing. She opened her eyes a little and saw that she was in a place that was very dark. She didn't recognize where she was. She cautiously moved her arms and legs, taking stock to see if she was injured anywhere, besides the throbbing ache in her shoulder. Moving her arm made her shoulder ache more, like a bad tooth. She stopped moving and tried to concentrate on remembering what had happened. She was very confused and tried to sort out all the thoughts running through her mind. Where was she? Why was her shoulder aching so badly? In the next instant total recall slammed into her mind, and she remembered everything. She sat up, so fast that her awareness started to fade, and she felt the blackness coming for her once again. She lowered her head and kept saying over and over in her mind, "I will not faint." As soon as she knew that the dizziness had passed and she wouldn't pass out, she started yelling in panic, "Joe. Oh my God, Joe. Where are you?"

She must be in the tornado shelter. Reaching out with her hand, she felt the post of a 2 x 4 frame. Yep, she was in the tornado shelter. She slowly scooted over to the table and turned on the battery-powered 300-lumen lantern. Her vision was still blurry, but she finally saw Joe lying on the floor a few feet to her left. She scooted over to him as fast as she could, ignoring the pain in her shoulder. She reached out hurriedly and ran her hand down his sweaty cheek to his neck and found a pulse. She relaxed a little and let out the breath she had been holding. Hot tears ran down her cheeks in relief. He was alive and that was the only thing that truly mattered at this moment in time. She continued to run her hand over his body, trying to check for injuries. Doing it one-handed was hard, and she was afraid she might miss something important. After determining that he didn't have any serious injuries, as far as she could tell, she glanced up at his face. Joe had his eyes open and was watching her run her hand over his body.

When she was finished he said, "Am I going to live, Doc?" Jane smacked him playfully on the top of his head and replied, "Maybe, I haven't decided yet."

He smiled and laughed as he said, "Uppity woman."

She smiled at him and said in mock severity, "And don't you forget it, mister."

Jane looked around and realized they were in the small steel-reinforced room in the basement that Joe had built for tornado protection. She hadn't been down here since he finished the project a few years ago. She had forgotten all about this room even being in the basement.

She gave him an intense look and said, "If I ever bitch about your stupid ideas and wasting money again, just tell me to shut up."

He said, "I will remember and hold you to that promise."

Jane asked, "What happened? I'm a little fuzzy on the details after I got shot." Joe looked around the room and was very glad that he had taken the time and money to build it. He had used quarter-inch steel on the ceiling, with steel support beams and posts. He built it for protection from tornadoes. This room had saved their lives. The room had everything they would need, even a two-burner cook stove.

He looked at Jane and answered, "Tim yelled on the radio that they were bringing the artillery cannons up closer. I grabbed you and dived into this room. I barely got the door shut before they shelled the house. I hit my head on the door and that's all I remember until you woke me up just a little while ago. We'll wait a few hours and, if we don't hear any noise from outside, then we'll get out of here."

Jane nodded her head and said, "All right. Do we have any water in here? I'm really thirsty." Joe got up stiffly, walked over to a shelf in the room, opened a box and pulled out two water bottles.

Every now and again Joe would sniff the air to check for fires outside their room. That was their worst danger. He knew fires would be burning whatever was left from the artillery round, which would complete the total destruction of the farmhouse. He prayed that the others had gotten out in time. He had yelled for everybody to retreat as he dived for the door down here and into the safety that the room would provide. He looked forlornly at the pieces of his radio that he had picked up, and which had been scattered around the room. He must have smashed it when he hit the ground as he dived into the room. There was no way to fix it. Jane's radio was still in her L.B.E. vest, which he had taken off to bandage her shoulder, and it was probably lying under who-knew-how-much rubble. He could kick himself for not storing extra radios down here. Now there was no way to contact anyone from their group to find out who had made it and who hadn't.

He was pretty sure that Preston had enough time to get Amy and himself far enough away to have survived the destruction of the farmhouse and barn. He had a sick feeling in the pit of his stomach about the rest of the group, who had been in the loft. There wouldn't have been time for them to get out if the enemy had fired both artillery cannons at the same time.

He got up and checked on Jane. She had instructed him on how to debride her shoulder properly, and he had stitched up the entry and exit holes the bullet had made. She started a fourteen-day dose of antibiotics and took some pain medication from the medical supplies that he had made sure to store down here, and she was now resting on one of the cots in the room. He would let her rest until it was time to leave. Who knew what they might face, or have to do to survive this, when they finally got out of here?

A few hours later, Joe woke Jane up. He helped her sit up and handed her a cup of hot coffee to drink. He sat on a five-gallon bucket across from her and drank his own cup of coffee. He looked her over, evaluating her condition, and said, "You don't look too bad. How does the shoulder feel?"

She eyed him like he had asked a very stupid question and said, "I feel like I got run over by a Mac truck and then someone decided to dig a hole in my shoulder. When the pain medication wears off, I'll let you know how I really feel."

He smiled at her and said, "That good, huh?"

She returned his smile a little and replied, "Are we getting out of here anytime soon?"

Joe turned around and reached behind him for two paper plates. Each plate had an M.R.E. on it. He turned back around to face her and said, "We'll eat first. Then we'll get out of here."

When they finished eating, Joe grabbed the plates and the various discarded package wrappers, putting them into a trash bag. He then stood up and said, "I'm going to go outside and look around, just to make sure it's safe. You stay here and rest. Lock the door after I'm out. I'll give you the signal when I come back, so you'll know it's me outside." Jane stood up with a worried look on her face and looked at the metal bar that pivoted up and down, which was the lock for the door. Joe grabbed his AR-15 and patted down his vest, making sure he had put all the magazines back after filling them up from one of the ammo cans he had down here. He had already checked his rifle over, making sure it was in top working condition. He leaned down and kissed Jane, saying confidently, "It'll be all right. We will make it through this."

He reached out for the metal bar and pulled it up to unlock the door. He had to struggle to get the bar all of the way up so that he could get the door open. When the shell had hit the house, it must have done a little damage to the doorframe, making the bar a tighter fit than it was meant to be. This wasn't a good sign. His heart started jumping around in his chest, flooding his body with adrenaline. He reached down, gripped the door handle tightly, and turned it to open the door. The door handle wouldn't turn or move at all. He drew a hasty breath, bracing himself, and gave the door handle a hard twist to the right. A popping sound was all that he heard. He twisted the door handle again, and it turned easily in his hand, right and left. The door handle had popped out of the mechanism and was freely turning, not connected to anything. He sighed and turned to look at Jane.

She said, "What? What's wrong?"

He said, "The door handle broke and it isn't connected to the mechanism that unlatches the door."

Jane looked startled and said breathlessly, "You can fix it, right? Tell me you will be able to open this damn door."

If Joe could have seen outside the door, he would have understood how big a mess they were in. The main twelve-by-eight-inch oak support beam for the house had fallen across the door at a ninety-degree angle, with one end still supported by the steel floor joist. When this had happened, it literally moved the wall that the door was on inward a little bit farther, jamming the steel door tighter into the frame. Debris and rubble were jammed tight all around the door and wall, holding it securely in place.

Joe looked at Jane and said, "Something must be jammed into the door frame and it's holding the door closed."

With an edge of panic in her voice, Jane said, "Preston does know to come look for us down here, right? You did tell him about this hidden room?" Joe looked away from the burning intensity of her accusing eyes. After being married for so many years, she knew what the answers to her questions were. Joe couldn't look her in the eyes. In full panic mode now, she cried out in a shrill voice that kept climbing higher and higher, "What the hell were you thinking not telling Preston about the room down here? You stupid bonehead, he's the only one that would even think to look for us down here."

The room they were in was behind where the house furnace was and completely hidden from sight. Joe had stacked old boxes along the wall to further make it look like there was nothing else back here, and now no one would even know to look for them here. They probably would have thought that both of them were dead and buried under the rubble of the house.

Tears ran rapidly down Jane's face, dripping off her chin. She was silent for a minute, absorbing this awful news, and then she started sobbing loudly. Her body was shaking in time with her deep sobs. She was finally able to say haltingly, "Great job, genius. Now this room will be our tomb." Her body just sort of collapsed and she lay down on the floor, almost in slow motion.

Her sobs were the only sounds that could be heard. This was the last straw for Jane. All they had faced and gone through today and since the world had ended paled in comparison to this latest disaster. Her shoulder throbbed and burned like fire, making her sob harder. It was all just way too much to handle right now. In her misery she realized that, even if Preston had known about this room, there was no guarantee that he had survived the army they had faced. Maybe none of them had survived and she and Joe were entombed down here, just dying a lot slower than they had. But she and Joe were dead now, too. There was no one that would even come looking for them, let alone help dig them out. Maybe they were already dead; this was hell and they would be entombed down here for all eternity, trying to get out of this room.

Chapter 2

On the Road

> "There was nowhere to go but everywhere, so just keep on rolling under the stars."
>
> ~Jack Kerouac

Preston, Amy and Michael used their normal tactic of traveling during the night. The countryside had changed and the atmosphere was tense in certain areas. Death hung in the air—literally in some areas—from the dead and dying, and the smell was overpowering. Disease was rampant. Cholera in the water, trench foot, infection and disease were the new norm.

They were taking a midnight break and whispering back and forth. Amy asked, "How many dead do you think are out there?"

Preston replied, "I'm not sure, somewhere between 75 to 90% of the population. Maybe more, there's no way to tell for sure. I would lean more towards the 90% side."

"Wow, what about all the dead bodies? Are we going to catch some disease and die?"

"The myth that dead bodies pose an urgent health threat is overblown. Survivors using polluted water are much more likely to be a source of disease outbreaks. We're avoiding the big cities, being careful where we gather water. All we can do is pray and take precautions. After the tsunami that hit southern Asia in December of 2004, this myth was passed on and even starving people would not eat fish caught from the ocean. The fish were perfectly safe to eat. The media loves to run with myths and they become urban legends. However, those handling the dead are open to certain types of infection and should take universal precautions."

"Really, I thought the same thing, but what about setting up cremation to clean up the area?"

"Of course that works, but people need to understand that cremation takes a lot of heat for a long period of time. Some experts suggest over 1600 degrees for 2½ to 3 hours."

Michael was in good shape, but Preston realized he could not keep up the speed he wanted. This meant they needed to slow down. The longer they were gypsies traveling on the road, the more likely something would go wrong.

They traveled most of the night, but had to take ten-to-fifteen minute breaks every hour. Just before first light they stopped for the day. They were near a stream with a drainage ditch running off from the road, which allowed the water to flow into the stream. The ditch was dry, but in the culvert nearest the stream there were fresh raccoon tracks. Amy pulled out her professional grade self-locking snares and quickly set one on each end. Preston stood guard over her, asking, "We have to leave just after dark. Do you think this is going to work?"

Amy said, "If we get lucky the coons might spend the day in this dry culvert, so they might be coming back shortly. We should set up on the hill, keeping our scent away from the area, and it will make it easier to watch."

"Ok, let's do it."

They needed food and a raccoon provided the most calories per pound than any other meat, about 1,250 calories per roasted pound. After being on the bikes all night, they really needed the calories quickly.

Amy stayed up on first watch to keep an eye on the snares and let the others get some sleep. About an hour later, in the predawn light, she saw a dark, roundish critter working its way up from the main stream. She thought, *Please stay on the path.*

Within five minutes, the coon was caught, fighting mad and hissing at the snare. She woke up Preston. "Come on. We have to go grab breakfast."

Preston smiled, "That's my girl. Sure glad you're here."

"We have to get this killed and back out of sight before someone sees us."

Using his short handle Estwing axe, Preston killed the coon quickly. They pulled the snares and ran back up the hill. It still wasn't full light yet and no one was in sight.

It wasn't a great big coon, only about sixteen pounds, a great roasting size.

Amy said, "Sleep will have to wait until we move off the road about a hundred yards and leave Michael on watch. You clean it, and we're not saving the fur. Just get me a whole, cleaned, ready-to-cook animal."

"What are you going to be doing?" Preston asked.

"Making the fire and getting the forked sticks set up so we can roast it."

Preston and Michael left to do their parts and Amy got to work getting the fire started. The luxuries of matches or a lighter were long forgotten now. Luckily, she had her trusty flint and steel.

Preston walked down to the stream and quickly cleaned the coon, burying the remains rather than tossing them in the stream, as he didn't want evidence floating downstream that might bring unwanted guests.

As he carried the coon back to Amy, he saw that she had a small but good fire going. He ran the small pole through the coon's body and propped it on the forked sticks above the flame.

She smiled, like a little girl in the candy store, "Fresh meat. I can't wait. How long before we can eat?"

"About an hour, maybe a little more," He replied.

"Ok, I'm going to keep an eye on Michael. You need anything?"

"No. Just stop and see me in thirty minutes, just so I can see your smile, ok?" She still got butterflies in her stomach when Preston walked in after being gone for a while.

Chapter 3

Freedom

"Sometimes life knocks you on your ass... get up, get up, get up!!! Happiness is not the absence of problems, it's the ability to deal with them."

~Steve Maraboli

Joe pulled out an axe. "I'm going to get us out of here."

He handed Jane a pair of hearing protectors. "It's going to be loud." He started working on the door and Jane groaned. Even with the hearing protection on, it still sounded like being locked up in hell.

Jane was depressed; feeling trapped like rats and now the constant ringing from the axe on the door were driving her insane. Finally Joe took a break and she poured him some water. He had worked up quite a sweat. "How's the war?" she asked, with a weary half smile.

Joe, trying to lighten the mood, responded, "It's the first quarter and the other side is not swinging back, so I think we're doing well. I checked all four corners and I think I can get us out. The top left side is giving a little and I'm just going to have to work hard on it."

Within an hour, Joe had the metal door bent down about two inches, just the top corner, and he could see daylight.

After four more hours, he had an opening almost large enough to squeeze out of. He was about to give up for the day, being worn out, but took a few more swings, when the handle shattered and the axe head flew off, clanging to the floor. He started swearing and the strain was showing in his face. Trapped like rats and the only tool that might get them out just broke.

Great… Just Great!

He gave up for the day—defeated depression setting in. The best laid plans of mice and men, he thought. Jane didn't say a word. She was happy the damn ringing had stopped. Joe was smart; he would figure something else out.

The next day, Joe was searching for something, anything, to work as a tool. He found an old half-inch steel pipe, about 33 feet long, that might work. He propped it in the opening, pulling down with his whole body weight, but the door didn't move and the pipe just bent down; it had folded like a cheap piece of plastic.

Now what? There had to be something they could use to get the door open. As they ate breakfast, at least they had plenty of coffee to drink.

Jane asked, "Why don't we try a 2 x 4?"

Joe smiled and said the steel pipe was stronger and it just bent; the 2 x 4 would just break.

Jane said, "Come on, we have to think of something. We are not going to die down here. You built this thing, so figure it out." Joe was leaning against a steel support, the type with the adjustable threaded ends, used to lift houses.

He looked at the pipe support and burst out laughing.

"What's so funny? Have you gone insane, or what?"

"I'm leaning on the answer right here," He said. Using the support pipe, he was able to force and bend the door down far enough for him to get out.

Once on the outside, he was able to clear the debris and open the door.

"Now what?" Jane asked, "Are we heading back to the camp to join the others?"

They walked out and surveyed the damage. Jane was softly crying; a lifetime of hard work had been wiped out in a single morning.

Walking up to the truck, he saw Preston's map. "They've already left. They must have figured we couldn't have survived the blast. We need to stay put and allow your arm to heal before we hit the road."

"What does it mean?" Jane asked.

Joe smiled, "It means MAP (Michael, Amy and Preston) left 6 June, outbound to hunting camp in Wisconsin."

MAP
O
6 JUNE

Chapter 4

A Stranger

Don't trust anyone. People will do anything just to survive.

Amy was bent over, slicing the rear leg of the raccoon open to see if it was cooked all of the way through. She never heard or saw the man until he spoke.

"Smells good; do you have any extra?"

Amy dropped the knife and whipped out her 9mm, pointing it directly at the guy. He was wearing dirty clothes, a torn and ragged coat and torn jeans. He had long stringy hair, a dirty beard and was filthy. He looked like he was homeless. He had no gun, just a belt knife.

"Whoa, easy lady. I'm just starving and wanted something to eat."

"Who else is with you?" She was searching all around, but still keeping an eye on him.

"Just little old me. I meant no harm. If you don't have any extra, I can just keep moving on."

"Wait. When was the last time you ate?"

"Two days ago. I hit a chipmunk with my slingshot."

"Slingshot? Where's your gun?"

"I traded it off for food this winter. I only had seven bullets left for it and it was just an old 30-30."

"Where's your slingshot?" Amy asked.

"It's in my back pocket."

"Just leave it there. How did you find me?"

"I smelled the meat cooking. If you don't mind me saying so, I suggest you turn it before it burns," he said, as he nodded towards the raccoon.

Amy glanced down, took four steps back and then said, "If you don't mind, you can finish cooking."

Then she added, "Wait." He froze as she walked back and picked up her knife. Backing away again, she said, "All right, you can finish cooking."

Just then Michael walked up. He was startled by the stranger and said, "Who is that?"

The stranger was bent over the fire, turning the raccoon meat slowly. He stood up and said, "My name is Luke Bradford."

Michael said, "Hi."

Amy asked, "Michael, are you hungry?" and he replied, "Of course."

"Luke," Amy said, still holding the gun on him. "Back away for a minute, please."

Amy handed Michael her knife and told him to go cut off a back leg and then bring the knife back to her. When he had, she said, "That's your breakfast. Now go on watch and tell Preston we have company."

"Luke, you can sit down on that side of the fire and break off a front leg for yourself."

Luke asked, "Why are you so cautious? I'm alone and unarmed."

She looked him straight in the eyes and said, "Better safe than sorry."

He attacked the meat like a starved animal, even cracking the bones open and sucking out the marrow.

Preston walked up as Luke devoured the leg.

He asked Amy who the stranger was, never taking his eyes off Luke. She told him what she knew, while also watching the stranger's every movement.

Preston grabbed a front leg and handed it to Amy, then he cut off the other back leg and sat down, his eyes never leaving the stranger.

The stranger pulled in everything at a glance. They had coffee and halfway clean clothes and were cooking meat. The lady was armed and trained. Her husband was a big guy, carrying his AR-15 with confidence, and their son was standing watch. Wow, he thought, these people don't mess around. The son was only carrying a little .22, but he seemed much older than his age. Too much weary wisdom was reflected in his eyes.

He was waiting for Preston to start talking.

Preston cleared his throat and whispered something to Amy. She got up and walked off. Luke thought, *Oh no, this is not going good.* He started talking, "Look mister, I don't want any trouble. I'll just be moving on." He started to stand up, but Preston had the AR-15 up in flash, saying "Sit down." His no nonsense tone made the man comply.

"You can relax. I'm not going to kill you, but I'm sure as heck not going to allow you to walk off while I'm sleeping. I'm sorry, but we're going to have to tie you up for the day, at least until we are ready to go."

The stranger protested, "What? I haven't done anything wrong. I'm not what you have to worry about."

Preston shot back, "Oh really? What *do* we have to worry about?

"There's a gang roaming the area and they have horse-drawn wagons with caged girls. They trade the women at an hourly rate for whatever they need. I'm telling you, they're twenty heavily-armed bad-asses and you three wouldn't stand a chance against them." Preston listened carefully, allowing the stranger to continue. "They have mountain bikes and horses. There are two wagons; one carries their food and supplies and the other the girls. They have a regular route set up and know where all the single guys are. They trade for food, ammo, silver and gold. They are always looking for new women. They would kill you for your young wife and cut your son's throat in a heartbeat."

Preston growled instinctively, "So where are these lowlifes right now?"

"They're supposed to be in the area this week. I'm not a threat to you, really."

"I'll tell you what, you're leaving and I'm escorting you out of the area. If I even see you turn around in the next two miles, you are a dead man. I'm sorry, but I'm going to look out for my family first."

Luke said, "No problem. I understand. Thank you for the food and I pray you make it through without any trouble."

Preston followed him out of the area for a mile. He told Amy to move camp and, when they did, she took watch and let Michael sleep. Amy was waiting for Preston and he was back within thirty minutes. He passed on what the stranger had told him, saying, "We need to get out of this area damn quick. We need to move hard and fast."

Amy nodded and said, "We can't push Michael any harder than we already are."

"I know. Damn, I am worried about you, too."

Amy responded, "Don't worry. I'm a pretty good shot, trust me."

"Twenty trained men against the three of us won't work. We're in the open and they could easily outflank us, taking us out."

"What's the plan then, boss?"

"You get some sleep. I have some thinking to do."

She thought, *Great, shake me up and then tell me to go back to sleep.* She climbed into her sleeping bag and was so very tired that sleep came easily for her.

She woke up at 2:00 and Preston was still on watch. She handed him a thermos of coffee and he smiled.

She said, "You are my awesome guy," and kissed him.

"Well, Mr. Awesome is going to sleep now. Wake me in 6 hours. I have a plan for tonight."

She anxiously asked, "Really, what's that?"

He responded, "I'll show you tonight."

Chapter 5

The Best of Plans

She believed that rape and the victims of rape were simply part of the madness of war – a chaos without rules or system.

"It has become more dangerous to be a woman fetching water or collecting firewood than a fighter on the front-line."

~UN Special Representative on Sexual Violence in Conflict, Ms. Margot Wallström, February 2012

Amy woke Preston up before dark. She was trying an old trick called slow cooking that she had learned when she was in the Girl Scouts. With this method it's very easy to cook, but without the smell and sign of having an open fire. This method is, quite simply, to dig a hole and then you fill the bottom with coals and place your pot inside. Cover the meat with water and whatever else you're going to add to it. Put the lid on the pot, place coals around the pot and on top of it, and then cover it with about six inches of dirt, burying the whole thing.

Six hours later, simply remove the pot. It had been cooking the whole time, almost like a natural slow cooker. Amy did not want to waste anything, because food was vital. To ensure they got all the nutrition they could from the raccoon, she had placed it in the pot, bones and all, and surrounded it with some cattail roots and dandelion greens. She was lucky to find some mint, which she also added into the pot. With this slow cooking for the whole day, the stew was mouthwatering, tender and unbelievably delicious.

Preston smiled as he took another bowl, saying, "Amy, you are one heck of a cook, even out in the middle of nowhere. The magic you do, not only being able to catch food when we desperately needed it, but to turn it into a delicious meal, is something I truly love about you."

Amy smiled, "Well, I guess all that training and practice is paying off now. What do you think our chances of actually making it up to Wisconsin are?"

Preston smiled, "I think we have a pretty fair chance of making it. The only thing I'm really worried about is running into that band of guys that are grabbing women. There's no way the three of us could hold off twenty highly-trained men that have been snatching women for the last year. Our best defense against those kinds of numbers is to sneak through this area as quietly and as quickly as possible."

Michael smiled, "Is there any more food? I'm starving."

"Why are you always thinking about food?" she replied.

They headed out into the darkness. It was a cloudy night, the kind where it was hard to make out the road in front of them. The darkness was truly their friend in these perilous times. If there was an enemy waiting to ambush them, they would be able to sneak by. That's exactly what Preston wanted to do.

The dread he was feeling, that they must clear this area quickly, and as quietly as possible, was brewing in the back of his mind. He just couldn't shake it. Just before light they stopped and set up camp.

No chance for a fire now, no hot meal, but they just needed to get a really good eight hours of sleep. Amy said she would take the first watch. They were running low on food. Food was their gasoline, for it powered their bodies, which powered the bikes. At two in the afternoon, Amy woke Preston up.

She smiled and handed him a cup of coffee.

"I told you no fires, but I'm glad you didn't listen to me. Nothing in the world is better than waking up to you and a hot cup of coffee."

Michael was still sleeping and she sighed, saying, "We did push him pretty hard."

Amy said, "All right, Mr. Tough Guy, there's a pond back behind us. Why don't you take the fishing equipment and go see if you can catch us dinner, while I get some sleep?"

Preston complained, "But who is going to stand guard and watch over you?"

"Oh don't worry; it's been as quiet as a church mouse out there. Nothing's going on."

"You're right. We haven't seen anyone and we haven't had any trouble. I'll sneak over there, rig me up a little fishing pole and see what we can catch for dinner."

"Sounds good to me. I'm going to get some much-needed sleep. Wake me up around 7:30."

Preston walked over to the pond, which was about half a mile away. It felt good to walk for a change instead of pumping the pedals on the bike.

After cutting about a 10-foot-long sapling with his knife, he went searching for bait, turning over old logs and leaves until he was able to find a couple of worms. Using his knife again, he was able to make a little bobber out of a stick. Cutting a groove around the center, he tied it to his line. From this, he attached a sinker at the bottom of the hook. The 10-foot pole was able to get out to the edge of the weed bed.

He was looking around for a place to sit down, when the bobber disappeared with a 'plop.' He was so excited and he jerked so hard, that the little bluegill came right out of the water flying straight at him. The fish smacked him in the chest and then fell to the ground. He reached down and grabbed it. Placing it on the ground, he quickly put his knife through the brain to kill it. Luckily he still had half of his worm left, and within ten minutes he had caught four more. None of them were huge, but now he had to stop fishing and go on another search for more worms.

Within two more hours, he had caught a half dozen more. It was when he was searching for more worms that he heard screaming. Dropping his pole, he took off at a fast run back to camp. By the time he had covered the half mile, it was all over. He raced to the road just in time to see the caravan moving away, with Amy in the back of a wagon with metal bars on the door. She was screaming, "Preston, kill me please! You promised!"

After what had happened to Vickie's friends, she had made Preston promise that, if she were ever taken, he would kill her, so that she wouldn't have to suffer being abused, raped and tortured. She had become adamant and insisted that, if he loved her, he would kill her and not let her suffer that fate.

He had prayed that this day would never come. He knew he could never fulfill his promise and shoot her. The men riding horses near the wagon looked around and thought she was bluffing. Before he could blink, they were out of sight.

Then he remembered, *My God, where's Michael?* He raced over and found Michael in a bloody heap. He was still breathing, but it was shallow. He must tend to Michael's wounds. He would have to rescue Amy at night.

All their supplies and guns were gone. The only thing that remained was Michael's sleeping bag. It appeared that they just walked up and butt-stroked him with their rifles. At least the stranger had been wrong about them slicing his throat. Preston still had his daypack on. He quickly removed it, grabbed the first aid kit and cleaned Michael's wounds. Michael woke up in a daze and mumbled, "What happened? What's going on? Why did you hit me?"

Preston said, "I didn't hit you. The Raiders came and they took Amy." Michael immediately sat up and said, "We have to go save her right now." Putting his hand to his head he groaned, "Oh my God, does that hurt!"

Preston told him to relax and lie down. "I'm going to set you up in a safe, hidden camp, away from the road. Once I know you're safe and okay, then I'm going after Amy, alone. Do you understand me?"

In a panic, Michael said, "No, no I'm not staying here. She means just as much to me as she does to you."

"I'm sorry, Michael, but you're just not big enough, strong enough, or fast enough right now. You must stay and regain your strength. I'm going to set you up with the fishing equipment and the frog spear. When I come back with Amy, I expect you to be well fed, have dried fish, and be ready to go."

"You can't take on that many guys alone," Michael protested.

"I don't have to; I just have to rescue her at night."

Reluctantly, Michael agreed, "Okay, then get me set up by the camp and go save Amy."

Preston took them back to the area and set up camp. "Now listen to me closely, Michael. I don't have time to worry about you, too. Therefore, you are going to listen to me and do exactly as I say. You are going to stay right here. Do not go anywhere near the road until

I return for you. If I'm not back with Amy in four days, you are going to be on your own. Here's my 9mm pistol, two extra magazines and two boxes of shells. You also have the fishing equipment and frog spear. Here's an extra flint and steel for you to start a fire. I promise I'll do everything in my power to be back with Amy in four days."

Chapter 6

Northbound

"No matter where you are, you're always a bit on your own, always an outsider."

~Banana Yoshimoto

Joe was all ready to go. They had everything they could carry. He made a cache inside the camp and stored the extra coffee. You never know if you might come back through somewhere sometime. The stuff would be worth its weight in gold.

The July heat was hitting them now, so it would be best to travel at night and try to find a cool spot during the day to rest.

"Where are we going?" Jane asked. "We're nomads, now that we've lost everything. Well, not everything," she smiled, "we're still armed."

Joe answered, "North, I told you, to the hunting camp in Wisconsin."

"Let's go." They headed out past the burned-out spot in the ground where her dream home had been. A single tear fell down her cheek as they headed past, maybe for the last time. She was numb. *We have a one-in-a-million chance of ever seeing Preston, Amy, and Michael again, let alone making it up to this hunting camp*, she thought.

After seven days on the road, they were out of food. Riding the bikes, they made about 30 miles per day, which was about 210 miles, and they still had over 120 miles to go. Four days with no food; they would never make it. They had crossed into Wisconsin early, thinking they would miss the main population centers around Minneapolis-St. Paul.

"We must find a way to resupply," Joe admitted. "I want to rest for a couple of days, but we must find a way to get supplies."

"I know that I need to rest for a couple of days, at least," Jane replied. "Food and rest: got it, Mister?"

Joe said, "Where am I going to find that?"

Jane shrugged her shoulders, "That's up to you, Mr. Know-it-all, but we better do something quick."

Joe found a secluded spot off the main road. They were both too tired and worn out from lack of food to make a proper camp. They just crawled under their sleeping bags and sleep overcame them quickly. Waking up about noon, Joe looked around. Something had wakened him. What was it? He searched the recesses of his mind. Was it a noise? Slowly he moved around, looking to identify what it was. Everything around them looked normal. He strained his ears, trying to pick up some noise. He could barely hear something clicking. What is that?

He slowly sat up, finding Jane sleeping beside him, and everything looked normal. The noise was gone now. He quickly got up, grabbed his rifle and sneaked out to the road. Way off in the distance, he could see a person on horseback.

He woke up Jane and told her what he saw. He said he was going to follow the person and maybe they could get lucky and find some food. They most certainly had enough coffee and that would make for easy trading or bartering. Jane told him to be careful and be back soon.

Joe told her, "No more than a few hours, I promise."

With that, he was off like a flash. He must catch up to this person before losing him. Riding the bike, he quickly caught up with the person on the horse. The person was unarmed and quite startled to see him.

"Who are you and what you want?" It was a guy in his thirties. His clothes looked halfway clean, but well worn. His beard was dark and of medium length. They both stopped and looked at each other from about twenty feet away.

Joe said, "I mean you no harm. We're running low on food and we'd like to trade or barter, if you have any to spare."

The man said, "You must not be from around this area if you still have guns."

Joe responded, "Still have guns? What do you mean? Are you out of ammo?"

"No, but the local warlord doesn't allow anybody to have guns except for his troops. If they catch you, they will kill you and take your guns for sure."

Joe smiled, "Not without a fight they won't. But that doesn't really matter right now. We just need some food and then we'll be traveling on."

The man asked, "What do you have to trade?"

Joe smiled and said, "Green coffee beans!"

In surprise, the man said, "Real honest to goodness coffee? Well, if that's true, what do you want to trade for?"

"We need food. Preferably rice, oatmeal and some meat; fish, or poultry. What do you have?"

The horseman said, "Follow me. I'll take you to the farm."

They turned off down the road and the man seemed quite at ease. Maybe this warlord is halfway fair. A few miles down the road, they turned onto a dirt road, heading off to the north. Soon they came up to a small homestead. There was a main house and what appeared to be two small guest cabins. There were probably 40 acres planted with a variety of different foods; corn, wheat, potatoes, tomatoes, squash, etc. and there was also an apple orchard.

There were children outside, running and playing. There were four people working out in the fields, pulling weeds. Joe scanned the area and, for the life of him, he couldn't see anybody with guns or any type of weapons anywhere.

An older man came out and said, "Jacob, who did you bring back with you?"

The horseman replied, "I'm sorry, I didn't catch his name. He is traveling through and wants to trade coffee, yes, real coffee, for some foodstuffs."

The older man looked at Joe and said, "Hello, my name's Philip. We need to get you out of sight, before the warlord's troops see that you're here with a gun."

"Hi, my name's Joe. I mean you no harm and don't wish to cause any problems for you by being here."

Philip said, "We need to hide your bike out back. If you insist on keeping your gun, then we have to get you inside and out of sight."

With that, Jacob said, "Follow me and I'll take you behind the house where you can put your bike." They placed Joe's bike out of sight behind a woodpile. Walking inside, the smell of fresh bread reminded Joe how hungry he truly was. But then the thought of Jane being just as hungry and waiting for him back at camp came bursting into his mind. He must make the trade and move on as fast as he could. Whoever this warlord and their troops were, he didn't want to find out. He wanted nothing more than to get out of this area.

An older lady was busy in the kitchen. She was preparing bread. Philip sat down at the table and pointed toward the empty seat. "Sorry, all we have is tea to offer you."

Joe replied, "Tea would be fine. Thank you for your kindness."

"So you have coffee? How much do you have and what would you like for it?"

"I have 2 pounds of green coffee beans. I would like to get 5 pounds of rice, 2 pounds of jerky, a pound of oatmeal, some fresh butter and bread. I think that would be an awesome deal."

Phillip said, "Wow, that's kind of a steep price for only 2 pounds of coffee, don't you think? But you can skip the rice; we don't have any. We do have dehydrated potatoes, would that work? We have the jerky and oatmeal and I do believe the wife has made some extra bread, so we could throw that in with a pound of butter. Would that work for you?"

Right then, the door burst wide open and Jacob came running in. He had a worried, stressed look on his face. He shouted, "You must hide right now."

Joe stood up, alarm showing on his face, "Why? What's going on?"

"Troops are coming and you can't be here with your guns, your camouflage and all of the gear you have. We have to hide you right now." Taking Joe by the arm, he said, "Quickly, we have a storm cellar. You can hide in there and don't make a sound." Philip and Jacob moved to opposite ends of the table. They lifted it and quickly moved the table out of the way. Philip grabbed the carpet and whipped it to the side. Underneath was a hatch. Philip opened the hatch and motioned for Joe to go quickly down the ladder.

Joe could hear the horses and the sound of the troops' footsteps. He glanced outside as he was on the stairs and could see them. There appeared to be at least 10 armed men. He walked down the narrow staircase and it was pitch black down there. He sat down on the stairs. The hatch was quickly closed and the carpet and table were set back in place.

The darkness was overwhelming and his only sense was his hearing. He heard the door open and footsteps walking inside. A muffled voice said, "Have you seen any new people in the area?" Joe believed it was Philip that answered.

"No, we've seen no one, and we've not heard of any in the area. Why do you ask?"

He heard the muffled deep voice again, "No reason. This time of year people are traveling and we like to keep tabs on who's traveling through our territory, that's all. From the looks of your crops, you should have no problem paying your taxes this year."

Joe was thinking, *Taxes? If money is worthless, what are they using to pay their taxes?* He then heard what sounded like a briefcase opening up and papers being shuffled. The voice said, "According to our reports, you have a girl coming of age before this winter. There won't be any problems like last year? Right?"

Philip replied, "As far as I know, there will be no problem."

The deep voice again replied, "That's good. We wouldn't want to kill too many of your men, otherwise you wouldn't have enough to keep growing our crops for us. You do enjoy our protection, don't you? Have there been any raids on your farm since we took control?"

Jacob replied, "No. There have not been any raids. Thank you for your help. Is there anything else we can help you with today?"

The deep voice replied, "No. We were just patrolling the area and stopped in to see how you're doing. That bread sure does smell good."

Philip replied this time, "The wife just finished a loaf. Would you like take it with you?"

"Yes I would. Well, we'll get out of your hair, so you can get back to farming. Motioning to Philip and Jacob, he said, "You two shouldn't be sitting around the house; you should be out working in the fields."

Jacob replied, "I was out for a morning ride and saw you were coming. So I informed my father that you would soon be here."

Joe heard footsteps above him and then, "Thank you for the loaf of bread. We'll be moving on now."

More sounds of footsteps walking away and then the sound of the front door opening. He could hear muffled voices, but couldn't make out what they were saying. And then, silence. Joe was wondering if they were giving him up. *Was this going to turn into a gun battle after all?* There was nothing he could do but sit and wait. Suddenly, the darkness felt overwhelming. Even though the basement was cool, he broke out in a cold sweat. *I should never have let them talk me into coming into the basement.* Just then he heard a teenage girl's voice whisper softly in the dark, "Who are you?"

Joe stood up quickly, smacking his head on the ceiling. He whispered back, "Where are you?" His mind was racing a million miles a minute. *What the heck is going on here?*

The girl whispered again, "My name's Mattie. I'm 15 and my dad's not going let them take me."

"Mattie, my name is Joe. What do you mean take you?" Joe whispered back.

The girl, still whispering, "You don't know that part of the taxes are that, once a girl reaches the age of 15, she must spend one year working for the warlord?"

Joe tried to wrap his mind around it. "Part of the taxes? What are the other parts?" He whispered back.

"We have to give them 20% of everything we grow. They come by once a month to collect eggs, butter and milk from us."

Before Joe could ask another question, he heard the furniture upstairs being moved. The door was pulled open. "Come on up Joe."

"What about Mattie? Is she allowed to come up?" He asked.

Philip replied, "Not until tomorrow. I'm sorry. I'll explain when you come up."

Joe climbed up, everything was put back in place and the door was sealed, with Mattie still in the basement, or root cellar, or whatever it was. Joe said, "What in the heck is going on around here?"

Philip told him to have a seat. "Well, I guess it's been almost a year since the world went dark. At first it was all chaos and killing around here. We quickly ran out of ammo. My sons, daughters and their friends came here to survive the chaos. We had a few guns, but very limited ammo. This warlord, a rich millionaire with a huge farm and 30 horses, formed this . . . I don't know what you would call it, a militia Sheriff's Department, whatever name you choose. They said they would protect us, as long as we agreed to pay taxes. Taxes are 20% of our crops, and all girls between the ages of 15 and 18 are drafted into one year of service at his farmstead."

Joe's mind was confused and he asked, "Why are you putting up with this? Why don't you just kill them and run your own lives?"

Philip looked deep into his eyes and Joe could see the strain on his face, the wrinkles hardening. "You don't think we would stand up and fight if we had the guns?"

Joe thought, *Should I get involved, or should I just make the trade and move on*? "How many men does this warlord have?"

"Counting himself, we believe he has around 30," Philip replied. "They normally do patrols in groups of 10. We have kept close watch on the different men. Our best educated guess is that it's roughly 30. Not sure how many he has at his place. I would guess maybe a few personal body guards, one or two men he highly trusts who stay with him at all times."

"How many men do you have here?"

"Counting myself, five. Do you have five extra rifles you can lend us?"

"No. I'm sorry; all we have are two rifles and two pistols. Do you want our help?"

"Who's we?" Phillip asked.

"My wife and I. She's just as much of a warrior as I am. But I must ask, what happened last year?"

Jacob sighed. "There was another family staying with us. The mother and father refused to turn over their 18-year-old daughter. They defended her with an axe and a pitchfork. The father was able to kill one with the axe and the mother stabbed one, before they were both shot down."

Philip interrupted, "And to teach us a lesson, they rounded us all up and forced us to look at their dead bodies. We had to watch them drag the bodies around the yard, with ropes around their necks, tied to their horses. We were warned that if anything ever happened again, all of the men here would be given the same treatment."

“I have to talk this over with my wife. But you need to understand - if we start this war with them, it’s going to be bloody and there will be losses. The price of freedom must be paid in blood.”

Philip replied, “We will talk it over with the others tonight. Please come back tomorrow and let us know what you and your wife want to do.” With that, Phillip’s wife handed a cloth bag to Joe. Joe handed her the 2 pounds of coffee and thanked her.

Chapter 7

Kidnapped

> "And then something happened. I let go. Lost in oblivion - dark and silent and complete. I found freedom. Losing all hope was freedom"
>
> ~Fight Club

Amy closed her eyes and prayed her death from Preston's bullet would come quickly. Before she knew it, they were out of sight. Shoulders dropping down, she felt defeated, and turned around to look at the other occupants in the wagon. Expecting to see women in torn and dirty clothes, with the thousand yard stare, the "just kill me, please" look, she was shocked to see that they were clean, well dressed and appeared to be semi-happy.

"Would you tell me what the heck is going on?" she asked in general.

A tall, redheaded woman stood up and said, "Have a seat, sister. You're one of us now. As long as you do what you're told, you'll be treated fairly and have plenty to eat, clean clothes and showers. You just have to lie on your back when they tell you to."

"What?" Amy was stuttering, "I am not lying on my back for anybody. This is my body and this is my choice."

They all started laughing at her. Different women were throwing in different comments. "Oh yes you will," said one. "She doesn't know how the game works yet," another said. More laughter.

The tall redhead began again, "But you see, this is how the game is played. You're their prisoner. You can have a good life, or you can have a bad life. If you choose the bad life, you'll be given rice, bread and water. No showers, no clean clothes and you'll be kept locked up in this wagon jail cell the whole time."

Amy was trying to get her head wrapped around this new nightmare and said, "Sorry, I'm not for sale at any price."

They all laughed and the redhead continued, "That's what we all said, sweetheart, but within 10 days you'll be begging to get released from this wagon. Look, it's not really all that bad. These guys protect us and make sure nobody hurts us. Of course, the best thing to do is get friendly with one of the guards. You take care of him, he takes care of you and it's a real simple life."

She glared at the redhead and asked, "Where are we going? Where are they taking us?"

The response was, "We are en route to a small compound of people. You see, this is how it works. We come to some place and they trade. The guys then come and pick who they want to sleep with. You don't have to do it. We normally spend 2 to 3 days at one camp. Then we go back to our place. We stay there sometimes up to a week. Some of the locals come to our main camp and trade for us there also."

Preston, no longer caring about being seen, rode the bike down the road to catch up with the wagons. It only took him about an hour. He could see them a half mile in front. He stayed way back and out of sight. He really didn't have a plan. His only hope was to be able to sneak in quietly at night and pull her out. This was a lot easier said than done. Twenty armed guys against just him.

For four hours he played this cat and mouse game. He almost lost them once when they turned off the main road, but found them again just before dark. They pulled up to what appeared to be a farmstead - old buildings with a main farmhouse, garage and barn - and all of it appeared to be well fortified. Barbed wire was strung everywhere, encircling the entire place. There was a main gate with two armed guards.

Preston stashed his bike in the woods, making sure it was well hidden. It was time to do some recon and figure out how to rescue Amy.

He slowly worked his way up to within 50 yards of the main gate. He could see that the horses were being taken into the barn. Two wagons were still out front, easy to see. *Was Amy still in the wagon, or was she in the house?*

Darkness was setting in. He sat for an hour and just watched the guards. Every hour, one of them did a patrol around the whole area. He saw the ladies being pulled out of the wagon, but he was pretty sure Amy was not one of them. Time to do a recon around the back and sides of this place.

Two hours after they arrived, Amy was pulled from the wagon and dragged into the house. Two big burly guys, one on each side, walked her inside, and took her up the stairs and into a bedroom. Candles lit the room.

As Amy entered the room, a man sitting in a chair spoke, "Welcome to your new life. Let me explain the rules to you." Interrupting him and glaring at the man, she said,

"I have already heard the rules and decided not to play your degrading little game."

The man broke out in laughter, saying, "You did notice there were 10 other women in that wagon, correct? Didn't all 10 of them tell you the same story? See, it's totally up to you. I do not believe in force or rape. You have the choice—good life, or a bad life."

Amy interrupted, "What the hell do you mean you don't believe in force? You took me forcefully. You stole all my guns! Did you kill Michael too?"

The man stood up and he was tall, probably 6 feet or more, with broad shoulders, a scar on one cheek, with his hair cut short. "Was that your little boy's name? No, we didn't kill him. I'm sure he's fine. He was simply knocked out."

Still glaring at him, she said, "Oh, just great, you left him knocked out, to starve to death all by himself. You know he's only 12 years old, right? He's never going to make it out there by himself. You need to let me go right now. I'm his mother, and I need to be with him."

The man held up his hands and laughed, "Look, I'm a businessman, you could say a commodity broker. You are a commodity, which is highly prized in this new world. I'm sure somebody will find and help your son, so stop worrying. Besides, you are my property now, you're my commodity. You were yelling for somebody to kill you. What was that all about?"

Amy, thinking quick on her feet, replied, "I was asking my son to kill me, because I'd rather be dead than be your property, or commodity, as you so rudely put it."

Smiling, he said, "So I take it your answer is that I won't be breaking you in tonight?"

"Not tonight, or any other night. I'd rather starve than let a thing like you touch me."

He turned to the door and shrugged, "Guards, take her back and throw her in the wagon. Maybe a night in the cold will teach her a lesson." With that, the door opened and the two big burly guards entered. Each grabbed one of Amy's arms and dragged her back out to the wagon.

When she returned to the wagon, she found she was the only one in it. No blanket, nothing but a cold, hard, wooden floor. *Where the hell is Preston?* She thought. She went to the far corner like a caged animal and sat down on the bench, where she curled up and started crying. She would not give them the satisfaction of seeing her cry. The temperatures were still in the 50s, but with no heat or blanket it was freezing inside the wagon. She hadn't noticed the cold before, with all the other women inside, but that was during the day, with the sun shining. She got control of her emotions and began thinking about how to escape from this wooden cage. The door was half wooden. The upper half held bars, spaced about 4 inches apart. The rest of the wagon was comprised of solid walls. First she checked the door. She reached her hand through the bars and felt the solid steel hasp, with the thick padlock that was holding her in.

It was too dark for her to check anything else. All she could do was curl up on the bench and try to sleep. She needed daylight. There must be some way to escape. She just had to figure it out. Who knew, maybe Preston was coming to save her right now?

Preston circled to the rear of the compound and found an easy place to enter. The barbed wire was only four strands and was designed more to keep cows in than people out.

He could smell the cows. He worked his way up to the edge of the house. There was no light coming from the house, so he was hidden by the darkness. He crawled underneath the hedges and lay down in a spot that allowed him to see the whole area. Now all he had to do was make sure nobody could see him and then save Amy. Hopefully she was still in the wagon. Just then the front doors opened. He could see two guys dragging a woman toward the wagon. His heart leapt when he saw in the moonlight that it was Amy.

You could hear the keys rattle in the night and he heard the lock open, then the door swing open. One of the guards said, "Hope you enjoy your cool night. Maybe it'll teach you to be a more warm and caring commodity." With that, the door was slammed shut and locked and the two men walked off laughing.

Preston thought, *Commodity? What the hell is he talking about?*

There were too many people walking around and he didn't want to be discovered. His best bet was to wait until way past midnight, when most of them would be asleep. Get the pattern of the guards. Make sure nobody else was coming out and checking. He only had one chance and he had better do it right.

Chapter 8

Decisions

"Doing nothing for others is the undoing of ourselves."
~Horace Mann

Joe returned to camp and, over the best meal they'd had in days, they discussed the problem. It was hard to concentrate, with the fresh bread and real butter. After they finished the meal, Jane said, "Okay, Superman, tell me how just the two of us are going to take on 30 men?"

"There have to be other farms in the area. There's no way the small farm that I saw could support 30 men. We need to form a volunteer army to stop this."

Jane sighed, "This is none of our business. You got us enough supplies to make it to where we're going, so we should just keep moving."

Joe looked at her, "We must face reality. Do you think Preston and Amy really made it? Maybe we can work out a deal, stay here with these folks. They seem to have it together. We could take over as sheriff and help protect them."

Jane chuckled, "Really, Sheriff? These people don't know us." She paused and then said, "But I don't like the thought of 15-year-old girls being dragged away for one year of service to a warlord. If you think you can make this work, without getting us killed, then let's look at the possibility."

The next morning, Joe and Jane rode over to the farm. They stashed their bikes in the woods and approached on foot. Philip was in the front yard when they approached.

"Please, come in so we can talk," he said, as he turned his head toward the barn and nodded.

Joe quickly looked and saw Jacob, who nodded back. He wondered what that was all about.

"Jacob's job today, while we're talking, is to make sure we're not interrupted like we were yesterday. He's going to go for a ride on his horse to make sure there are no close patrols."

Joe nodded and said, "Sounds good." They entered the house and again the overwhelming great smell of fresh bread hit their nostrils. Jane set her beloved .22-250 against the wall. Joe kept his rifle at his side. They all sat down at the kitchen table.

"What have you decided?" Joe asked.

"We want your help, but how are we going to take out a patrol of 10 men with only four guns? Then, what are we going to do if they bring 20 more and kill us all?"

Joe responded, "Well, I thought about this most of the night. There have to be other homesteads in the area. Are there others who are willing to help and stand up to this warlord? If we could get some more men, then we would have a fighting chance."

"Yes, there are several farms, but we have some traitors in those other groups. Men have visited and traded for, how do I put this, to be with one of the young girls. I don't trust some of them," Philip said.

"You must know the men that you can truly trust. If this is going to work, we must set up an ambush area. Away from anybody's homestead. If anything goes wrong, nobody will be to blame. You must have bows and arrows, maybe crossbows. Does anybody else have guns stashed?"

"Yes, we have some bows and arrows, but how are bows and crossbows going to be effective against semiautomatic rifles?"

Joe looked Philip in the eyes and asked, "Have you studied any war tactics in your life?"

Philip let out a strained laugh and said, "No. That should be no surprise, I'm a simple farmer."

"Sun Tzu, in the *Art* of *War*, teaches that you must appear weak before you strike; for this allows your enemy to have the arrogance of the quick and sure win. That part has already been accomplished. Your next main goal is to pick the means we are going to use to accomplish this; we must be training as a unit. We must become a band of brothers. I would prefer 20 men; that way we have two-to-one odds. Every two men would be assigned one target. We pick an ambush site. We make straw men as targets and we practice from our hidden positions, until everybody is trained and ready to kill."

Philip had a look of amazement on his face. "How long would this take?"

"A week, maybe two. If we could train a couple of hours each day, say an hour to set up the targets, an hour to practice and then clean up and go home. Is this something your people are willing to do?" Joe studied Philip's face as he thought about the question.

Philip smiled and said, "I think that sounds like a plan. Jacob will take you back to our hunting/fishing camp. It's about 5 miles from here. You can stay there and give me 5 or 6 days while I talk to others. I'll let you know how many men I can muster." Philip stood up and so did Joe. They smiled and shook hands.

Jane nodded her approval and Joe said, "Then we'll talk to you in a week, or hopefully sooner."

They walked into the woods and retrieved their bikes. Jacob came riding up on his horse saying, "Follow me." He took them down a two-track dirt road. In about an hour they could hear the stream flowing. They turned off the main trail and, within a quarter of a mile, came to the camp: a small, maybe 12 x 20 hunting lodge, situated near the stream.

Jacob showed them around, saying, "You can cook on the wood stove. You have bunks to sleep in and the fishing equipment to keep you entertained. There should be enough food to last you a week and plenty of wood to burn."

Joe thanked Jacob and said, "Please come back in four days or so and let us know how it's going."

"I will. I promise." And he rode off.

Joe looked around and said to Jane, "Well, you got your wish. You can rest, eat meat, and fish for the next couple of days. We can even have fresh trout for dinner tonight.

Jane smiled and looked at him, then, with a put-on frown, said, "Don't just stand there. Get out and catch some fish. While you're gone, I'll make this place livable."

With that, Joe walked over to the fishing equipment and grabbed a pole, choosing a Panther Martin spinner with a red tail. He had a big smile on his face, saying, "I'll be back with trout for sure."

Jane had a broom in her hand and pretended to swat at him, saying, "You'd better Mister; I need some fresh food. Now get out of here."

The stream was only about 10 feet wide, with lots of brush overhanging and brush piles in the water, giving plenty of cover for the trout to hide. He sneaked up to the first hole and cast his bait right in front of a fallen log. He retrieved the lure, but nothing, no fish following it. *Oh no, maybe I shouldn't have been bragging so quick*ly, he thought.

An hour later he finally caught his first fish, a beautiful 12-inch brook trout. Joe breathed a sigh of relief. He sure didn't want to hear from Jane all night long about what a lousy fisherman he was.

A half hour later he caught another one about 10 inches long. *Well that's good enough for tonight,* he thought. *At least we have one whole fish each to eat.*

Chapter 9

Amy's Rescue

"Having a sense of purpose is having a sense of self. A course to plot is a destination to hope for."
~Bryant McGill

Preston needed to find something to pry the hasp off the wagon door. The guards were pretty easy to figure out. They must not have had any problems for months, because they were very relaxed. Once an hour they took a walk around. One stayed in the gatehouse, while one walked the perimeter of the compound. They walked right by the wagon several times. It was time to go into the barn and try to find a pry bar of some type.

It shouldn't be too hard, as the barn was also a little workshop. Preston opened the door and entered, listening for a while, and then quietly closed the door behind him. No flashlight, so he would have to use his hands and try to find something by feel. He had to move very slowly, as he couldn't afford to knock something over and make a bunch of noise. He wanted a long pry bar, but he would settle for anything that he could use to pry the hasp off. A claw hammer, a big wrench, a pipe wrench, a crescent wrench, or large channel locks would work. There had to be something in the barn that he could use.

It was difficult in the dark and he fumbled around, slowly moving his hands around the workbench. He found small wrenches, screws, nuts, bolts and pieces of wood, everything but what he was trying to find. He worked slowly along the bench, coming to a toolbox on the end. Inside, he found what he was looking for: a claw hammer and a large cold chisel. He grabbed them both and was so excited that he swung his hand to the side too quickly, knocking over a can of nuts and bolts. As it hit the concrete floor, it bounced and scattered the bolts and nuts everywhere. It sounded really loud to him and he quickly shoved the cold chisel in his pocket, pushing the hammer down along his belt. He raised his rifle, pointing it at the door, waiting for the guards to come bursting in.

His heart was racing and the adrenaline pump hit him, causing his hands to shake. *Some rescue this is turning out to be*, he thought. He waited, straining his ears to hear the sound of running footsteps and shouting, but there wasn't a sound. He lifted his foot to take a step and kicked the can. It rattled along the concrete floor, making yet more noise. He told himself to calm down and stop acting like a rank amateur.

Slowly he crept to the door, being careful not to trip on the scattered nuts and bolts. His whole plan was based on his doing this quietly. He couldn't let Amy down. He couldn't have been inside for more than 10 minutes. He should still have plenty of time before the next patrol. He opened the door a crack, peeked outside and breathed a sigh of relief. Everything was as quiet as before. He had gotten lucky. He stepped outside, turned around slowly and, turning the handle, he quietly closed the door. Once the door was shut, he allowed the handle to turn back slowly, so there was no loud click.

He looked up to the gatehouse and the two guards were standing around joking, not really paying attention at all. He slipped behind the barn and stayed in the darkness until he worked his way back over to the house.

It was almost midnight by now and he guessed that they would probably be changing guards at midnight. He wanted to wait until the guards had changed and give the new guards a couple of hours to relax before he made his move. He had just crawled back under the hedges next to the house, when he heard the front door open. He panicked a little, wondering if someone had seen him. He raised his rifle up, ready for trouble. Two men came out and stepped onto the porch. They looked around and stretched, "Another long, cold, lonely night, hey?" one of them said.

The other replied, "Yeah, it sure was hard leaving Lisa in that nice warm bed. But she'll be waiting for me in the morning when we get off."

They started walking towards the gatehouse. Preston thought, *Good. Hopefully they are worn out and tired*. He couldn't hear what they were saying when they approached the other guards, but, after a few words, they relieved them. The two that were getting off watch quickly entered the house.

Now the waiting game had started. The only problem was that the rear of the wagon was facing the front gate. He wouldn't be able to use a hammer and chisel without alerting the guards. He was going to have to take them out. He didn't want to kill them, as chances were they were just guards for the compound. They had nothing to do with kidnapping Amy or hurting Michael. He would just use the hammer and knock them out. He would turn the hammer sideways, smack them hard against the head and then gag and tie them to a tree. Now he only needed to worry about the roaming guards.

He crawled back out and picked a dark corner where the guards couldn't see him. He gave them about 15 minutes to settle down and then sneaked off behind the barn. That was the darkest and farthest part that the guards patrolled. The only thing he was worried about was that the guards tended to be lazy at night. He was worried the guys might not do the full patrol. That's why he must strike on the first round. Chances were the guy would be lazy on the next one. He found a spot halfway along the barn, where there was a hay-baling machine. It was perfect to hide behind. His plan was simple: let the guy walk out, smack him in the head with a hammer and then gag and tie him up.

Setting his rifle down, he practiced stepping out and striking. This practice was so he could clear anything that might make noise, like branches, tall grass, or anything else. He practiced over and over and over again. And it was good thing, because there were sticks that snapped under his feet and one lone beer can in his way. Once everything was clear, he was 100% positive he could approach the man without making a sound. He waited for the patrol and the waiting was killing him. The sooner he could free her, the sooner they could put miles behind them. He thought about Michael and prayed he was okay. He prayed that Amy would be in good enough shape to run. With the waiting and the darkness, his doubts and insecurities came flooding in. *What if this doesn't work? What if the other guard kills me before I can knock him out? What if someone sees me? What if I can't get the hasp to break?* Question after question popped into his head. *Stop!* He told himself. *Focus and do your job and it will work.* He gave himself a pep talk, but the doubts kept coming back. *What if that stranger returned to their camp, killing Michael and stealing everything they had left?* His stomach grumbled. He had not eaten in hours. He had taken two of the fish with him, skinned them and eaten them raw, but that was late afternoon and he hadn't had anything since. *Man-up*, he told himself. *There'll be time to eat later.*

He peeked around the corner and saw the guard coming. The guy was walking slowly and he was almost to Preston, when he stopped. *Damn. What's the matter now?* Preston thought. *Does he have night vision? Did I make a mistake? Was that empty beer can used as a marker? Was he really this sharp?* Preston strained his ears, trying to hear something. He kept his breathing shallow and quiet. Come on already, buddy, make a decision. His mind was racing. *What if the guy turned around and left? Should he take a chance and try to take him out?* He heard a zipper open, followed by the sound of water running on the ground. *Oh, that explains what's going on,* Preston thought, *Hurry up and finish already.* He heard the zipper closing and footsteps coming closer and he was almost there. As he walked past, Preston stepped out and hit the guy really hard with the hammer. The guy crumpled to the ground like a piece of paper. Quickly, jumping on top of him in a flash, he grabbed his head and lifted it up. He was knocked out cold, but still breathing. Using the nylon baling twine, he shoved a rag in the guy's mouth and tied it securely in place. He then tied his hands behind his back, dragged him over to the far wheel of the bailing wagon and tied him to the axle. He stripped the man of his rifle and ammo. *Good, at least Amy can be armed now*, he thought.

Preston sneaked back beside the house, stashed the gun and ammo in the brush and, wearing the guard's coat and hat, he could casually walk up to the last guard. Keeping his head down, he walked up to the front gate. The hammer was in his right hand, behind his back. The other guard turned back around. "What took you so long?" Ignoring the question, he kept his pace slow and steady. When he could see the guy's feet, he looked up and said, "Your friend is tied up." It was a shocked look on the guard's face. Preston jumped, swinging the hammer down, but the guy had pulled back. The hammer didn't connect with the full force. The guy fell back on the ground. Begging for his life, he cried, "Don't kill me." Preston hit him again with the hammer, knocking him out cold. Same as before, he gagged and tied him up. Propping the guard up to a post, Preston thought it would give the appearance he was still standing duty, just sitting down for a break. Good deal of time to get Amy free now. He looked around. All the lights were out in the house. At a fast walk, he made it to the wagon.

Upon reaching the wagon he whispered, “Amy, are you in there?” Silence. “Amy?” he said a little louder. He heard rustling. “Amy, is that you?” He heard mumbling as Amy woke up.

“Preston? Is it really you? Am I dreaming?” He whispered for Amy to be quiet “Preston, is it really you? You’re really here. Please, get me out of here.”

Preston whispered, “What do you think I’m trying to do?” She moved to the door and asked,

“What’s the plan?”

“I’m going to see if I can break this hasp off.” Using the claw part of the hammer, he jammed it between the top of the hasp and the door. Bending down, using his full weight as he did so, he expected the hasp to break off, or the screws to pull out, but they didn’t. He could hear the screws starting to pull out, but he needed to put more pressure on the hammer. He repositioned the claw at the bottom of the hasp and, as he strained with it, he felt something give and heard a loud snap, as the claw of the hammer broke off, causing him to smash his knuckles against the door.

He wanted to swear. He wanted to cuss like a drunken sailor, but knew he couldn’t. *Damn, that really hurt*. Amy said in the darkness, “What happened?”

He whispered, “The hammer broke.”

“Can you get me out?” she said in a near panic.

“Hang on.” He pulled the cold chisel from his pocket and, with the screws pulled out almost an inch, he thought he could get enough leverage to pull them loose. Setting the hammer down, he placed the chisel between the door and the hasp. This time he pulled downward. Putting one foot against the door and using all his weight, he pulled for all he was worth. The hasp gave way suddenly, causing him to fall on his butt.

The door swung open and Amy jumped out. Helping him up, she then jumped into his arms, kissing him and whispering, “Thank you, for saving me.”

"It's not over yet. We still have to get out of here." She started toward the front gate, but Preston grabbed her arm, pulling her back, "Over this way. I have a rifle and ammo for you."

"Oh, you think of everything," she whispered. He retrieved the gun and ammo pouch from the bush and she quickly put them on. He handed her the guard's coat, which he had been wearing over his, and gave her the hat.

They walked right out of the front gate. The guards were still knocked out cold. *So far, so good,* he thought. Once they reached the bike, Amy asked, "Where's Michael? Is he okay?"

"Yes. He has a nasty bruise on his head, but he was doing fine when I left him."

Amy smacked him, "What! You mean you left him?"

Preston said, with some exasperation, "We can talk about this later. Right now we have miles to cover."

Amy whispered back, "You'd better believe we are going to talk about this, Mister."

Preston was about to remind her that he wanted to stand guard over her, but she insisted he go fishing, which is what put them in this mess, but thought better of it.

"Fine. But right now, shut up and get on the back of the bike. We have miles to cover." She did so with a pout and they were back on the road.

Each mile traveled, they felt more and more relief. No pursuit, no sign that anybody even knew she'd escaped . . . yet. With any luck, they wouldn't know until morning that she was gone. By then, they should be back with Michael and moving on. After two hours, they stopped for a break. They had covered at least 15 miles.

Amy was still mad at him and said, "What's going on? How dare you leave Michael all by himself? You should've brought him with you. What were you thinking?"

Preston said, "Keep it down. I moved him back by the pond and I'm sure he's fine. There was no way I could take him with me. He was injured and couldn't have kept up to catch the wagon and save you. You sure are being ungrateful."

She hung her head down, "I'm sorry, I know. I'm just worried about him." She kissed him again, saying, "Thank you for saving me." And then she slugged him in the arm saying, "You promised you would kill me and not let me be taken."

Preston winced, "I'm sorry. I didn't get there in time," he lied and then jokingly said, "The way you're behaving, I'll seriously consider it, if there is ever a next time." Amy paused and then giggled quietly, hugging him tighter.

"Do you have anything to eat? I'm starving."

"Sorry. They stole your pack and I left mine back at camp. I had to travel fast and light."

They made it back to the pond about an hour after daybreak, but there was no sign of Michael. They could see that he'd built a lean-to and the fish smoker had fish in it.

Amy looked at Preston, "Where is he?" She looked around.

Preston was also scanning the area and said, "I have no idea. He has to be around here somewhere. I told him I would be back within 4 days. Maybe he got lost."

In a panic, Amy said, "Oh my God. What if somebody took him?"

Chapter 10

The Training

"Wars may be fought with weapons, but they are won by men."

~Gen. George S. Patton Jr.

On the third day, Joe was getting impatient and, as Jane cleaned some more fish, he said, "We should be training people. We should be finding ambush spots." And he paced the floor.

Jane told him to just relax already. "Can't you just enjoy the free time that we have?"

"I know, I know. I'm sorry. I just want to get this going already."

With a smirk on her face, Jane stood up, wiped her hands on a towel and started unbuttoning her blouse. "Well, I can think of something to take your mind off everything."

Joe looked up, "Oh, whatever do you mean, my dear?" He smiled with a devilish grin.

Later that afternoon, when Joe was outside splitting kindling, he heard a horse riding up. He retrieved his rifle, which he had hidden behind a woodpile, and within a few minutes Jacob appeared. Joe stepped out to greet him. "Good to see you."

Jacob smiled and said, "I have good news. We have 15 men, plus you two, which would make a total of 17 altogether. That should be enough to get the job done, don't you think?"

"Yes. That should work. Are these all trustworthy men?"

"Yes. I can vouch for each and every one of them. I just came back to let you know that there's a meeting at the house tonight. Come up just before dark."

"Thanks Jacob. Would you like to come in for a cup coffee before you head back?"

"I'd love to, but I just don't have the time. I have a few others to visit before I head home. I'll see you tonight." With that being said, he turned the horse around and left.

That evening they all met. There were 15 men, ranging in age from 18 to 45. Joe started the meeting by asking, "Do any of you have any military experience?"

Six of the men said they had. "Have the rest of you hunted before?" All but 4 of them raised their hands. "Good. Here's the plan. We need to pick an ambush spot, one that's not near anyone's homestead, far enough away that we won't be found out and no one person or family can be blamed. We practice for a week or two, until everyone is very efficient and knows what to do. We use bait to lure them into the trap. We kill them all. We take no prisoners. No one can escape. Does anybody have a problem with this?"

The room erupted and it was hard to make out what people were saying. The overall consensus was that they were fed up with being pushed around. They were sick and tired of paying taxes, giving their daughters and sisters up to be whores for the warlord and being under his constant thumb.

"Okay. Okay, everybody settle down. What do we have for weapons? Please, one at a time, starting with you, Philip."

Philip said, "We have two compound bows and plenty of arrows." He turned and looked at the next guy.

"We have one double-barreled 12-gauge shotgun and a box of double-aught shells."

The next man said, "We have one crossbow and several shafts," another said,

"We have a single-shot 410 shotgun and some shot and slugs."

The next one said, "We have axes, machetes and pitchforks." That was it. Just a half dozen weapons, plus what Joe and Jane had. It would have to do.

Joe asked. "Have any of you heard of the term *slam shotgun?"* Not waiting for an answer, he continued. "It's a simple concept. Take a three-quarter-inch steel pipe and a 12-gauge shell fits perfectly in it. This fits inside a 1-inch steel pipe that has a metal screw on cap, with a tack soldered in the center. You make the 1-inch steel pipe 6 to 8 inches long. You file the three-quarter-inch pipe all the way around until it easily slides in and out. When you're ready to fire, you simply slam them together. They're not very accurate and are extremely close range weapons. But, if you make the three-quarter-inch pipe about

20 inches long and mount it on a homemade stock, you have a fairly accurate shotgun. The only problem with this is reloading. You have to take it all apart, pry out the 12-gauge empty shell and insert a new one before you're ready to fire again. It can be done, but it's not as easy as you think. The brass on the 12-gauge shell expands tight to the three-quarter-inch pipe. But for our purposes, it will be a great one-shot weapon."

"Do we have a plumber in the house?" Joe asked. Everybody pointed to one man.

A man stood up. "My name's Mike. I used to run a plumbing supply and repair business. I believe I have everything to make what you're talking about."

Joe replied, "Great, Mike, that's your main job this week. I'd like everybody to have a gun. You think you have enough supplies to make 10 of them?"

"I don't know for sure, but I would guess I do."

One asked, "What did you mean about bait? How is this going to work?"

Joe smiled. "Now, we know their weakness is young women, correct? We have to lure them into a trap on our terms, where we have the total advantage. The best way to do that is to use bait. Have a young female lead them right into our trap. It will be an ambush site and we'll all be completely hidden. Without breaking our cover, we kill them all."

Philip interrupted, shouting, "You're NOT using my daughter as bait."

Joe said, "We have to. It's the only way to make it work. We put her on horseback and we have her ride right through the ambush site. As soon as she's out of the way and completely safe, we start our attack. Talk it over with your family and your daughter. If not, it's going to be so much harder." He looked around. "I must warn you all, this is a fight to the death. This is not playing at war and it is not a game. Once we start this, we have to finish it. There's no backing out. They patrol on horseback, correct? We kill them all, take their bodies way off into the woods and bury them, kill all of the horses and eat the meat to hide the evidence. That way, the remaining forces have no clue what's going on. You go back to your lives and make it appear as if everything is normal. If we get extremely lucky, we can take out two patrols, leaving only 10 men at the main house. We then form a plan and take them out, too. Do you all agree to this?"

Philip asked, "Okay, but what's in it for you two?"

"My wife and I would like to be your new sheriffs. Of course, we would work on the farm and do whatever we had to do. We'd also do patrols and keep things in line. We could train anyone who's willing to be trained. That way we would have a mutually assisting, well established, volunteer army for any new threats."

Philip spoke up and said, "I'll talk to my family and, while I can't speak for everybody, I can say for myself that I will agree to your terms."

Joe looked over the room and asked, "What about the rest of you?"

Everyone nodded their heads in agreement. "Good," Joe continued, "I know what I want for an ambush spot and Jacob has offered to take me around and show me the countryside. I don't know how big this area is and it might take me 2 or 3 days to find what I'm looking for, but we'll move forward with the plan. Unless there is other business, I bid you a good night." They all left the house and Joe rode back to the camp. Once inside, Jane asked him how it went.

"Fairly well. If we can get set up right, it shouldn't be a problem. Jacob is coming by in the morning and we're going to do a recon in the area to find the perfect ambush spot."

She asked, "What would you like me to do while you're gone?"

"You could spend some time with the women up at the homestead. Find out who has nursing or doctor skills in the area. Find out what they have for antibiotics, bandages and tourniquets, and make up some first-aid kits for the battlefield."

The next morning Jacob was there at the crack of dawn and had a cup of coffee before they left. Once Jane was at the homestead and had hidden her bike, she met with some of the women.

Jacob asked Joe what he was looking for, hoping to save them some time.

"Well, first off, the place must be far away from anybody's homestead. It should be a trail, or a real narrow dirt road, preferably something with a hill where, at the bottom, we could set up some old cars or trucks on each side of the road, leaving a narrow opening so they would have to go single file. We then build blinds on the side of the road and we can have people hidden in the bed of the pickups, too. That's where we'll put the guys with the shotguns. I'm thinking it's going to take about 8 to 10 vehicles to do this. We'll set up a rope or cable at the end. This will be yanked up after the bait, excuse me, the young lady, clears the area, just in time to trip the lead horse. That will be the signal for everybody to open fire. We really must take the time to make this first strike perfect. If anyone escapes, it could turn into a long bloody war. Plus, success will really boost the morale and give us 10 more rifles and ammunition."

Jacob thought for a moment and then said, "I have a spot in mind that I think would work perfectly."

"Good. Let's check that out first." They rode until they were about 6 miles away from the homestead. Jacob turned down a dirt road. Joe thought it was a little too wide to his liking, but that soon changed. There was one lone house off to the right. Once past the house, it turned into a very narrow, two-track road and up over a hill the road went, down into a valley with a tiny creek.

Right at the creek, there was a lone culvert that was a perfect spot to make a very narrow opening, but it was mostly open hardwoods without enough brush to conceal everybody, like Joe had been hoping for.

Joe said, "This spot is okay, but I want something with denser brush and more cover on both sides of the road."

Jacob was disappointed. He thought this was the perfect location, but okay then, off to the next one.

They spent the rest of the day looking and looking for the right spot. Finally, a couple of hours before dark, they hit it. It was a super narrow road with dense brush on both sides and a really sharp turn, down a slight hill, right into the ambush zone. This would put them about 10 miles from any of the homesteads.

Joe was a little concerned that the warlords patrol may know this area and would be instantly alerted to the changes they planned to make. Jacob told him that he had never seen a patrol go down this road, as it was a dead-end at an abandoned house. They would just have to chance it and hope for success.

As they rode back, Joe was trying to formulate everything they would have to do to prepare the spot. First, they had to get the vehicles there. There were enough horses around that they could rig up some way to tow the vehicles there. Building brush blinds to hide in shouldn't be a problem. Last, but most important, was practicing and learning to work as a team. He hoped he could pull it off in 2 weeks.

At the meeting that night, he laid out the plan. He drew it all out, crudely, on a piece of paper. Now the work began.

The next day, using two teams of horses, they started towing vehicles back to the ambush spot. As soon as they had eight vehicles there, they started building the brush blinds along the side of the road. This all took over a week to get prepared, but they had learned to work as a team, as a unit. Now they had to practice as a unit.

Chapter 11

The Reunion

"The sweetness of reunion is the joy of heaven."
~Richard Paul Evans

After they had both scanned the area, Amy slugged Preston in the arm. "What were you thinking of, leaving him here alone?"

"Calm down. He's probably out fishing and it's the best time to be out. Maybe he's looking for bait. Just calm down, relax."

She marched straight up and into his face. "He had better be all right."

"Come on, let's go look for him. I'm sure he's fine. I'm sure he didn't expect us to be back so soon."

They split up and started searching along the edge of the lake, one on each side. They were almost to the back side of the lake, where a small stream was flowing out, when Preston spotted Michael.

Preston called out, "Michael, are you okay?" Michael looked up with a big grin on his face. "Sure I am. I just caught me a nice big 5-pound pike." Preston motioned for him to come and said, "Grab your stuff and let's go. Amy is worried sick about you."

As Michael picked up his equipment, he said, "You saved her? Is she okay? Is everything all right?"

Preston nodded, "Yes, but she's just worried about you right now. We need to get you back quickly, so she can see that you're okay."

Michael came running up, with his pole in one hand and a stringer of fish in the other. Preston waited for him to catch up to him. He looked towards the other side, getting Amy's attention, and pointed back toward camp. When she saw Michael, she started running towards camp. "Michael, hand me that stuff and you run back and tell Amy that you're fine. Let her see that nothing's wrong."

Michael handed everything to Preston, with a confused look on his face, and said, "Of course I'm all right. What is she worried about?"

Preston grinned and said, "Because she knows you were hit in the head and because women always worry about their children. Now just run."

Michael turned to head towards the camp and said, "I'm not a child. I'm almost 13."

Laughing, he replied, "Yes, but she's going to worry about you for the rest your life, so just get used to it. Now run over there and tell her everything's fine."

"Well of course, it's fine," he said confidently, in his young voice. "But I do want to make sure *she's* okay." And with that, he was off in a flash.

Preston started walking, looking at the stringer of fish: a couple of bluegills and two nice-looking perch, but they all looked dinky compared to the big pike. He smiled about that and thought that at least they would have a really good breakfast. He walked over and snapped off the pollen on cattail stems. It would make a good substitute to use for breading the fish. When he reached the camp, he had enough pollen to coat each fish.

Amy was crying and smiling at the same time, as she was so happy that they were all back together and nobody was seriously hurt. Preston walked up and said, "Enough of the mushy stuff, let's get cooking breakfast." Amy looked up, tears streaming down her face,

"Oh, just shut up, Preston." She saw the stringer of fish and told him to go clean them and get them ready for cooking. Michael, pulling back from her embrace, said with an excited voice, "Did you see that monster I caught? We'll be eating well this morning."

Amy hugged him closer, "I saw what you did and the smoker you built. You did a great job. Thank you. You did all of that while injured too and I'm proud of you. You're well on your way to becoming a true warrior." He was beaming at the praise. He wanted to be just like Joe and Preston.

Michael had been taught how to collect dried wood. This was wood with no bark and preferably from a tree that had fallen. Only the bone-dry upper limbs were used. It made a quick and almost perfect fire, with little or no smoke. Preston came back with the cleaned fillets. He pulled out the cattail pollen and smiled, "We can even have it breaded." Amy prepared the food, and they quickly ate, enjoying every crumb. After cleaning up, they were all ready for some much needed sleep. Michael took the first watch. They had been lucky that their bikes had been hidden far enough away from camp to not be found or stolen. Tonight they would ride like the wind and leave this area once and for all. Preston knew that the men would come looking for them and they would most likely head straight to the spot where they had kidnapped Amy, knowing the boy they knocked out was there. He was counting on them not coming until the tied-up guards had been found, which should give them several hours.

Both he and Amy needed some sleep if they were going to ride the bikes hard. As soon as it began getting dark, Michael woke them and they packed the bikes and got ready to leave. That night they rode like the devil himself was chasing them.

Little did they know that there were four patrols searching for them, each made up of five men. They didn't think they would still be back where they had captured the woman, so they had been concentrating on wider grids of the area.

Just before light they started to pull off the road, when Preston looked up on a hill that was about a mile away. In the predawn light he could make out what he thought were five shadowy figures on horses. He told Amy and Michael to follow him and they quickly went up a small hill and lay down. He told them to be ready to shoot it out, in case they had been seen. Within five minutes, the men were even with them, having stayed on the road. They stopped right in front of them. They heard one say, "We're never going to find them. This is fruitless and we're just wasting time and energy. Do you know how many side and dirt roads that they could have easily escaped on? And where do we patrol? On the main roads, like they'd be stupid enough to ever use these again?"

Another man spoke, "You need to just shut up. You're not in charge; I am. The boss says this is what we patrol and that's our job. If you don't like it, you're free to leave."

The first man said, "I'm just offering suggestions. I think we would be far better off on dirt roads and searching there, instead of looking on the main road. That's all I'm saying."

"Well, lucky for us, you're not in charge. Come on, let's move out." They rode off into the dreary predawn light. Preston breathed a sigh of relief. At least, with only five of them, they would have a fighting chance. Amy whispered, "What should we do?"

Preston thought for a minute and then said, "We should stay right here and get some sleep. We'll stay with our plan to travel at night. Get some sleep and I'll take the first watch."

Michael whispered, "Wake me up next. I'll take the second watch and let Amy sleep."

"Okay, both of you get some sleep."

They didn't bother to make a camp and just lay in the grass to sleep. Thanks to Michael, they had dried fish to eat. That would give them enough food for today and tomorrow. They knew that they had to use that to their advantage and cover as much ground as they could. Preston checked the map. Thirty miles, maybe thirty-five, and they would be at the camp.

That night, as they walked their bikes down to the road, they heard a yell in the distance. "There they are!" The sound of charging horses clacking on the pavement echoed across the valley. Preston whipped around quickly and told Michael and Amy to follow him. They ran up the hill and, laying their bikes down, turned the rifles back towards the road. The bright moonlight had given them up.

"Listen to me. Don't shoot until they're almost on top of us. We can't afford to be wasting any ammo. Shoot the horses; they're bigger targets and it will put the men down on the ground." But before the men reached them, out of nowhere, ten rifles opened up, with flashlights turned on the approaching horsemen. Someone was yelling for them to open fire and kill them all. Three were shot off of their horses and the other two turned around and retreated.

A voice off in the distance called out, "Are you three friendly?"

Preston thought, *What in the heck is going on?* He yelled out, "Who wants to know?" The answer was, "The Wisconsin voluntary militia. We knew they were looking for somebody, but we had no idea what was going on." Preston whispered to the others to stay where they were and he would go find out what the heck was going on. He stood and walked over to meet a big man on the side of the road. He was giving out orders for his men to go collect the three horses and weapons. Preston walked up and extended his hand, saying, "Thank you for your help."

"No. I should be the one thanking you. You set them up perfectly to bring them right into our trap." He was a large man, and, even in the dark, he looked to be a little taller and about 20 pounds heavier than Preston. He grabbed Preston's hand with a firm, honest grip and shook it. "The name's Fred. And you are?"

"I'm Preston and *darn* glad to meet you."

"Well, Preston, I'm glad to meet you, too. Now, what's your story and what can you tell us about these guys?"

"We were traveling to our camp in the north and these guys kidnapped my wife. They travel with two wagons and 20 armed men on horses. They travel to homesteads and barter sex with the women they have kidnapped, in exchange for food and trade items. I managed to follow them to their compound and broke her out, freeing her that first night. That was the night before last and now they've come looking for us.

Fred asked, "Did you kill any of theirs? What kind of weapons do they have?" and "Where is their base of operations?"

Preston responded, "No, I didn't kill any, but I knocked two of them out. They have an assortment of different weapons. I didn't get a real good look, but I thought they were mostly AR-15s, or AR-15 platforms. The homestead is about 15 miles north of here. It's a large white farm house with a barn and some out buildings, surrounded by barbed wire and well guarded."

"Good. Thanks for the information. So where are you heading now?"

"We are going to the Three Bear Hunting Lodge."

"The one up by Little Creek?"

"That would be the one. Is it still open?"

"As far as I know, it is. Why are you coming up here? Did you have trouble back at your place?"

Preston began telling the story, "Yes. We were overrun by a group of fanatics that call themselves the Rainbow Warriors. They're a bunch of nut cases and are killing anyone that refuses to believe what they believe. They have two 105 artillery cannons and blew our farm to pieces, killing my friends. We think we're all that's left of our group. If any of the others survived, they know to meet us at the lodge, so that's why we're on the road. After I get my family set up and secure,

I'd like to join forces so we can take these nut cases out once and for all."

"You sound like our kind of man. Come on, we'll escort you through the area and get you to the camp."

"That would be great, but don't you have to finish your mission?"

Fred smiled and, with a raised eyebrow, said, "*Mission*? You must be ex-military. Well, our mission was accomplished. It was to stop those that were chasing you and, if you were good people, to help you get through the area. I was also to grab Intel on what we're up against, which we have now."

Preston volunteered, "Yes, I'm retired Army. What about you?"

"I did four years as an Army Ranger," Fred replied.

It was almost full daylight now. After Preston called Michael and Amy over, introducing them, they rode north together. The cool morning dew sparkled in the sunlight and it looked like it was going to be a great day after all.

Chapter 12

The Practice

"A pint of sweat will save a gallon of blood."
~Gen. George S. Patton

The first day of practice was a real eye-opener. They had set up square bales of hay, to the height of a horse, and then put a straw man on top of each one. Each one represented one of the enemy horsemen. When they had all of them set up, they had the targets they needed to practice on. They put two of the straw men on the ground, as if the men were taking cover, having been knocked off their horses by the rope. The idea was simple; the men with axes would take out the two men on the ground. They would be wearing Gillie suits and lying on the ground next to the road. They would jump up, take those two out as quickly as possible and grab their guns. The two men with shotguns would be hiding under a tarp in the bed of the first pickup and their job was to make sure nobody escaped to the rear. The men with bows and crossbows were to take out the men in the middle that were left on their horses. Ammo was too precious to waste in practice, but they did come up with a few Red Ryder BB guns to replace Joe and Jane's rifles, so they could practice shooting the targets.

Joe said, "This is our first practice, so things are going to go wrong. That's not a problem and we expect that. We have to find out our flaws and learn from them. Now, does everybody understand what his field of fire is? It's very important that everybody understands this, as we don't want any friendly fire accidents. I'm going to start this by pulling on the rope, yelling, and screaming. When you hear that, do your assigned jobs. Are there questions before we start?" No one responded, so, when they were in position, Joe yanked on the rope and started yelling, "Kill them all." The two guys with axes jumped up and charged their opponents. The guy on the left tripped and fell, dropping his axe, which bounced off into the woods. The other man delivered his blows and, like a good warrior, took one more step and hit the other one.

The arrows flew all over the place, but only one hit a target. The two men with the BB guns managed to hit one, but missed the others completely.

Out of the ten opponents, only four had been hit. Joe said, “Okay, let’s review our actions.” He gathered everybody around. He looked at the man that had tripped and lost his axe, saying, “This is why we practice. Accidents happen and not everything works out the way you plan. So what you have to do now is adapt and overcome. After you lost your weapon, you did nothing. What you should’ve done was pulled your belt knife and started stabbing.” Joe looked at his partner and said, “You did the correct thing. You took out the first opponent and then quickly moved on to the second. That’s how we all have to be. Don’t get in that mindset of ‘*it’s not my job*’.

“Okay, you guys with the bows. I think what we need to do is allow you 30 minutes of practice. At the same time, you guys with the BB guns practice coming out from under the tarp and hitting your targets. You should all try to practice at home as much as possible. We are only going to get one chance at this. Now, in real life, you get to keep shooting until all your opponents are down, not just hit, but down and out of the fight for good. You also have to remember that a battle plan works perfectly, until you engage an enemy. So that means that, no matter what happens, you just adapt to the new situation and keep fighting; you keep shooting until it’s over, or you’re dead. Does everybody understand?” Everyone nodded. “Good, then let’s get started.”

Joe spent his time watching the men shoot with their bows and crossbows and he asked each one: which was their best shooting position, sitting or standing? If it was standing, then they needed to add more brush for them to hide behind. He then walked over to the guys with the shotguns and said, “Okay, I’m going to show you an old hunting trick. You, with a single-shot, let me see it for a second.” Taking the gun, Joe looked it over and said, “This is an H&R and has the barrel release lever right next to your thumb, so what you need to practice is hooking the shells in between the fingers of your left hand, like this.” He demonstrated. “Now, from inside the truck, you have to practice this. Don’t actually fire, but hit the release button, ejecting the shell, and then take one of the shells and slip it into the chamber, close it and you can shoot again. Just practice that, so you can do it in your sleep, and the same goes for you with the double-barreled 12-gauge. It's a little harder for you because you have to get two shells lined up, but, with enough practice, you should be able to do it in your sleep. This is where I'll teach you what's called muscle memory. If you do something thousands of times, in the heat of battle your muscle memory will take over and you'll reload without even thinking about it."

The guy looked up confused. "A thousand times?" The other guy looked at him and said, "I think I had it down after a hundred." Joe turned to him and asked, "Have you ever been in the heat of battle?"

The man answered, "Well no, I haven't. But I've hunted for years."

Joe tried to explain, "Well, it's sort of like that, except now *your* life is on the line and your adrenaline is pumping, with your heart racing at 900 miles a minute. People are screaming and yelling. People are begging for help. It's chaos at its finest. The only way you can function effectively in that environment is if you've practiced enough to have muscle memory. In your first combat, you'll probably get tunnel vision, only seeing what's directly in front of you. It will just be you and whoever is trying to kill you; the rest of the world will fade away and so will your hearing. You'll feel like you're moving in slow motion and your mind will be screaming at you to shoot faster. It's surreal and that's why we train and practice. Once this battle starts, the dress rehearsal is over and there will be no second chances, no do-over, no reset and play the game again. You must take this deadly serious, because *everyone's* life is going to be on the line.

They finished practicing and called it a night. While Jacob was riding back with Joe, he asked, "So, are we ready?"

"No, not even close, but I expected mistakes because they are going to happen. What we have to do is make sure everybody's covered. Do we have anybody that has experience throwing axes?"

"Yes. I think we do. I never even thought of that. The only problem - it's a young boy of only 14."

"I'd like to meet him tomorrow. He may be too young to take into battle, but maybe he could teach a few of the men how to throw. I'll tell you this, if everybody keeps practicing, and we keep working as a team, we'll be ready to take them on next week."

Jacob smiled. Let the fun begin.

"How is Mike coming on the slam shotguns?"

"When I talked to him earlier he said he had all the pipes, but wanted your help to make sure he is doing everything right."

"Okay, then that will be my project for tomorrow."

Chapter 13

The Hunting Camp

"Sometimes good things fall apart so better things can fall together. Every story has an end, but in life every end is just a new beginning."

~Unknown

Just before dark, Preston, Amy, Michael and their escorts reached the hunting camp. Along the driveway, Preston stopped, leaned down and picked up a small rock, Turning it upside down, he moved a cover and retrieved the key to the camp.

Fred said, "So, you do belong here."

Preston laughed, "I sure as heck wouldn't travel that many miles if I didn't." And they all entered the camp. There was nothing special about it, just a small 16' x 24' hunting lodge. When Preston unlocked and opened the door, they all went inside. The musty smell from being closed up so long was immediately noticeable.

Fred looked around and then said, "Well, good deal. I'll leave you folks to it. When you're ready, come down for a visit. We're 10 miles east of here, just past the Little Creek turn off."

Preston smiled and shook his hand, "Thank you for helping us make it here."

"No problem. We're glad to be of assistance. See you in a week or so." With that, Fred mounted his horse and the volunteer militia rode off.

Preston turned around and went back inside.

Amy was busy opening up all the windows. She told Michael to go cut kindling and get a fire going. She turned to Preston and said, "Don't just stand there; make yourself useful."

Preston laughed, "Can't a guy just sit down and relax, enjoying a few minutes of peace?"

"Not until you help clean this place up and we get it aired out." He looked around and noticed there was a thin layer of dust on every flat surface.

This was his favorite hunting camp and it had a shallow well, with a hand driven old-style hand pump, which fed directly into the sink. He walked over and started pumping it. Nobody had been here for a while and he hoped the leather seals were not worn out and cracked. He had never repaired a pump before, but he would have to figure it out if he couldn't get the water going.

He used some water from his canteen to prime it and, about a minute later, the pump pressure changed and he could feel the water starting to flow out. Amy had just walked in and saw the rusty, dirty water coming out. She exclaimed, "Oh my God. That is so disgusting. We're not going to drink that, are we?"

"Relax. It's just rust from the pipe and will clear out within a minute," Preston explained and then said, "The water is super good here. You'll really like it."

Amy wrinkled her nose, "Not if it looks like that, I won't."

Preston ignored her and just kept pumping. Soon the water was coming out crystal-clear. He grabbed a glass and filled it up, handed it to her and said, "Would you like to try it now?"

She wrinkled her nose again and said, "Nope. You're the taste tester. You try it."

With that, he drank the whole glass down. He pretended to be choking and, while making a terrible face, said in a raspy voice, "Oh my God. It's poison," and then he started laughing.

Amy said, "That's so not funny. Now quit clowning around and get to work." She smacked his arm. "Come on. I want to eat dinner and go to bed already."

As soon as the place was dusted and swept out, Preston cleaned the ashes from the wood stove and started a fire with the wood Michael had brought in. Before long, the entire cabin room took on a soft, warm glow from the fire. Amy began cooking some Zatarain's Jambalaya Mix, adding bottled water, as she was still unsure of the pump water.

After dinner, Michael asked who was taking the first watch.

Amy looked over to Preston. Preston said, "I think we should just bring the bikes in here and close the place up. The windows have solid wooden shutters, with metal on the outside to prevent bears from breaking in. We have a solid industrial-strength metal door on the front. I say we all get some much-needed sleep and not worry about watches tonight."

Preston was lying in bed staring at the ceiling. Now, what did they have to do to survive the brutal winter that was coming? They had one heck of a lot of firewood to cut and, without the luxury of a chainsaw, or a truck to haul it, there was going be a heck of a lot of real work to collect it.

The next morning, over breakfast, they talked about what needed to be done to get ready for winter. Amy got up and walked over to the kitchen cupboards and started opening them up. She looked over at Preston and said, "Best I can figure, we have maybe 2 weeks' worth of food. So tell me again, why did you bring us here?"

Preston chuckled, and said, "Oh, ye of little faith. We have a root cellar below us, with enough food for four guys to survive twelve months. Mind you, it's nothing special: rice, beans, oatmeal, wheat berries, honey, sugar and, you guessed it, a 50-pound bag of green coffee beans," laughing out loud. "And, with a little luck, we can get deer and maybe even a bear for meat. We can fish and gather from the old orchards and farms in the area. We might, if we're really lucky, stretch it out to two years."

He went on, "There's also a .22 single-shot rifle with 5,000 rounds of ammo, a thousand rounds of .223 and two hundred rounds of .22-250. We have a gillnet and other fishing supplies and, if I recall correctly, solar battery chargers with nickel-hydrate batteries and flashlights. There's enough kerosene to feed the lamps for a year. We have the really good Aladdin lamps, which are equivalent to 60 watt light bulbs."

Preston added, "My main concern is getting all of the firewood we'll need."

"Just like last year at the farm," Michael said. "Well, at least we have plenty of practice doing it."

Above the door going outside was a decorative saw with a painting on it. "My first job," pointing up to the saw, "is to get that sharpened."

Amy asked, "Before you get started, could you bring me up a bucket of wheat berries? Do we have hard red winter wheat? Oh, and did you guys put any of the white wheat away? You know, the kind to make white flour with?"

Preston thought for a moment, "I think so. Why? Are you going to start grinding flour right away?" Amy replied, "Yes, that too, but I was thinking that I would do some sprouts right away. We need the extra vitamins and nutrition that sprouts will give us."

Preston chuckled, "Oh great, you're one of those. They taste horrible. Well, maybe not horrible, they're just bland."

Amy said, "It doesn't matter what they taste like. We have to eat them to stay healthy. I'll mix them in with other food so you won't have to eat them all by themselves, you big baby." Michael asked, "So, what do they taste like?"

Preston said, "On a good day they taste like cardboard," laughing, "and on a bad day, you don't want to know."

Amy said, "Would you just knock it off and get to work already?"

Preston looked at Michael and said, "The general has spoken. I want you to start scouting for dead downed trees around the camp. That doesn't mean go traipsing all over the place. I want you to do about a 100-yard circle around the camp. And carry your rifle."

Preston hauled the wheat buckets up from the root cellar for Amy and they all got to work. The cabin was small, with one lone bedroom and a couch in the living room that pulled out into a bed. No bathroom, but the wood stove had a water heating jacket on it. There was a shower stall where you could fill up a bucket of hot water and wash yourself off. Not the best, but beat the heck out of not having hot water for a shower. After all, it was just a hunting camp. And there was an outhouse, which got mighty cold in the winter.

At least they had shelter and a good fighting chance. Thank God they had been smart enough to buy their food insurance and store their supplies ahead of time. They were definitely worth their weight in gold now.

After the first week, they had not seen one person. Preston thought that was very unusual, but they were far off the beaten trail. He calculated how long it was going to take him to get in at least six full cords of firewood. He was thinking about 6 weeks.

As for foraging for foods, the good news was that there was a clear-cut area a couple of miles away that was loaded with blackberries, plus he knew a good blueberry spot, too, and in the spring they could make maple syrup. He hoped they'd be able to get enough from the land to survive and carve a life out for them here.

One day, when they were cutting firewood, three cows with two calves walked through the area. Preston and Michael tried to corral them, but these cows had turned feral and were quite wild. They easily outran them and crashed off into the woods.

Michael and Preston were panting and sweating. Preston said, "Well, I hope they are around just before winter sets in, as we could shoot one of the younger ones and put up a winter supply of meat.

Michael asked, "How in the world are we going to catch them?"

Preston laughed, "I think a bullet to the head would do it. Can't run off when you're dead, don't you think?"

Michael laughed, saying, "That just doesn't seem right."

"Right or not, I'm sure those T-bones will taste mighty good come January. But they're feral now and there's no way we'll be able to catch them. It sure would be nice to get a milk cow, but I don't think there's enough grass in the area to support them, let alone to feed them all summer and then have enough put up to feed them all winter." But it was a good pipe dream.

Michael was licking his lips and said, "Fresh milk would be so good right about now."

"Yes, it would, but we have work to do, so let's leave the day-dreams behind and start cutting more firewood."

That evening, as they were approaching the camp, they saw Fred talking to Amy on the front porch. Preston was pushing the wheel-barrow full of cut wood and Michael was carrying the saw and axe.

As they approached, Fred said, "Why are you doing it the hard way? We have a regular woodcutting crew: wagons with horses to haul out the large trees and we have a whole team of people that are experts at doing it. If we help you with that, it would mean you would have to pay back by working on everybody else's place."

Preston was sweating and stopped, looked up and said, "You have what? Oh my God. That sounds like a dream come true. Yes, we all have to learn to work together as a community to survive."

Changing the subject, Fred asked them, "How you folks doing on food?"

"Amy said we're good for at least a year."

Michael was petting the muzzle of Fred's horse and asked, "Can I ride the horses when they're here?"

Fred laughed, "I'm sure you can. You folks need to come down tomorrow and see what we have set up and how everything's working for us. We have a pretty good co-op system. For instance, if you want milk and cheese, then you work the field with the hand sickle, cutting hay for the cows to survive the winter. If you want fresh eggs, then you work in the wheat or corn fields."

"It sure sounds like you people really have it together up here."

Fred replied, "Well, it's not perfect, but it works for us and, if you do become part of the community, you'll be required to do patrols. But the main reason I came here is to ask a question." Looking at Preston he asked, "Would you help lead a patrol down to the fortified homestead? Are you willing to do that?"

Preston smiled, "Willing? I'd love too. When are we going?"

Fred was obviously pleased and said, "Good deal. That's all I need to know. Come down tomorrow and I'll show you around and let you know how we're working things. We can discuss all of it tomorrow."

Amy asked if he would like stay for dinner, but he declined, saying, "Thank you, ma'am, but I must decline your lovely offer. We'll see all of you tomorrow." He climbed back on his horse and said, "See you around eight?"

Preston said, "We don't have a watch, but we'll try to get there around that time."

Chapter 14

The Encounter

> "I firmly believe that any man's finest hour, the greatest fulfillment of all that he holds dear, is that moment when he has worked his heart out in a good cause and lies exhausted on the field of battle - victorious."
>
> ~Vince Lombardi

Joe spent the next 3 days working with Mike and his son Chris making the homemade slam shotguns. Chris was his woodworker; his job was to make a crude rifle stock. He took 2 x 4s forming the stock. Nothing fancy, it would be held on the bottom with the right hand. The left-hand would hold the barrel, slamming it back into it. They were going to have to make a prototype first. Luckily, Mike had hand pipe-threading dies. Using a hacksaw, they cut the 1-inch pipe and threaded the ends. The only problem was that they only had 7 1-inch steel caps. Seven more shotguns were better than none; it would have to do.

For the backing to hold the 1-inch pipe in place, they used an angle iron with two holes drilled in it. This was held in place with 2-inch-long wood screws. They had to drill the holes by hand using a brace. Power tools were surely missed in this long slow process. Chris had to whittle a notch for the steel cap so the pipe would lay flat and even with the stock. The piece of angle iron was mounted behind the steel cap to prevent the pipe from flying backwards, hitting the shooter in the face. With a lot of filing, cussing, and persuading, the three-quarter-inch pipe was rounded out enough to fit inside the 1-inch pipe.

They were ready to test fire their first prototype. They rode horses deep into the woods so the shot could not be heard by anybody and set up a 5-gallon bucket as a target. Using a tree for cover, they put the stock against it, reached around and slam fired. They missed the bucket completely, but this was a safety test to make sure the angle iron and 2 screws were strong enough to protect the shooter from a fatal failure.

It worked like a champ. Joe then put it up to his shoulder and, aiming low on the bucket, he fired. He hit the bucket high. But it worked.

Mike jumped in and said, "All right, my turn." They reloaded and Joe warned him to aim very low. He fired, knocking the bucket off the stump. With a big grin on his face he said, "By God, I think we got it worked out! I have a box of number four shot. It's not the best, but at close range it will definitely do the trick."

Joe asked, "Do you have any more like number eight skeet shot; something we could let these guys at least practice one shot with?"

"No, but I do know somebody that should have a box."

After four more days of practice, everybody was learning to work as a team. Everyone's shooting skills had vastly improved. On the fifth day, he changed everything up. He arranged the straw men so that the two men in front were still on horseback, the six in the middle, kneeling or lying down, and the two at the far end still on their horses.

Everybody was wondering why the change. Joe explained that they simply had no idea how this was going to play out, but they did know one thing for certain – it wasn't going to go exactly as planned. He told them they needed to practice different scenarios; they would be better prepared.

He had instructed the guys with the shotguns to take some empty shells and reload them, but with no powder or new primers, just the weight of the lead. This time they were able to practice shooting and reloading. Since he had extra men, he had them build homemade spears.

The 14-year-old boy that was good at throwing axes had taught two men how to throw properly and they were pretty good with them.

They began again and the two men at the end with axes jumped up, charging the men on horses and hitting them in the stomach area with their axes. But then an accident happened. One of the men with a bow was shooting at too much of an angle. His arrow ricocheted off a car and hit one of the men holding an axe in the leg. He went down, screaming in pain. Joe called out for a medic and told the rest to keep practicing and firing. "This is just like a real battle, so don't stop and keep fighting," he said.

He let everybody keep shooting for a few more rounds before he called a halt. He could tell they were all greatly upset and worried about their friend. Everybody ran over, surrounding the man lying on the ground. Luckily they were using practice arrows with target tips. It hadn't hit the bone or any vital area, so the arrow was removed and the wound was wrapped with bandages.

Joe said, "Two of you men go with the medic and take him back to camp. The rest of you must do it again. The more we practice, the better we become."

Jacob interrupted, "Joe, everybody is upset by the accident. We should wrap it up and call it a night."

Joe shook his head. "This is exactly why we need to keep practicing. Friends might get killed or wounded when the real fight goes down and people must learn to overcome their emotions and keep fighting. This is not a game. His wounds are not serious and he'll heal up in 3 weeks and be fine. So we do it again."

Joe was trying hard to hold his temper because he knew these men weren't battle hardened and didn't understand what it was like to be in a life or death fight, but they soon would.

As everybody walked back to their positions, Philip walked beside Joe and quietly said, "You can be one cold, hard son of a bitch, can't you?"

He stopped and turned toward Philip. "I have to be. We're practicing, right? If we allow people to break ranks and run to a fallen friend during battle, we'll be cut to ribbons. Remember when I said that, in the heat of battle, you would fight the way that you practice? Well, if we allowed the men to break ranks now, they would do the exact same thing in the heat of battle, when it really counted. It may seem cold and heartless, but we have to get that mindset. Do you understand?"

Philip replied, "Yes, I do, but it doesn't mean I have to like it."

Joe said, "It doesn't matter if you like it or not. My job is to make sure we win and keep as many of you alive as possible."

After practice was over, Joe gathered the men that would be using the slam shotguns to explain how they would be using them in the upcoming battle. He said, "Now, the 7 men with the slam shotguns will be given a chance to test fire them once. This is empty, see?" He held the three-quarter-inch pipe out. "The three-quarter-inch barrel slides underneath the pipe strapping back to the 1-inch pipe. You hold it like this: using your right hand and holding it tight against your shoulder, aim and slam back, fast and hard. The trick is slamming hard enough to fire the shell, but not so hard it throws your aim off."

Joe continued, "Chris has whittled you guys dowel rods. Your dowel rod is buried in the ground, standing straight up to about 3 feet long. You fire your first shot. You pull out the three-quarter-inch pipe, slamming down the dowel rod. This knocks out the empty shell. You have another shell in your pocket; quickly replace, put the pipe back into the stock and then you can fire again. You each will be given three shells. If you're lucky, you should be able to get all three shots off. But the most important thing for you men to remember is to make that first shot count. Don't worry about the follow-up shots. If we all do our job, it should only take one shot."

The men each fired one shot, ammo was way too precious for any more practice, but they at least had a good idea how to work the homemade shotgun.

After 3 more days, no matter what position Joe put the straw men in, everybody was hitting their target. He called everybody together and said, "Now, are you ready to do this?" Everybody nodded their heads, saying they were ready and shouting, "Let's do it!"

Standing in the back of a pickup, Joe said, "Okay, tomorrow the patrol should pass through this area." He turned to Mattie, "Are you ready do your job?"

Mattie responded with a nervous voice, "Yes. As ready as I'll ever be."

Joe went on, "Good. If they follow their normal pattern, they should be coming by this road at about 2:30. Things change, patterns change, so I think we should be here at eleven o'clock. We'll use 2 scouts to find their location. When they've been located, one will stay just in front of them and the other will come back to tell Mattie and the rest of us where they are. His job will be running back and forth with updates."

The next day was foggy and the temperature was a cool 55°F. This could work to their advantage, but it could also work against them. It might be almost impossible for the scouts to find them in the fog. Over breakfast at Phillip's house, they talked about calling it off.

Joe said, "I don't think so. This fog normally burns off when the sun comes out, so by eleven o'clock we are moving into position. It should be breaking up by the time they come through and it shouldn't be a problem."

Philip said, "I've seen this fog rolling in before. Sometimes it breaks up, just like you say, and other times it lasts for a day."

Joe responded, "I say we go for it. If the weather doesn't break, if the fog stays bad, then we'll call it off."

By 10:00 that morning the fog was already starting to break up. At 11:00 they were all set up. Mattie and the two scouts went out to the road. Mattie was briefed on how to act like a scared girl, new to the area. Her shirt was tied up Daisy Duke style, knotted below her breasts, to add a little incentive to be chased. Her job was to stay at least 100 yards in front of them. Her little Mustang was a short horse, not a thoroughbred like the ones that would be chasing her, but he made up for it with plenty of heart and spirit.

Everybody was in position, sitting and thinking that they had two-and-a-half hours to wait, when the scout came racing back. "Oh my God, they're only 2 miles down the road," he yelled, before racing back.

The camp became electrified. You could feel it; the moment of truth would soon be upon them. The sun broke through and was warming the day, burning off the fog.

Joe walked around and calmly told everybody to just relax and do what they'd been trained to do and everything would be fine. He walked back to his position and Jane looked over at him. "You sure this is going to work?"

He gave her a weak smile and said, "Yup, I'm sure everything will work out just fine."

Ten minutes later, the first scout arrived back and said they were within a half a mile. He quickly hid his horse and took up his position. A few minutes later the other scout raced in, saying they were almost to Mattie's position.

Mattie was to be dismounted, with her horse feeding in the ditch. She was to let them get to within 150 yards, watching them out of the corner of her eye. They had positioned a car as a marker and, once the patrol was even with that, it was her signal to jump on her horse and race off, screaming in fear. She was nervous and scared to death of being caught and when they were 300 yards away, she wanted so badly to just get on the horse and race off, but she didn't think they had seen her yet, as they had not changed their speed.

At 200 yards, still no noticeable change from the patrol. Mattie started edging her horse up towards the road. She thought, "Jesus, are these guys blind or just half-asleep?"

At 150 yards, still no noticeable change. "Close enough," Mattie thought, as she swung the reins around the neck of the horse, put her foot in the stirrup and swung her leg over. When she was mounted, she heard somebody yell, "Halt!"

She looked in that direction and, seeing the full patrol of the men starting to charge her, she raced off down the road.

Her little horse went into a trot, not really running. She looked over her shoulder and screamed. They were gaining quickly and they were only about 75 yards behind her. She leaned down, dug her heels into the horse's hindquarters and yelled, "Run baby, run." The horse, sensing her urgency, kicked it into high gear and was at a full gallop.

She quickly made it to the road and turned towards the waiting ambush. That's when she heard the first rifle shot. "Oh My God. They're shooting at me!" She leaned down even closer on the horse. The bullet was high overhead, but the sound of the high-speed snap spooked the little horse. He was almost in full panic, running for fear. Mattie had a heck of a time just hanging on. She raced down the road and luckily the trees blocked any further shots, until they caught up to the road she was on. The horse was more confident on the dirt road and he surged forward at an even faster speed.

Another shot rang out as she raced by the old house. "Another high shot," she thought, "they must be trying to frighten me into stopping." She dared a quick glance over her shoulder to see where they were — about 60 yards behind her and still gaining. She was almost to the final turn. "It's going to work. It's going to work. Come on, horse," she whispered. The horse had run its initial panic out. She reined in to slow the horse down for the final turn. She turned and looked; they were only 40 yards away. God, their horses were fast. Pushing forward another 100 yards and her job was done, and then it was up to the men to save her.

Two more quick shots over her head. Thank God, they're not shooting at her or the horse. She could hear the men yelling behind her, ordering her to stop and shouting that she was going to pay dearly for running. *Not this time*, she thought, *you are the ones that are going to pay dearly.*

Down the hill and through the trap and she raced out of sight. The plan worked perfectly. Like hound dogs on the hot scent of their prey, the men didn't even notice they were riding right into a deadly trap. When the lead horse was about two car lengths away, Joe yanked the rope up, which was hooked onto the tow ball of a truck. Before the lead guy could rein in, his horse tripped over it and he went flying. So did the second, third and fourth guys, causing the others to stop. Joe stood up and started shooting. Jane opened up and the arrows started flying. The screaming and crying began. The two men in the Gillie suits jumped up and quickly dispatched the first two, but before the other two could be killed, they managed to fire a couple of shots. Joe and Jane, hearing the shooting behind them, swung around and dropped both of them, quickly turning back around, looking for new targets.

Horses were running around in panic, but he saw one lone guy make it past the guys with shotguns. They shot at him, and he slumped over, but kept on riding. It looked like an ancient battlefield, with spears and arrows stuck in the downed men. The men knocked off their horses never even got a chance to retrieve their rifles. Their horses had run off in a panic. The last two men standing still had rifles, but tossed them to the ground and stood up, saying they surrendered. Before Joe could do anything, Philip and Jacob walked up to the two men and said, "You're the two that laughed about taking my daughter. Remember that?"

Sheer panic quickly crossed their faces and they both knew what was coming next. They made a desperate dive to retrieve their rifles, but father and son buried their axes into the backs of the men's heads. Joe thought that it was righteous anger. There were three more men lying on the ground wounded, with either a spear or an arrow in them. One was begging for mercy, pleading with them to allow him to live. Joe walked up to them and calmly shot each man in the head. Then he yelled out, "Rodney, Ed, get on your horses and make sure that lone man doesn't make it back to his camp." They mounted and rode off. Joe looked at two of their own dead and shook his head. *We should have had more men at this end*, he thought.

Everyone came from their positions and down to the battlefield. They all cheered and then turned and saw their own dead men. The shock of what had really happened started to sink in. Seeing the blood and gore of their enemy caused two men to run off and get sick in the woods.

Joe barked out orders, trying to snap the men out of their shock, "All right, you men, we still have work to do. Quickly gather up all their arms and ammunition and anything else useful. Pile it all in the back of this pickup and then get some horses to drag these bodies to the pre-dug graves and get them buried."

Mattie came back with three of the four horses that had come up to her. She broke down when she saw two of their own lying dead.

Joe turned to Philip and said, "You should take Mattie and go home."

Philip disagreed, "No, we have work to do. Mattie, tie them horses off, then head on home and get cleaned up." Before long, everything was cleaned but the blood and gore. They wrapped their dead in tarps, preparing to take them home. Soon the area was cleaned up. For the next ambush, they would be on equal footing with the 11 rifles they now had.

Joe told the men to gather up all of the horses, as they needed to get rid of the horses that had been wounded during the battle. They were quickly put out of their misery and dragged out of sight. The blood was covered up with dirt and the area was restored almost back to way it looked before the battle began.

The original plan was to slaughter all of the horses and eat the meat, thereby getting rid of all the evidence that they were involved, but one of the men offered a suggestion, "I know where there is a corral and good pasture land. We really should keep these horses."

Philip added that it would nice to have some extra horses, once they had gotten rid of the other assholes.

Joe thought about that for a minute and said, "If they can be well hidden and not connected to anyone, then maybe it would be okay, but it means someone has to feed and care for them."

Several of the men volunteered, so the uninjured horses were spared and would be taken to the unknown location.

They started heading back and Philip rode up beside Joe. "It sure wasn't like I thought it was going to be. I know it never is, but . . . still."

Joe replied, "It never is. Humans, deep down, know it's morally wrong to kill their own. The only problem is that sometimes we have no choice."

Philip asked, "How do you deal with it? I could have gone my whole life without killing another human being. You think God will forgive us?"

"I don't know. I can't speak for God, but I do know there are many wars in the Bible that God did condone."

Philip quickly interjected, "But the Ten Commandments say 'thou shall not kill.'"

"You know, that was poorly translated. In the Hebrew text, the correct translation is 'thou shall not murder.' And what is the definition of murder? It is the unlawful, premeditated killing of one human being by another."

"But that's exactly what we did. We carefully planned and trained to murder those men."

Joe took a deep breath and said, "Okay, let's analyze this. Who drew first blood? They did. Anywhere in the Bible does it say 'give up your daughters and allow them to become whores as part of your taxes'? What lawful and legal authority does this warlord have to rule over you?"

Philip understood, when it was put that way, "I understand. They did draw first blood, as well as stealing from us and abusing our daughters."

"Exactly. This was clearly self-defense. You have the moral high ground. And if you look it up in the Bible, what do they say about thieves?"

Philip thought for a moment and said, "I don't remember exactly what it says, but it's something like 'if thieves enter your house at night, they should be there in the morning'."

Joe smiled and added, "Right. Now why would a thief still be there in the morning? Because you defended your family and the thief would be dead, therefore he would still be there in the morning."

"I understand what you're saying, but I still don't feel right."

"Philip, you have to remember that you're an American. This country was born out of blood. Force and coercion is not rule of law. It's not the color of law; therefore, everything they were doing was immoral, unjust and reprehensible. If you are really religious, I suggest you pray about it. You'll find the answer you're looking for. I think every man has to come to peace with it in their own way."

Philip nodded and seemed in quiet reflection of Joe's words.

"Remember, I did warn you that once this started, there's no turning back. If this warlord's truly a millionaire, that means he's not stupid. He will assume his patrol got taken out. He just doesn't know if it was from you, that he considers peasants, or if there's a new force in the area. Either way, I fully expect them to retaliate in some fashion, because he will assume somebody knows the truth. The only question that remains is how long before he reacts and what form will that action take?

Chapter 15

The Farm Visit

> "All labor that uplifts humanity has dignity and importance and should be undertaken with painstaking excellence."
>
> ~Martin Luther King, Jr.

Preston, Amy, and Michael rode their bikes down to Fred's house. He had a really nice dairy farm, with a nice house and a modern insulated metal barn. He had pastureland for the cows, plus a huge area for growing crops.

Fred said, "Amy, why don't you go inside? My wife and daughter would love to meet you. I'll take these two around and teach them the ropes. You can put your bikes over here," as he pointed to a spot next to the barn.

Fred turned to Michael with a smile on his face and said, "I've got a horse for you to ride. Would you like that?"

Michael grinned like he was in a candy store. "Oh yes sir, I sure would. Thank you."

"I have a job for you, too. I'd like you to ride the fence. Do you know what that means?"

Michael had a confused look and said, "Is that like riding on the fence?"

Both men burst out laughing. Fred said, "No, son. What it means is you ride the horse along the fence to see if there are any breaks in the fence. There's a scabbard on the side of your saddle, for your rifle. Your job as a ranch hand is to shoot any coyotes, wolves, dogs, foxes, or any other predator that could hurt our cows or chickens. Think you can handle that?"

Michael grinned from ear to ear and said, "Yes sir, I would love to do that."

"Okay, here's your horse. Her name is Star, because she was my star quarter horse in her time. She's an old mare now, but she's in good shape and very friendly to first-time riders. I want you to go through the gate and work your way around the whole 80 acres. That means the section where the food crops are. Go out the gate on the far corner and make sure you close it behind you. Check all the fences where the cows are. Can you do that for me?"

"Yes sir," Michael said, as he was helped up onto the horse. Michael carefully put his rifle into the scabbard and headed for the first gate.

Preston asked Fred if it was safe for a boy Michael's age to ride out alone. Fred assured him that his ranch hands were out in the fields and would keep an eye on him. If there was any trouble, they would be there in a matter of minutes. Preston breathed a sigh of relief.

Fred motioned for Preston to follow him and said, "Let me show you around." Fred led him into the barn and showed him the milk stalls. "We're running 20 head of milk cows and have one bull. We get right around 20 gallons of milk a day. The heavy cream is separated and we make butter out of that." He led them through a door to a side section and took him to the chicken pen. "We have about 50 chickens. They provide us with eggs and meat." He pointed to the field out back. "We plant extra corn for animal feed and also soybeans because of the high protein count."

Preston asked, "How many people does your farm support?"

"Well, aside from my family and hands, we support many people. We're part of a larger community. We either trade or barter for the things we don't produce ourselves. There are other farms that produce things we don't produce. One is a pig farm, with a smokehouse. They produce the ham, bacon and pork chops. Another specializes in honey crisp apples. If you're not familiar with them, they're a hybrid apple. I believe they were developed by the University of Minnesota and are one of the best tasting apples around. They can withstand the harsh cold weather of northern Minnesota. That farm also keeps bees to pollinate their crops, so they trade honey, too."

They walked around to the back of the barn and Fred showed him his collection. "I collected old farm equipment for years. You see that," pointing to a machine, "that's an early 1900s hay cutter. Without that, it would be very hard to get our winter hay in for the cows. Over there," pointing now to the wagon with some type of disc on the back, "do you know what that is?"

Preston looked at him like he was crazy. "Of course I do. It's a wagon."

Fred burst out laughing. "Well, you're right, it is a wagon, but it's an early 1900s manure spreader. That's how we fertilize the fields." He then pointed to a plow and said, "And, of course, we have horse-drawn plows to till the fields."

Preston told Fred how impressed he was with all of it and asked, "How do you get water for the cows?"

Fred just pointed to a windmill standing out in the field. "That, my friend, is how the ranchers and farmers got their water before electricity."

"What, that powers an electric pump?" Preston asked.

Fred laughed, "No, it's on a cam and, as the wind turns the windmill, it works the pump up and down to pump the water into that tank."

"What do you do in the winter?"

Fred said, "We teach the cows how to eat snow and there's no shortage of snow around these parts," as he chuckled.

"We also have a blacksmith, a very talented one I might add. He can make just about anything you need and is indispensable at keeping all this equipment up and running."

"Tell me how you guys all came together and formed this community," Preston asked.

"Well, after things ended, we went through a pretty tough winter. People understood that we must come together if we wanted to survive. It's kind of like a tribe, but not like that hippie commune nonsense. It's more like the Amish, where we work together for the benefit of all."

Preston had to ask, "Have you had any problem with the Rainbow Warriors?"

"None. About 50 miles east of here, there were some coming, but they were persuaded to turn around and go back to Green Bay. We haven't heard of any trouble from them since. Generally, all we had to do was clean out the dog packs; the small gangs and other assorted lowlifes. When we came together as a community, those who were prepared to work and earn their keep found various spots to work. We even have a 78-year-old lady that still earns her keep by doing all the sewing. It's a simple concept and everybody works. We also have an electrical engineer who is trying to get five monster electric-producing windmills up and running. He has two former linesmen that think they might be able to get them up and running on a small grid. That would provide the hundred households that we have with electricity."

Preston smiled, "That's very impressive. Do you really think they'll be able to repair those windmills? What about the months when the wind isn't blowing?"

"He tells us that he's got a real good chance to get them up and running. They were enclosed in steel and grounded and he's taking what parts he needs from other windmills, ones that were down for a repair when the EMP hit. Winds coming off Lake Superior should give us electricity for at least eight months out of the year. Granted, it's not perfect, but we should be able to at least enjoy lights and electricity in the winter months."

"That's great. So how do we fit in?"

"You are in great shape and, with your military background, we definitely want you for patrols. We need people for all kinds of work. As long as you're willing to work, you and the family are more than welcome here."

"Here? You mean move into the farm with you?" Preston asked.

"No. You don't understand. You can stay where you are, or you can go on patrol tomorrow and see if you can find a nicer, vacant place that would be on the grid when the power is turned on. That's up to you."

"We thank you. Of course we will jump right in and help.

You've already put Michael to work," he said with a laugh. "I know we need to rebuild, so what would you like me to do first?"

Fred smiled as he handed Preston a hoe and then grabbed one for himself. "There's no shortage of weeds." They spent the rest of the morning going through the cornrows, hoeing weeds. Just before they broke for lunch, Preston looked around and thought that this was really good. For the first time since the end of the world happened, he felt uplifted and had a sense of community. It was a smart move coming up here. He would have to talk it over with Amy and Michael and decide if they should look for a better house, or stay in the camp. Decisions, Decisions.

Amy fit right in and became friends with Fred's wife, Molly, like they had known each other for years. Today they were canning blackberry jam. Amy asked, "How many lids do you have and what will you do when they are used up?"

Molly laughed, "Well, I've been kind of frugal my whole life and I just hated the thought of buying canning lids every year, so thanks to the wonders of the Internet, I was able to find reusable canning lids. They were really hard to find and just one small company made them. I believe they were out of Denver, Colorado somewhere. I think their name was Reusable Canning Lids LLC. We've never been really well off as farmers and we've had good years, along with some bad years. So anyway, I would try to help save money everywhere I could and it really helped us survive."

Amy said, "So really, the end of the world didn't change your life much."

Molly responded, "But I do miss going to the store and just grabbing what we need. Canning salt for pickling is the only thing that I believe we'll run out of and I haven't been able to come up with a substitute for it yet."

Amy said, "Well, I guess we'll just have to get used to life without salt. And besides, it will probably help us keep our girly figures," she laughed.

"Yes, but our bodies need salt."

Amy responded, "That's true, but how did the Indians survive all those thousands of years without salt? It must come naturally in the foods and we just don't taste it."

Changing the subject, Molly asked, "Are you folks going to stay around? We'd sure like to have you in our community."

Amy replied, "I guess that's going to be up to Preston. He has kept us alive this far, so I will abide by his wishes, but I do hope we can stay."

Molly was a little hesitant when she asked, "Tell me about your son, Michael. You look a little young to have a son that old, if you don't mind me saying."

Amy laughed, "Well, technically, he's not my son. I've never had any children myself. It's a long story but, in a nutshell, his mother and he were traveling through our area and, unfortunately, she was killed. Michael was left an orphan, so we sort of adopted him and he's been with us ever since."

Molly said, "Oh my, that's horrible. So Preston's not his real father?"

"No. Preston and I got together a few days after the lights went out," she laughed, remembering Sharon. "Preston was with this super skinny model type and I lived in the apartment across the hall from him. The little "Princess" could not come to terms with what happened and flipped out. Preston did everything in the world to look out for her, trying to save her. We planned on riding bikes to his friends' place, Joe and Jane. That night Sharon sneaked out of the apartment and left. To this day we don't know what happened to her. She was being totally unreasonable. Anyways, that's how Preston and I got together, because it was the end of the world. I guess it's not the most romantic story out there, is it?"

Molly laughed, "I don't know. It does have a romantic tone to it. Big strapping guy saves damsel in distress."

Amy, in her own defense, said, "Well, I'm not exactly helpless, but I sure am glad I met Preston. By the way, is there a preacher around? Preston and I would like to get officially married. We had planned to do it during the fall harvest, before our place was wiped out and all our friends killed." Her eyes teared up, remembering the battle scene. She turned away and Molly walked over to give her a hug.

"We've all lost dear and good friends during these trying times."

Amy gathered herself together. "I'm sorry. I didn't mean to break down; it's just been a long time since I had another woman to talk to."

"That's all right. Come on, we have more work to do. Those blackberries aren't going to turn into delicious jam all by themselves."

After giving it some thought, Molly said, "There is a preacher over in the next county. Maybe we could get him to come over and marry you two."

Amy was beaming and in quiet thought about having a ceremony.

For lunch, they made peanut butter and blackberry jam sandwiches. Before the EMP, Molly had bought dehydrated peanut butter on a whim. It was another of Molly's ways to try and save money. With food prices constantly rising, she thought storing a case of number ten cans of it just made good practical sense.

Michael had safely returned from riding the fence, reporting no damage and no predators. After he groomed the horse and put her out in the pasture, he helped Fred and Preston weed the rows, until the women called them in for lunch.

At lunch, all Michael could talk about was getting a horse of his own. He was so excited about his ride that the others could barely get a word in edgewise.

After lunch, they all went back to work. When the day was finished and the goodbyes said, they headed home with fresh butter and eggs.

In the morning Preston rode out to the main road to join the men patrolling the area.

The man in charge was about 5'9," 200 pounds and had a full beard. As Preston got off his bike the man said, "You can leave your bike here; we brought an extra horse for you. You do know how to ride, don't you?"

Preston laughed, "No, not really."

"Well, there's no time like the present. You'll get the hang of it."

After Preston got mounted, they rode off and the man introduced himself as Scott. He stopped and turned his horse around and rattled off a bunch of names, introducing everybody. Preston thought, *Maybe in a COUPLE of weeks, I might have all their names down.*

"Our job is to keep the riffraff out. We don't interrupt people when they're working, unless, of course, they're offering us something to drink or eat. We try not to impose on people. We pack our own lunch. We've not had any real problems in this area. We'd heard about that gang down where we helped you out, but there's nothing coming through our area. After that first winter, those who weren't prepared perished. What we are facing when strangers do come through are more vicious and well-organized gangs. They've already seen the blood and the guts. They're tough, hard-working units, but even those we haven't seen since June, I believe."

Preston nodded and said, "How often do you guys patrol?"

"Every other day, but we have been talking about moving to every three days. I believe we'll have to go down and clean out the rest of those men that took your wife, but, other than that, I think we will be able to concentrate more on rebuilding our community."

Preston said, "I think we should stick with every other day, at least for this year. We're spread pretty far apart and it would be easy for a small gang to come in and take one homestead at a time. There would be no time to call out any extra support, at least until this year is over. After this coming winter, we should be able to go to patrols once every 3 days."

Scott looked at Preston and thought for a minute. "You make a good point. I, for one, will feel a lot better once that gang is cleaned out."

They patrolled more or less in a square and, if they didn't see anybody around a homestead, they would ride up to the house until somebody let them know everything was okay. It was just a good neighbor policy.

They stopped by a pond to have lunch, letting their horses drink and graze in the lush grass near the water. The talk among the men was mostly about hope that the electricity got turned back on and girlfriends or wife problems. It might be the end of the world, but life keeps turning as normal in so many aspects. After lunch, as they were finishing the patrol, they ran into two lone men pushing a shopping cart. They rode up, surrounding them, with their rifles drawn. It was clear they had been on the road for a long time. They looked homeless and dirty, with filthy, torn clothes. One had a rifle slung on his back and the other had a double barrel shotgun lying on top of the shopping cart.

Scott demanded, "What are you two doing in this area?"

"We're just traveling through. We mean you no harm. Please don't rob us; these are all the supplies that we have."

Scott said, "We aren't bandits and won't hurt you unless you give us cause. Where are you heading?"

"We're coming from Duluth. Those crazy Rainbow Warriors took over the whole city. We swung this way to avoid them and then we planned on heading south."

"We'll escort you through, but give us your weapons until we're clear of the area. And understand that you are to keep going and never come back. Do you understand?"

"Kind of harsh, don't you think? We haven't caused you any trouble and we haven't harmed a soul. We're just traveling through. And why do you want our weapons? We don't give them up to nobody."

Scott responded, "We only want to hold on to your weapons for our own safety. We'll give them back when we are out of the area. If you cooperate, then there won't be any problems."

The man looked frightened and asked, "Do you guys have any food that you can spare? We don't have much."

"Sorry, we have none to spare, but will escort you through the area so no harm will come to you." He then assigned four men escort duty. The men turned over their guns and the rest of the patrol turned around to backtrack, making sure that these two had caused no harm to anyone in their community. It was better to be safe than sorry.

Preston asked, "Why didn't you talk to him more? They might have valuable skills that the community could use."

Scott responded, "That may be true, but we have standards. Those two were not keeping proper hygiene. It's the end of the world and the best they can come up with is a shopping cart? Don't you think somebody that was smart enough to have valuable skills would have found a better way to travel?"

"Good point. So why did you allow us in?"

"Because you were clean and you obviously had the skills to rescue your wife. You knew the area and you had hidden food. All moves of a smart and capable person."

"How did you know about the food?"

Scott smiled and said, "That was just a guess, but we figured a man like you wouldn't risk traveling with his family unless he had a place in mind with supplies already stashed."

Preston nodded. He was impressed with Scott's deductive reasoning and how he was able to size up people and the situation.

The patrol backtracked, stopping at different houses and farmsteads, making sure all the people were okay. Everyone reported the same thing: that the two didn't stop and were just traveling through.

Once they were sure the two guys hadn't caused any problems in the community, Scott dismissed the rest of the men.

He asked Preston to ride with him, saying, "I know of a house I think you might be very interested in. It's a little off the beaten trail but, once we get power on, it would be perfect for you and your family. It has a well and a garden area, with a few fruit trees. It's not perfect by any means, but it should work out well for you."

They rode up to a nice three-bedroom ranch style house that was a couple 0f miles from the main highway. The main advantage was that it had a rocket stove. Rocket stoves were invented in the 1980s for use in the Third World countries and were simple, highly efficient designs that create a virtually smokeless fire.

The house was well built for the area, with six-inch walls and new insulation sprayed into them, making a total barrier. There were highly efficient three-pane windows and heavy insulation in the ceiling. The only disadvantage was that there was no way to get water without electricity.

Preston said "Did you ever watch that TV show, The Colony?"

Scott said, "I saw the one set in Louisiana. Those people would have starved to death if they hadn't sent in that recon Marine to help them out."

Preston shook his head and said, "No. I'm talking about the one they did in Los Angeles. They had a generator and were able to design a wood gasifier to use as fuel for the generator. What they didn't explain in the show was that the barrel they created the wood gas in needed to be piped so many feet over to the generator. Now the trick to this is to cool the wood gas to the right temperature in order for it to work. It's going take some playing around to get the correct distance and temperature, but once it's up and running it should run a generator and be a very good system to have."

Scott looked at him in amazement, "You know how to do that? Wow...it would be great if you could set all of us up like that."

"Well, I don't see why not. Fred said we have an electrical engineer, right? I heard that just about all of the farms have generators and it doesn't have to be anything special; I mean really, what do you truly need? Water to wash your clothes, a freezer to keep things frozen and a battery charger to charge batteries for running lights at night. I think this is very doable. Once we get the first one figured out, we should be able to duplicate it for everybody's place, but, and this is a very big but, I've never done it before and it's going to take some playing around to get everything correct."

Scott was very excited. "Really, if we can do this, it means we can take it to the next step. We can get some of the older tractors and convert them to run on wood gas. Heck, we could even rig up trucks to run on it. Oh my God, this would be great. D you know how much better all our lives would be?"

"Well, this is going to be a huge learning curve, but now we need to find all the supplies. We need some metal 55-gallon barrels, piping, generators for everybody, battery chargers and batteries, all kinds of pipe fittings, a gas and oxygen torch and the tools."

Scott was so excited as he said, "We'll figure it all out. Wow, I'm so glad you came up here."

"Hang on a minute, don't get all excited and tell everybody I can do this, until we get one up and running. It seemed to me, when I watched the show, that they had quite a problem getting everything set up just right for it to work."

That night, back at their place, Preston talked it over with Amy and Michael. Amy was very excited, saying, "Do you know how much better our life will be if you can do this magic trick?"

Preston laughed, "It's not a magic trick. It's science. I just hope we can run into somebody who has the actual book or plans on how to make one."

Michael had a big smile on his face. "You mean we'll be able to put meat and fish away without drying them? No more trying to make jerky taste good? No more dried fish? We can live like real people again?"

Preston laughed out loud, "Okay, okay. You two need to calm down. I only watched it on a TV show; that doesn't mean I can magically make one. I know it's possible, but we just need to get everybody together, put our heads together and make it work."

Michael asked, "Why did this all happen? I just don't understand."

Preston said, "Because we sat back for too long and allowed the control freaks to ruin America. Government was crushing small business."

Michael was confused, "What does that have to do with an EMP and whoever fired it?"

"Our government was warned and told it could happen, but they ignored it and took no preventative steps to save our electrical grid. We were due for some form of collapse, either the dollar going under, too many natural disasters, or an EMP taking America out. What we have as a result should teach the new generation the evils of big Government. For example, say you own a small ranch that you raise cattle on. Our government allowed the control freaks in the animal rights movement to set policy for people that owned private land."

"What?" Michael said, "What right do they have to tell someone how to use their land?"

"Exactly. That's what I'm talking about. See, you're smart and catching on. I read about different farmers and ranchers being taken to court for the Clean Water Act requirements. They went after ranchers, even when their property was about five miles from a stream, not hurting the stream one little bit. Lots of these regulations were based on Agenda 21."

"Agenda 21? What's that?"

"A power grab by the UN and their supporters. They were the control freaks. They wanted to transform America into a big National Park, where all the animals had more rights than people. They wanted about 90% of the land to be turned back over to the animals."

Michael asked, "Are they the Rainbow Warriors?"

"Maybe. It's all the same thinking. Animals have equal rights to people. Total insanity."

"Why didn't they want the cows drinking the water?"

"Because the cattle pooped in the water and they had some crazy theory that the feces in the water would hurt the native fish and animals."

Michael added, "Wait a minute...I learned in school that there used to be millions of buffalo. Did they hurt the water too?"

"Good question, Michael. You are smart for someone your age. Yes, there used to be 40-60 million buffalo, which is the best guess from the experts. And yes, they were leaving feces in the water too, and there are only about 31.5 million cows in America. It was all a lie to force ranchers out of business. They also blamed cows farting and belching, saying it was hurting the atmosphere. There is no end to what they came up with to pass their agendas."

"Why would the Government want to force people out of business?"

"You see, Michael, our government was slowly and quietly taken over from the inside. Some were like the Rainbow Warriors, psychopaths using the eco propaganda as an excuse to murder millions. Others were idealists that believed animals were more important than people. The rest were just control freaks that wanted power and everyone under their thumb."

"So, if I'm the future, what do I have to guard against?"

"We must teach everyone that people come first. Never allow the government to get too large. Allow the states to use their power to control themselves. All laws must be written for the common man to easily understand and we need to go back to an honest court system."

"Court system?"

"That's a long topic that we can save for another time."

Chapter 16

Retaliation

"The best fighter is never angry."

~Lao Tzu

The men raced after the wounded survivor of the battle. They occasionally caught glimpses of blood on the road. They knew he was wounded, but how badly? That was the big question preying on their minds. The thoroughbred horse was panicked and racing for his life. The smell of blood and screams of panic told him not to stop until he was safely back in his own barn. His rider was not giving him any commands, so he ran for safety; he ran from fear; he ran to survive.

The two men tracking him were never able to get closer than a mile from him. Their horses were no match for a thoroughbred, whose main purpose in life was to race. All they could report was that the man was leaned over in the saddle and the blood traces became more evident. When they were within a couple of miles of the millionaire's farmstead, they slowed down and started sneaking along the edge of the road. The wounded man made it to the farmstead. They had failed in their duties to stop him. Pulling out binoculars, they watched men race up to the wounded man.

That was all they needed to see, so they sneaked back until they were out of sight. They rode hard and fast, back to warn the others. They didn't catch up to Joe until they got to Phillip's homestead. Joe started barking commands, "We need two men up in that barn loft. Put some square bales of hay in front of you to help protect against bullets and open the door to make sure you have clean targets. Wait until we start shooting down here, before you open up. Do you understand?" The men nodded and raced off. "You two men, go gather everybody else and don't stop until you get back here. Make it quick! If the battle has already started, listen to me carefully, you'll sneak into a good covered position and together you open up on them, as a team. Do you understand?" The men both nodded at once. Joe said, "Good. Now get out of here."

He turned to Philip and said, "Get your house sealed up and have Mattie run food and water up to the men in the loft. Jacob, I want you to be our sniper. Get up in one of these trees, preferably a thick spruce tree. You'll need a good field of fire, giving yourself plenty of camouflage. You don't start shooting until the battle begins. Space your shots out so they can't zero in on where you are. Make sure you grab some jerky and a canteen of water to take with you." Jacob nodded and headed towards the house to get his ammo, jerky and a canteen.

There were 6 men, armed and ready for what might come, and they waited. Their minds were racing. Would they be facing 10 men, 20 men, or more? Joe was extremely worried that these men weren't really trained soldiers and didn't know how to fight. Were they confident in using an AR 15? Waiting for someone else to react and trying to plan for it is an impossible task. There are just too many variables.

The minutes ticked by and the tension built, as the anxiety mounted. Where were they? How long would it take for them to get there?

An hour later, the rest of the men arrived. Joe spaced them out, hidden in the woods, but still nothing.

Another hour went by and still nothing. Joe walked outside and up to the two scouts. "Get two fresh horses. We need recon to find out what's going on. Do not engage. As soon as you have any information, come back and report."

It was 2:34 in the afternoon and there was plenty of daylight left.

At the warlord's place, the guards saw the horse and wounded man coming. They opened the gate and allowed the horse in, which headed straight for the barn. The horse stopped in front of the barn and the man slid off, falling to the ground. The men started yelling for a medic and raced to the wounded man's side. He was unconscious, but still breathing. The warlord, unable to get any information, had a second patrol assembled and sent them out, with strict orders to find out what happened to the other men - by any means necessary.

The gloves were off. If these peasants wanted an uprising, they would have a war. He wanted to find out who the leader was and kill all that stood with him. The millionaire told his men before they left, that they were free to rape, murder and pillage the closest homestead to find out what was going on. He wanted a full report before dark.

The nearest homestead was the Johnson farm, which Mr. Johnson had inherited only a couple of years ago. Being so close to the warlord's property, the others didn't trust him. He had no idea what was going on.

Mrs. Johnson was a good-looking 36-year-old woman, with a 14-year-old daughter and a 12-year-old son. The troops raced into the yard and Mr. Johnson had no clue what was going on. He walked out of the barn as he heard the horses, wiping his hands on a rag. As he looked up, 2 men raced towards him, shooting him in the chest. These men were mercenaries with no moral compass and, once off their leash of control, they lost their humanity. Several of the men went into the house and they all took turns raping the mother and fourteen-year-old daughter. Afterwards, they dragged them out into the yard naked. Through her bruised face and tears, she saw her husband lying in a pool of blood. They kept demanding to know who was in charge and who had killed their men?

Neither she nor her daughter could answer their questions. They threatened to burn her house to the ground if she didn't answer. She begged and she pleaded, telling them repeatedly that she had no idea what they were talking about. Naked, bruised and beaten, her whole world had just been destroyed and now they were going to take her beloved house. She begged over and over again for them to not burn her house. The man in charge told her, as her house was set aflame, "Go to your friends. Tell them what happened here and find out who killed our men. Tell them that if we don't have an answer by tonight, this is what will happen to the rest of them." Her twelve-year-old son had been hiding inside and came running out when the flames began engulfing the house. He made it as far as the front steps before the man shot him.

The merc and his men herded the naked women down the road. They stopped about a half mile from the next farm and told them, "You tell them we're coming. Tell them what happened to you and your farm. Warn them - this is what happens to peasants who dare challenge us." The men then turned and rode back to the warlord's place. They were confident that they would have an answer by nightfall. They were convinced that the "*sheep*" would start bleating and spill the beans.

The warlord wondered what happened to his other nine men and wondered if there was a new threat moving into the area. If so, what they just did could very well backfire on them. He dismissed that, having no signs or rumors of any large group in the area. It had to just be these uppity sheep. It had to be, he kept telling himself.

The scouts found the mother and daughter and quickly covered the women with their coats, taking them back to Phillip's homestead.

News of what had happened spread quickly. Joe angrily said, "Gather every man, boy and woman that's willing to fight and bring them all here. That warlord wanted an answer by tonight. By God, we will give him our answer with hot lead." Jane reminded Joe to calm down and not let his anger do his thinking. He took a deep breath and said, "You're right. I need to put together a plan that will keep all of our people safe."

By darkness, the army of people they had gathered was half a mile from the warlord's farmstead. They were 50 strong, each with righteous anger seething inside them.

Joe gathered the people and said, "The plan is simple and this will be our ambush zone. As they come down this little dip, they won't be able to see the rope and we'll do the exact same thing as before. We use bait to race through this area and then we yank the rope up and slaughter all of them, to the last man."

Philip said, "You really think this is going to work twice?"

Joe responded, "We don't know what they know and don't know right now, but they're very arrogant and I believe we've got a good chance. You two scouts sneak down and tie your horses a couple hundred yards from the front gate. Sneak down, try to take out two of the guards and then get to your horses, ride off and lead them back here. Fire about 10 rounds each. That should get everyone's attention."

"I know it's night and you might not be able to use your sights very well. Your job is not to necessarily kill them. If you can hit them, great, but your job is to lure them to us."

This time they didn't have the luxury of positioning vehicles to narrow the roadway, but, if the rope was staked off and held in place by logs, they probably wouldn't see it until it was too late. There was only one way to find out if they were stupid enough to do it again . . . try it and hope for the best. He told everybody, "We'll wait until they hit the rope and, in the darkness and confusion, the guns won't be very beneficial to them, so we'll rise up out of the ditch and charge in force. We don't stop until all of them are dead."

Two men sneaked up to within about 50 yards of the guardhouse and each fired 10 rounds, then took off running. No one was hit and the returned fire was not very accurate, so they easily made it back to their horses unscathed. They raced off down the road, but there was no pursuit. They watched; they waited - nothing. Joe thought the wounded man must've warned them about the ambush, or they were just being extra cautious.

He found one of his men that had been on the warlord's property before and had him explain the layout of the land and where he believed the troops were. He could send in a small recon crew to set everything they could on fire, or they could try to take it by force, but they were still desperately outgunned. If the mercs were halfway proficient, they wouldn't stand a chance. They still had 20 trained and fully armed men in fortified positions. He had to think and be smart, not letting his anger and emotions cloud his judgment.

He pulled Philip aside. "We need to pick the battleground and I'm thinking we should let them come to us. We don't do anything more tonight and chances are they'll come out in the morning. We just don't know what they're going to do and all we can do is guess. It's too dangerous for us to try to make a full raid on the homestead, especially in the dark. Everybody's mad and not thinking clearly. We could get cut to ribbons if we try it. I have an idea that we have enough manpower and horsepower for here, so let's block up this road and give us a fortified position to fight behind, take away their advantage and make them come to us."

Philip agreed, and they made up teams of men to make the blockade.

They used the horses to pull abandoned vehicles to the area, blocking the whole road. They then took logs and filled up the empty spaces between the vehicles, allowing more protection from bullets. They even positioned logs underneath the vehicles and did everything they could to prevent anybody from getting hit.

Now they waited for daybreak. Joe had most of the people sleep and he sent others back for food and water. All they could do was wait. He paced back and forth. He made sure that everybody that had military training was armed with an AR-15 and had plenty of ammo.

Jane touched Joe's shoulder and said, "You really should get some sleep. Nothing is going to happen until daybreak. You're tired and not thinking clearly, so go get some sleep."

Joe had been running on adrenaline and anger, but knew he needed to be fresh for battle. "You're right. I think they're waiting for us to try an attack."

He climbed into the back of a truck and crawled into a sleeping bag. Worn out from the exhaustion of the day's events, he fell into a deep sleep.

Jane woke him up as it was getting light and they could see something going on. He got up and went to the barricades. Grabbing a cup of coffee, he asked Philip, "What's going on?"

Philip said that it appeared they were getting ready for something, as there was a lot of movement at their place.

The millionaire came out, riding his prized horse, a thoroughbred that had once raced in the Kentucky Derby. He was carrying a pole with a white flag attached. He rode up to within 50 yards of the barricade and stopped.

Looking around, he recognized most of the people. He was right; it was just a peasant uprising and not some unknown new force taking control of the area. He breathed a sigh of relief. His mercs would quickly take care of this rabble.

He looked at the people and said, "My name is Brad Bowerman. You people know me and know that you've had a good thing going here. There have been no raids on your farms since I took control. We have provided you with safety and looked out for you and this is how you repay me?"

Joe replied, "No one appointed you king of the land and these people are done with you robbing their sons and daughters of their youth and innocence. You're finished taxing and stealing from them because you're too lazy to do your own work. Might doesn't make right. We will give you the option to surrender and leave this county, or face the consequences."

Brad laughed, "Who are you, little man, to demand anything of me?"

Ignoring Joe, he looked at everyone else and said, "The rest of you have a choice. You can tell this newcomer to get out of our county and then all will be forgiven. You will turn over the rifles that you stole from my men and then things will go back to normal. If you choose to ignore me and stay with this rabble," pointing to Joe, "then I'll be forced to teach you a very vicious lesson. My men, who will have no problem whatsoever robbing, raping and pillaging your little homesteads, outgun you. If you truly want this lesson to be taught to you, they will be more than willing to do it. Now, for the last time, leave your weapons here and return to your homesteads and all will be forgiven."

Joe, who was feeling the tension and knew some of them might be willing to give up, laughed loudly, saying, "Hey, Mr. Silver Spoon brat, if you haven't noticed, you are 10 short. We aim to clean you out. We will kill your mercenaries to the last man, including you. This is YOUR last chance to surrender, disband your mercs and leave this county forever."

Brad laughed back at him saying, "You and your rabble of farmers with pitchforks are going to take on my highly-trained mercs? I've given you my terms and you will regret this every day if you do not disband right now." With that, he turned around and rode off.

Everyone surrounded Joe, asking what they should do. Someone said, "He did say all will be forgiven and we can all go back to how it had been. Maybe we should take him up on his offer?" Another said, "No, we should stand and fight. We need this to end now."

Joe looked at everybody with a frown on his face. "I told you from the beginning this was not a game. Once we started, we had to finish. Do you honestly believe that all will be forgiven? Once he disarms you, he will, and trust me on this, make you regret you ever stood up to him. He will break you down until you have no hope left. Is that the world you want to leave for your sons and daughters? You are no different than slaves working on a plantation. The master works your sons to death in the fields and uses your daughters as whores. If that's the way you wish to live, then we will leave right now."

Philip and Jacob spoke up first; "We stand with you Joe - to the end." Several others shouted in agreement.

"If you all feel that way, I want everybody to get back in their positions. I believe that he's going to try and attack. He thinks his highly-trained mercs can take all of us out."

Everybody returned to their positions and waited. They didn't have long to wait. Eight of the community's daughters, ages 15 to 18, all stripped naked, were marched out with a merc standing behind each one, pointing the muzzles of their rifles against the backs of their heads. Behind them were 12 armed men on horses. They marched the girls towards the barricade. The girls were shaking in fear and crying, with tears streaming down their faces.

Joe and the crowd were almost in shock and it felt like a punch in the stomach. Everybody was looking at Joe and asking what they should do.

Joe raised his voice and said, "I told you that freedom isn't free, and it comes at the price of blood. There are your friends and daughters, so you must decide for yourselves. If we flee, they will cut us to ribbons. This is our chance to end this once and for all. If you agree to do it, we have to concentrate our firepower on the mercs behind the women. We do not stop until every one of them is dead."

There was hesitation in the crowd and Philip said, with a rage seething from his voice, "One of them is my daughter, Mary, and I say we fight, and end this at once, today, right now." Others agreed, and Joe sent a message to the men that were hidden in the forest with their bows and crossbows.

Once they got into range, their job was to first shoot the mercs behind the women and then concentrate their firepower on the men on horseback, shooting the horses out from under them. Joe was aware that only seventeen of the men had been trained and had experienced combat before, but he hoped that anger and adrenaline would help the others contend with what was about to happen. It was going to be a bloody tragedy, no matter what they did now. There was no way to save all the girls. He shared a look of understanding with Jane. She also knew what was about to happen.

"Nobody fires until I fire the first shot. Let them get close and think they have the advantage."

Once the mercs had marched the girls to within 100 yards of the barricade, one of the girls started pleading and begging. "Please, Daddy, drop your guns and go home. He will forgive you. Don't let them kill me."

Joe whispered to Jane, "Once the shooting starts, you take your 22-250 and make a head shot on Brad. No matter what happens, that arrogant SOB will never see the light of day again."

Jane replied, "My pleasure."

The closer they got, the more intense the pleading from the girls became. They were shaking in fear and it was heart wrenching.

Joe picked the biggest, mean looking merc standing behind one of the innocent girls. He shot him in the head and the battle had begun. There was no turning back now. Everyone else opened up, but before all the mercs were killed, two of the girls were shot in the back of the head. Some of the girls, when they realized no one was behind them, ran for the barricades, while the others just stood in shock, screaming in fear.

Jane dropped the man that had caused all of this, with her first shot. He had a look of amazement on his face, as his eyes glazed over and he fell from his horse. The millionaire didn't look so big and mighty now.

She looked for new targets. Two more of the young innocent girls were shot down by the mercs on the horses. She fired and dropped one of them and then the arrows started flying out of the woods. Men charged forward with axes, spears and pitchforks. Everyone opened up on the enemy and the blood, screams and panic made it a true battlefield.

Four girls reached safety and were pushed down behind the barricades.

Five of the remaining mercs broke off and turned tail, running back towards the farm. The rest of them had been cut to ribbons. Joe calmly walked up, pulled a pistol from one of the dead mercs' hand, a .40 caliber Smith & Wesson, and then calmly and methodically walked to each merc and put a bullet in their heads.

Joe gathered the men and said, "It's time to finish this. We take Brad's homestead now. We can't allow any of these animals to survive."

He sent two men on horses to collect the other horses. He wanted some of his men on horseback. He ordered the other men, that didn't have firearms, to pick up the weapons and ammunition.

They marched forward like a mob. In a lot of ways they were an uncontrolled mob. After almost one year of being controlled and told what to do, they wouldn't take it anymore. After all the abuses they had suffered, it was payback time.

They surged forward through the gates, looking for targets, but found none. They saw the five remaining mercs hightailing it out the back and across the field. The crowd surged forward and charged towards them. Several men on horseback chased after the mercs. Joe had lost control of them, but knew they needed this, so he didn't try to stop them. They were now a mob, hell bent on revenge. They stormed the merc barracks, grabbing any useful gear, and then set it ablaze.

Joe had to stop them from burning down the main mansion. There was food, ammunition, medical supplies and much-needed items for all of them. He could not allow it to all be burned to the ground.

One of the fathers, filled with rage and anger, marched straight up to Joe and said, "It wasn't your daughter who just died, it was mine, and I'm going to burn this evil place right to the ground."

Joe stood taller than the man and looked him in the eye, "After we remove everything that's useful, you can burn it to the ground, but not until then. Do you understand?"

The man threw down his gun and took a swing at Joe. Joe back stepped, but the blow still connected to his jaw, hitting with a glancing blow. He knew the man was emotionally out of his mind and he didn't want to hurt him. He dropped his rifle and ducked down, giving him his best uppercut. He heard the solid slam of the bottom jaw smashing in to the top jaw. The man fell back, surprised at how quickly Joe had recovered. Joe stepped in again and, with one more blow to the nose, knocked the man to the ground. Blood spurted out and he yelled at Joe, "You have no right."

The others had surrounded them, like a high school fight. Joe looked at Philip and Jacob saying, "Take your man for a walk and let him cool off, and then take him to his daughter's body so he can show her proper respect."

He turned to the others and said, "The rest of you men find a wagon. We need to load up the supplies and split them with everybody who fought." He had managed to defuse the situation.

The barracks was ablaze and the flames danced in the sky as pieces of ash floated in the air. The men were calming down and started to think rationally again. He heard the man he had hit wailing in the background, "She was my only daughter. She was my Princess and now she's dead because of him. I should've killed him."

As Joe walked into the house, he was amazed at the marble floor and double half-rounded staircase leading upstairs. He started checking rooms and finally found what he was looking for - the Armory. The only problem was that it was a large, thick, metal door. This appeared to be the entrance into a room. It was one of those old-style metal doors, with a combination lock and a big silver metal handle on front that turned to unlock the door.

He pulled on the door, hoping it would still be unlocked, but was quickly disappointed to learn that it was still locked. It was going to be a challenge to get into the armory.

Chapter 17

The Gasifier

> "Great spirits have always encountered violent opposition from mediocre minds."

The next morning, as they were eating breakfast, they heard the patrol riding into their yard. Preston glanced out and recognized the men. He stepped out onto the porch and asked, "How can I help you guys?"

Scott said, "The guys with the wagon are going to collect your winter firewood, while you and I are going to go meet Brett Wiserman, the electrical engineer. You two are going to come up with a solution to get the gas generators working for all of us. That is, if you don't mind."

Overhearing Scott's comments, Amy stepped out on the porch and said, "You guys are wonderful thank you." She gave Preston a little push and said, "Don't just stand there Preston, get ready and go get us some electricity."

Preston turned to her with a smile and said, "You know what, you are starting a sound like a nagging wife and we're not even married yet. If you keep this up girl...never mind."

Amy had a hurt look on her face, but soon smiled and both of them laughed.

He turned back to Scott and said, "All right guys, hang on a second, let me get my stuff, and then we can go meet Brett."

He opened the door and called out to Michael. "Can you help these men collect the firewood and show him where and how we want it stacked around the cabin?"

Scott and Preston headed for Brett's place. Scott said, "You know, everybody's talking about you and can't wait to get electricity again."

Preston wrinkled his brow and said, "I wish you hadn't told everybody. I only saw it on a TV show and I'm not sure I can build it. There's still a big learning curve to getting this just right and working."

Scott replied, "Sure, but you'll figure it out. We all have faith in you."

They rode for a couple of hours and finally pulled up to Brett's house. It was a nice looking, single level, ranch-style house.

Scott said, "I should warn you, Brett is little different. He's one of those guys with a super high IQ and sometimes has trouble communicating with people. I hope you can work with him."

Preston smiled. "I'll do my best."

They walked up and knocked on the door. A heavyset man answered. After opening the door, he simply stared at them. He had glasses and was balding. At first glance, he reminded Preston of the professor from Back to the Future, but heavier.

Preston was waiting for him to say, "Marty, we only have to get 1.21 gigawatts," or something along those lines.

Scott introduced Preston to him. Preston smiled and stuck his hand out in the customary fashion. Brett just stared at him, evidently not accustomed to greeting people; or maybe he was germaphobic.

To ease the apparent tension, Scott quickly said, "Brett, this fellow says there's a way to rig up generators to run on wood gas. We were wondering if you had any information, or if you could help him."

Brett seemed to come out of his trance and said, "Gentlemen, gentlemen, I'm sorry, please come in."

They entered and followed Brett into the kitchen. The table was covered with electronic parts. There was a soldering gun plugged into an inverter, wired to a battery, which in turn was rigged up to a bicycle driven alternator.

Brett said, "Don't mind the mess. I've been working for weeks, robbing components to get a switchboard operational for the windmills. As for your gasifier, I have the answer in my library."

"The answer? Sorry, but you lost me." Scott said. "What's in your library?"

"I have the FEMA handbook on how wood gasification works and how to use it to run cars, tractors, and generators." He looked at Preston and smiled, "Where were you last winter when we really needed you? Oh my God, this could be so easy. Why didn't I think of this before? All we need are barrels, piping and generators." He rushed off and said, "Follow me, gentlemen."

They followed him into what used to be a bedroom, but was now a complete library, with a desk in the middle, covered with papers and open books.

Brett started shuffling through the books and was thinking aloud, "Now I just have to remember what binder I put that printout of the PDF in."

One whole bookcase was dedicated just to binders. There was a slip of paper, listing all of the books and which binders they were in.

"You see gentlemen, I never trusted important documents to computer hard drives or disks. I always printed everything out and put it into my binders." As he continued to look through the binders, he said, "I was so stuck trying to figure out how to make the windmills work, because they would produce an incredible amount of electricity, that I spent months and months trying to get at least one up and working. This whole time we could have been rigging tractors, trucks and generators to wood gasifiers for everybody's houses."

He continued in sort of a mumble, his mind going a million miles a minute. He turned around, all excited, and looked at them. "Now, from what I can remember, charcoal works better than wood. Of course you can use wood, but it needs to be chips. You understand it's not like burning in a wood stove, it's different." He turned back to the bookshelf, scanning quickly and still mumbling to himself.

Preston looked over at Scott with the 'I see what you mean' look. Scott smiled and shrugged.

He said, "Brett, are you sure you printed it out?"

Brett swung around, "Of course I printed it out. Do you think I would trust a computer, or my failing memory, to something this important? Do you gentleman understand pyrolysis? It means to break down a compound by heating it in an anaerobic atmosphere, thus producing a gas."

Preston said, "In layman's terms, please."

"We have to heat the wood, without combustion, which breaks down the compounds, releasing the wood gas. It's really not that complicated; it just sounds complex. It's really quite simple once it's set up. Wood gas was used during World War II to operate cars, althoughy they used charcoal instead of wood, so that they could skip the pyrolytic phase and minimize the size of the generator."

Preston looked at Scott and asked, "Is there a coal mine anywhere around here?"

"I have no idea," Scott replied.

Preston asked the Professor, "So if we could find coal, it would make the refining process easier. Is that what you're saying? How much coal do you think we would need, say, per household, or per year? A ton of coal, two tons of coal?"

The professor turned around from the bookcase and looked at Preston, "Well, I don't know for sure. It all depends on how much they run their generators per day. If we can rig up batteries, they would only have to run it 2 or 3 hours a day. That's just for generators. Now vehicles, that would be something totally different. Why, do you have an idea where we can get coal?"

Preston responded, "Well, this is a long shot, but I do know that the trains that traveled through this area in the fall carried large shipments of Wyoming coal. It was shipped back east and mixed with eastern coal to meet EPA standards for emissions. Now, I looked into this once and I'm just going by memory, of course, but it seems to me that each train car held like 30 tons. If we got lucky and one of those train shipments broke down close to here, we could be sitting on a year's supply of coal.

Brett said, "All right gentlemen, I'll find this book." Looking at Scott, he said, "You need to put together a scavenging team, send them out to collect barrels, piping, generators, battery chargers, any good batteries they can find and we'll need inverters too."

After a pause, Brett said, "Oh, I almost forgot, we'll need plenty of wire. Now get out of here while I look for that book. I'll write down a plan for home generators first." Then, turning toward Preston he said, "Why don't you and another team go and search the train tracks? If you could find coal, it would make my job that much easier. Good day, gentlemen." With that, he abruptly turned around and went searching for the book.

Preston looked at Scott and Scott nodded toward the door. They walked outside and climbed on their horses. Scott chuckled, "I told you he was a little different. I did warn you, but he's a super great guy when he gets on a project like this. It's best just to leave him alone to work on it."

Preston smiled, "Actually, I'm very grateful to him. Now the pressure is off of me and it's on him to make it work. He's one of those guys that are perfect for helping to rebuild society."

As they rode away Scott said, "Tomorrow, we will put together teams to look for the items we need. I'll be with the scavenging team assigned to find the materials and I will assign one man down with you, plus you can take Michael to look for the coal. The man I assign can bring you extra horses so you guys can search the train tracks. Sound good?"

"That sounds like a plan. You know, if it involves horses, Michael's going to love it. Thank you for the use of them."

Scott smiled, "Heck, you're only a kid once. It will be good for him to get out in the woods." He stopped his horse and pulled out a map. Pointing to a spot, he said, "Just south of here is the main railroad tracks. If you remember, we crossed them a couple of miles from where we rescued you guys. I would say, as a suggestion, you go down and ride west for four hours the first day and then turn around and come back. If you haven't found any coal, then spend the next day going east."

"That sounds like a really good plan. Thank you. I was wondering how the horses are on train tracks."

"We don't ride them on the tracks; ride beside them, on the shoulder."

The next morning, Preston and Michael were up early and ready to go. A man rode in with two saddled horses behind him. They went out and greeted him.

The man's name was Barry and he seemed like a user-friendly kind of young man. He was about 28, had a young wife and two children. He liked Michael and they instantly hit it off. The road down to the railroad tracks seemed to take forever, as it was a hot July day, even for northern Wisconsin.

After arriving at the railroad tracks, they rode down the shoulder of them without a problem, but, when they had to cross a bridge, it became a problem. The railroad bridges had steel pilings that the railroad beams sat on and you could see clear down to the stream. They had no choice but to go down and cross the creek or ravine bottom.

When it came to crossing a small river, Barry knew just how to do it. They carefully led the horses down and rode them across. They were slow moving streams and one side was shallow, so crossing them wasn't too bad.

The miles clicked by and there was nothing, just empty track for mile after mile.

When they came up to another stream at noon, they stopped for lunch. After they had eaten the sandwiches Amy had packed for them, Michael interrupted their conversation and said, "While you two old men are sitting around talking, can I go fishing?"

Preston looked up with a surprised look and said, "You brought the fishing equipment with you?"

Michael laughed, "What have you always taught me? Be prepared. I have my survival kit with me."

Preston laughed, "Okay, good job. You can fish for an hour. Barry and I will ride the tracks for another half hour, and then turn around and come back. When we return, you be ready to go, right?"

"Of course I'll be ready to go, with the whole stringer of fresh fish."

Barry laughed, "Pretty confident for such a young man, aren't you."

Michael looked up and said, "I sure am. I caught a 5-pound Pike all by myself," looking at Preston for confirmation, "didn't I, Preston?"

Preston nodded, "Yes, you sure did. You're a great fisherman. We'll see you in an hour, so stay out of trouble."

Barry and Preston mounted their horses and rode back up to the railroad tracks, continuing westward.

They returned an hour later and Michael was ready to go. He had one 12-inch smallmouth bass. He showed it to Barry and Preston, saying, "You should've seen the monster that got away," and he stretched out his hands about 2 feet wide, "it was the biggest bass ever seen in my life. He spit the hook out just when I reached down to grab him."

Barry laughed. "Here we go with the monster that got away. He was 9 feet long, right?"

Michael looked frustrated and said, "I'm serious. He was huge. A great big fat bass."

Preston chuckled. "I believe you, now come on. We have to get back and have a lot of ground to cover."

They arrived back at the cabin around six o'clock. Michael jumped off his horse, grabbed his rifle and, holding the fish right in front of him, raced toward the door.

Preston said, "Whoa there, son, aren't you forgetting something?"

Michael stopped on the porch, turned around with a quizzical look, and said, "What?"

"I think you should thank Barry for bringing you a horse to ride, don't you?"

Michael looked at Barry and said, "Sorry. Yes sir. Thank you for letting me ride your horse."

With that, he ran inside yelling for Amy. "Look what I got us. A fresh fish for dinner."

Preston asked Barry if he needed any help taking the horses back and then asked if he would like stay for dinner.

"Thank you, but no. The wife is waiting for me. I'll take care of the horses and see you in the morning." Preston handed him the reins to the two horses they had ridden.

"Okay, my friend. I'll see you in the morning." He grabbed his rifle and started walking toward the house.

Suddenly, he heard the loud crack of a rifle shot, followed by the smack of a bullet hitting flesh. He reacted from years of training, without even thinking. He flipped the safety off as he brought his rifle up to his shoulder and swung in the direction the sound had come from.

He saw 10 men on horseback bearing down on them. He shot the lead two horses that crumpled and fell, tossing their riders on the ground. He fired five more shots at the remaining riders and they broke off the attack, stopping their horses and running for cover. He ran over and helped Barry up. He supported him with his left arm while he fired one-handed, as they ran toward the door.

Bullets were flying and snapping all around him as they dove in the door. Amy was already armed and standing by the door. She quickly shut and locked the door.

Preston yelled out for Amy to patch Barry's wound and Michael to close the shutters. Like a well-oiled machine, they automatically went to work and the house was secured.

Amy was using Kotex maxi pads for a battle dressing, stopping the bleeding. She said, "He must've been turning on the horse because the bullet hit him in the left arm and exited the back, going clear through."

Earlier, Michael had followed Preston's direction and had the men stack the firewood all around the cabin. This created 16 inches of wood, giving them some bullet protection. It was stacked 4 feet high, so they just had to keep their heads down and let the bullets pass over them. The shooting was intense for a few minutes, breaking bottles, pictures and putting holes through walls and then silence.

They heard a voice call out. "We want the girl. There'll be no more bloodshed if you just give us the girl. She's my commodity. I own her."

Preston responded, "Like hell we will." He then told Barry that it was the guy that had kidnapped Amy.

"Look, you don't stand a chance. I'm a retired lieutenant from the Sheriff's Department and was in charge of our SWAT team. We're experts at breaching houses."

Preston yelled back, "To protect and serve, eh. Well there's only one way to deal with crooked cops like you and that's to put them down like a rabid dog."

The response was, "Okay. We tried to be nice about this. Now we're going to burn you out."

They heard something crash on the roof. They heard a bottle breaking and the flames erupt with a whoosh.

Amy, with a frightened look on her face, looked at Preston, "What are we going to do now?"

Preston smiled, "You did notice we have a metal roof, right? It was painted with the new outdoor fireproof paint, released in 2013. The whole outside of the camp is painted with the same stuff. They're just wasting their time."

The fire burned for a few minutes and then nothing. Preston pulled a board off the wall, revealing a 12" x 8" shooting port. Looking for targets, he scanned the front lawn and noticed that the horses had run off.

Just then, a man came running up, holding a Molotov cocktail with the rag ablaze. Preston dropped him in his tracks with one shot. Another man ran up and, as he reached to pick up the bottle, Preston shot it, shattering the glass. Gasoline flew everywhere, bursting into flames and engulfing the man. He did not waste another bullet on the man.

The man was running and screaming in pain, flames shooting out behind him as two men raced over to help him. Preston dropped both of them. Nobody else moved and the man on fire fell over. Soon the screaming stopped.

"Hey SWAT boy. Looks like your team isn't doing too well, is it?"

The man responded, "More men will be arriving soon. We are going enjoy cutting you to pieces."

Preston yelled, "I suggest you retreat while you still can."

Preston's comment was answered with a flood of bullets. He ducked down laughing.

Amy demanded, "What the hell is so funny?"

"He just lost four men and it's my guess he probably doesn't have very many Molotov cocktails left. It would be kind of dangerous to be traveling on horseback with them, don't you think?"

The shooting died down. The stovepipe had been hit several times. These guys must be fools or have an unlimited supply of ammo to be wasting so much.

Barry had lost quite a bit of blood, but was still ready to fight. His rifle was still in the scabbard on his horse, so he asked Amy, "Do you have another rifle I can use?"

Amy handed a rifle to Barry and he moved to the front wall of the cabin, ready to follow Preston's orders.

Preston told Amy to keep her head down, but look out the kitchen window and tell him what she saw. He told Michael to do the same on the other wall. He told Barry where the shooting port in the back of the cabin was and he went to check for movement at the rear. Preston kept looking out through his shooting port.

Amy called out she couldn't see anything and nobody was moving around. Michael reported the same thing. Preston could see some movement, but nothing to shoot at. They were still there and probably trying to figure out their next move, just trying to come up with a plan.

Amy yelled out, "Oh no you don't." And she fired through the shooting port on the kitchen side. She was too late. Preston saw the Molotov cocktail fly through the air and crash on the porch, just below his shooting port. That wasn't good. If that caught the firewood on fire, they could be in serious trouble.

Chapter 18

The Armory Safe

"No problem can withstand the assault of sustained thinking."

~Voltaire

Joe walked into the other room and looked at the wall protecting the safe. *Wonder how thick this steel is and how in the world are we going to get in there?* He thought.

Thinking to himself, he noted that there were six sides total. *There has to be a weak spot somewhere.* He walked back into the hallway, deep in thought. The armory might be holding what they really need. It sure would be nice to find the blueprints, but nobody would be careless enough to leave those lying around. *Maybe we could use a blow torch. This might take a few days to figure out.* He walked back out to the entryway and saw men carrying food out to the wagon and then he remembered the five mercs that had escaped.

He started thinking, *I bet they didn't have time to grab everything they wanted. They are most likely watching the place and plan on coming back.*

He found Philip and Jacob, saying, "I have an idea that those remaining mercs might want to come back and grab more stuff before they leave. Tell everybody quietly that the three of us are going to stay. If we get lucky, they'll come back. Hopefully one of them knows how to open up the armory. Either way, I would feel better if all five of them were dead."

Within an hour everything was loaded into the wagons and everyone left. The three of them found places to hide in the library. Joe felt certain that they would try to sneak back at nighttime, so one stayed on watch while the other two slept. The hours ticked by. There was not a sound and finally the sun started going down. They closed all the drapes so they could move around and not be seen, trying to be as quite as church mice, in case the men were listening.

Once darkness had set in, they waited restlessly. Jacob whispered to Joe, "I don't think this is going to work. We should get back to our families."

Joe whispered back, "Sorry, but we're spending the night. If those men are still in the area, we need to finish them off." He continued, "The rest of the men will be back in the morning to finish loading up what's left. If nothing happens by then, we can assume they have left the area. Just relax and get comfortable."

Joe was getting restless. It was 10:15 and completely dark, but still nobody had come. He sneaked to the front of the house and peeked out the drapes. His heart leapt as, by the light of the moon, he saw one man on a horse, holding the reins to four other horses. He heard the front door creak open. *Damn it!* He thought, *I should have stayed put.*

He quickly stepped behind the drapes, hiding from view. He could hear the men whispering back and forth. Joe and Jacob had spread out cans, buckets, and steel dust pans, along with assorted other noisemakers. He heard one of the cans get kicked and roll across the floor. Hopefully that was enough of a signal to put Philip and Jacob into action.

Flashlights turned on and the mercs swept the house. Within a few minutes, one of them spoke in a normal voice, loud enough for all to hear. "You two go stock up on all the food you can carry."

Joe prayed that Philip and Jacob would follow the plan, and let them open up the armory door, and then kill them.

"Gary, you're with me." He heard one of them say. And then he heard them walk off.

He sneaked out from behind the drapes and carefully avoided the noisemakers, walking quietly over to the other wall. He would have to wait for Philip and Jacob to start shooting, before he could take out these three. He doubted that they were willing to fight; they just wanted supplies and would most likely just run off, especially the one holding the other's horses.

Philip and Jacob had heard the can get knocked over. One hid underneath the desk and the other behind a couch, as the men made their sweep through the room.

The library had double sliding doors. The mercs that checked this room had left them partially open, so they each sneaked up, one on each side of the doors, waiting for them to return. As they waited, their anxiety mounted and then they heard the two men approach.

They had previously worked out a plan on how to shoot the men. Jacob would stay high and Philip would kneel down, making sure neither of them would be in the direct line of fire.

The mercs walked straight up to the safe and one shone his flashlight on the upper wall. They heard one of the men say, "I kept seeing Brad look up here for the combination. I just never could figure it out." He looked at the stamped numerals in the molding. He knew it was a three number combination and had to be entered correctly.

Joe watched the other men carry out some food. They were filling up their saddlebags and backpacks. There was nothing he could do but wait. Once the shooting started, his job was to keep these three out of the fight.

Before long, they had finished loading the food. He heard the two walking back in and one said, "Let's see if the two geniuses figured out how to open up the safe." They walked to the library and, as they approached the safe, one asked, "Any luck?"

One of the men said, "I can't figure it out. Do you know what Roman numerals stand for?"

One of the men said, "I recognize up to about number five, but that's not going to help us with this." He looked up and read the letters; MCMX, MCMLIV, MMXII. Is that supposed to be three different numbers?"

Another one said, "I vaguely remember this from school."

The other said, "I have no idea what it's supposed to be. I thought it was simple, like the last two numbers. I think MX stands for 110, IV, stands for 15, and II stands for 22. The only problem is the safe only goes up to 90."

One of them suggested, "What if it's the first two? M stands for one, and C stands for one, so the first number would be eleven. M stands for one, D stands for 50, so the second number, I don't know, maybe 51? And if MM stands for 22, then try 11-51-22."

The man at the combination tried it and grabbed the handle, hoping it would swing open, but it stayed rigidly locked in place.

The man that appeared to be their leader said, "All right, I think we've wasted enough time. Let's just get outa here."

"You're right. This is a waste of time. We should just get out." said another one, adding, "Where do you think we should go?"

The man that seemed to be in charge, said, "We're going to Kentucky. I have an old friend there. He has a really nice setup. He's been storing supplies for years. He should be a great guy to work for."

Another said, "Are we going to pay these peasants back?"

"No, we've lost enough good men over this place. It's time to move on."

Philip had second thoughts about killing these men. He thought they should just let these men go. There's been enough killing. But Jacob had other ideas. He was still in the revenge mode.

As the men started walking down the hallway, he stepped out and started firing. Philip had no choice but to join in.

They dropped two of them, but the other two ran for the door. Joe was waiting and cut both of them down. He ran for the front door to get the man on the horse and had his rifle to his shoulder. He looked out until he could see the man. The man was ready for him and opened up as he dove for cover.

He heard the horses gallop off. Stepping out on the porch, he emptied his magazine at the man, but, in the darkness and with the muzzle flash, he was unable see if he had got him. He saw the man racing out the front gate down the road. The other horses scattered in the yard.

Going back into the house, Joe called down the hall, "Jacob, Philip, are you all right?"

They replied, "Yes, we're fine."

He walked down the hall and made sure all four men were dead.

He anxiously asked, "Did they get it open?"

Philip said, "No, but we did learn something." Grabbing one of the dead mercs' flashlights, he shone the light up on the symbols. "They have something to do with the combination."

Joe studied the inscription and asked, "Roman numbers? But what do they mean?"

Phillip said, "We overheard one of the mercs say that Brad kept looking up at those numerals when he opened the safe."

Joe said, "It would sure make our life easier if we could just open it up. Otherwise we are going to have to go through one of the walls from the back, top, sides, or the bottom, but we'll worry about it tomorrow, when we have full daylight." Pointing to the Roman numerals, he said, "Somebody's got to know what these stand for."

They dragged the bodies out into the woods and gathered the horses they could find, taking them to Philip's place.

The next day, Jane and Joe came back to the mansion and together they searched the library, trying to find an encyclopedia or something that would explain the Roman numerals. They finally found one.

They read that I equals one, V equals five, X equals 10, L equals 50, C equals 100, D equals 500, and M equals 1,000.

The numbers inscribed above the safe, MCMX is 1910, MCMLIV stand for 1954, and MMXII is 2012.

They looked at each other, both perplexed as to how those dates would represent the safe's combination.

Jane said, "This could take us days to figure out. Maybe it's just the middle number of each date, 1-5-1?"

They tried it no luck. Philip walked in and asked, "HHH HH-Hhhhjjkow is the mystery coming?"

"Not so well." Jane sighed, "We figured out what the Roman numerals mean, but none of them work. We have tried 1-9-10, 1-9-54 and 2-0-12, all with no luck."

Philip shook his head in disgust. "Well, I have more bad news. Back before the world ended, one of our guys was part of the original construction crew here. He said this part of the house is built on a solid slab of 2-feet thick, reinforced concrete and there is no basement. They had to hire a special crane to put this monster safe in place. It's 10' x 15' and has 2-inch thick steel armor plating. It takes a special torch to cut into it. I think we might have to give up on this if you can't figure it out."

Joe said, "It must be pretty darn important for him to spend that kind of money. Something that's worth our time to figure out. We are just going to have to figure it out, even if it takes us days or even weeks."

Philip told them, "Okay, I'm going to supervise the distribution of all the supplies that we have already taken. You two stay here as long as it takes, or until you give up, it's up to you, and I hope you figure it out. I'll be back in the morning to check on things."

Jane found a piece of paper and a pen. "All right, honey, from now on, we'll write down every number we try. That way we're not wasting time retrying the same numbers."

Joe agreed and said, "Okay, let's try it backwards this time. You write and I'll try the numbers: 0 – 9 – 91." Joe cussed, "Damn it. All of this is so frustrating. The dial only goes to 90, so that can't be it."

Jane told him to calm down. "It's all right. That's a good idea, but try the next one; 4 – 5 – 19. If 91 won't work, maybe 19 will."

Joe tried it, no luck.

"Okay, try 0 – one – 10."

Again Joe tried it without any luck.

Jane shook her head, "Do you think it's got some kind of failsafe built in? Like, after three failed attempts it won't open, even with the right combination?"

Joe looked at her with a frown, "You just had to throw that in there, didn't you? But how would it work if there's no electricity?"

"I have no idea. I'm not a professional safecracker," Jane said. "Let's give it a break and then try three combinations every hour."

They found a grandfather clock in the hallway, the type with a bell that rang on the hour, so they set the time for one hour from then. They figured out three more combinations to try for the next hour: 9 – 54 – 90, 10 – 54 – 19, and the last one 10 – 19 – 90, all with the same results. They did not unlock the safe. The day clicked by and every hour they tried a new set of three combinations.

They started wandering around the mansion, both too worked up and frustrated. It was time to walk away. Too many numbers, too many combinations.

They explored the master bedroom and found a king size bed with a canopy and fancy silk hanging on the corners. It looked like something you would expect to find in some castle for kings and queens.

Jane looked at Joe, saying, "It's almost dark out and I've always wanted to feel like a queen. Why don't you go find a tux to wear? Get cleaned up and look like a king. I'll look around and see if I can find a beautiful dress for me to wear. Let's pretend we're rich and everything's fine for this evening."

Joe smiled, nodded his head and went towards what must be a dressing room. Jane found a beautiful long flowing dress that Brad must have had for one of his mistresses. She sat down, fixed her makeup, put on some expensive French perfume, piled her hair on top of her head, with tendrils framing her face, and then admired herself in the mirror.

Joe found a nice tux and discovered that there was pressurized water in the bathroom. It probably came from gravity flow from a storage tank somewhere. He took a shower, shaved and got dressed in a nice tux, putting on some cologne he found in the bathroom and combing his hair in a fashionable style.

He met Jane for dinner in the master dining room. Jane had found some MRE's, put them on the fancy plates and served them dinner with the fine crystal and real silver tableware. She had found the wine cabinet and opened a bottle of wine to have with dinner.

She said, "I'm sorry, sir, but it's the maid's night off." She giggled like a little girl playing dress-up.

Joe said, "That's quite okay, my dear, I wouldn't want anybody to distract me from your beauty."

They drank the wine and Joe laughed, saying that it was probably some $2,000.00 a bottle wine. They drank and laughed and spent the evening enjoying each other's company. They retired to the master bedroom to fulfill Jane's dream of being a queen.

About 6:30 that morning, shaking him, Jane woke Joe up, "I figured it out. I know what we did wrong."

Joe, still half-asleep, said, "I don't know about you, but I don't think we did anything wrong last night. Didn't you have a good time? I know I did."

"Not that, silly! I know what we're doing wrong with the safe combination. It's not Roman numerals; it's our alphabet, using numbers."

She jumped out of bed, naked and shivering, and started quickly throwing on her clothes. "Come on, come on, get up. I've got it figured out. This is going to work, I just know it will. This is the answer, trust me."

"God, lady, would you at least make me some coffee first, before you start on this?"

"Go make it yourself; I have to go figure this out. That's why you brought me here, isn't it?"

"Okay, okay, lady. I'm moving." Joe stumbled downstairs and met her in front of the safe. "All right, what's this big master plan?"

Jane smiled as she jotted down something on the paper. "It's so simple. I should have figured it out sooner. You take our alphabet and assign it a number in order. The letter A equals one, B equals two, and so on, all the way to Z."

"So, using MCMX, MCMLIV and MMXII, I would use the last number from all three, so we just have to figure out what X, V, and I equals in our alphabet, and I'll bet you that's it." She started writing the numbers down next to the letters, mumbling as she did it.

A – 1, B – 2, C-3, D-4, E-5, F-6, G-7, H-8, I-9, J-10, K-11, L-12, M-13, N-14, O-15, P-16, Q-17, R-18, S-19, T-20, U-21, V-22, W-23, X-24, Y-25 and Z-26.

"V equals 22, X equals 24, and I equals 9."

Joe dialed the numbers and then yanked on the handle. Nothing. "See, I told you, coffee first."

"No no no. This has to be it. We just have to play with this idea." Jane was sure this was the answer and that they just had to play with the combinations of numbers.

Joe stumbled off to the kitchen. "I'm making coffee. Don't bother me until I've had at least one cup."

Most of the food and supplies had been removed, but there was a pantry that hadn't been cleaned out yet and Joe found coffee and a stove-top coffee pot. The stove still worked, as it was a gas stove and there was a large propane storage tank outside.

Jane thought, *Fine. I'll do it myself.* It would have to be something simple that would be easy to remember by just glancing at the inscription. It had to be just one of the three. She picked up her pad and wrote down 24-22-9, it failed. Using the third letters this time she tried 13-13-24. It also failed. Using the second letters this time, she tried 3-3-13. She grabbed the handle and pulled . . . to her amazement, it dropped down and opened. She thought, *Oh my God. I was righ*t. She did a little dance and hopped around in delight.

She had to contain her joy and didn't want to scream out to Joe, just yet.

She glanced inside, seeing racks of pistols, shotguns, rifles, cases of ammo and much more. She smiled and smugly thought, *Ha, ha, Joe. I'm the smart one.*

She walked up behind him, wrapped her arms around his waist from the back and said, "Smells great. When is it going to be ready?"

"Oh my God," Joe said, as he turned around. "Mr. Rich guy has real coffee, Colombian supreme, a hand crank coffee mill and tons of Mountain House food. We are going to live like kings and queens, if we stay here this winter."

"Great," said Jane, "That food and coffee sure does smell good."

She smiled and said, "I wonder what he has locked up in that safe? I bet it's something really good and important." She was bursting to tell him, but waited.

Joe pulled the skillet off the propane stove, dished up a serving for each of them and filled up their coffee cups.

"Let's eat and then go play with numbers and combinations."

They finished breakfast, walked back to the library and over to the safe. Jane still had not said a word. The handle was still down. Joe didn't notice and asked her what combination he should try next.

She started giggling and then burst out laughing. "I don't know, honey. What number would you like to try?" Laughing even harder.

He looked at her and frowned, "What has gotten into you, woman? Did you put laughing sugar in your coffee?"

Jane was still giggling. Trying to sound like a rough, tough guy, she said, "What is it that you always tell your trainees? You must always be aware of your surroundings and, if something changes, you should to be the first to notice."

Joe was starting to get angry. He looked all around the room. He looked at all the numbers and then he finally looked at the safe, noticing the handle was down. "Oh my God. You figured it out and didn't say a word to me."

Jane was still laughing. "I told you that I was right. It was the second letters."

After she let him absorb that, she said, "Wait until you see what is inside." She pulled open the heavy metal door and automatic LED lights lit up the inside of the room.

As Joe looked around the room he exclaimed, "It's a dream come true. Thank God for paranoid millionaires."

There had to be at least 25 AR-15s and hundreds of magazines. A table in the center of the room was loaded with ammo stripper clips and assorted other goodies and there were 10 Kel-Tec KSG 15-round shotguns. They were bullpup design, pump-action, 12-gauge, combat shotguns used for urban tactical operations. Talk about space-age-looking weapons.

Joe couldn't believe what he was looking at. Wow, they had hit the mother lode. He also discovered, in a special case, a McMillan Tac-50 Tactical Rifle. It is a .50 caliber sniper's dream rifle. It's capable of engaging targets beyond 2,000 meters. This bolt-action rifle has superior accuracy, compared to the other semi-automatic rifles.

Joe said, "If we only had this when facing the Rainbow Warriors, we could have sniped their whole artillery crew. This is a dream come true. I can't wait to show off everything."

And Jane said with a smug smile, "Well, make sure you tell everybody who figured the combination out."

Joe smiled and said, "I'm sure you'll be glad to fill everybody in with those details."

Chapter 19

Praying for Reinforcement

"While there's life, there's hope."
~Marcus Tullius Cicero

The fire on the porch was gaining hold and Preston ran over to the wall and unhooked the fire extinguisher. He pulled the safety pin and put the plastic funnel outside, spraying almost straight down onto the fire. He managed to quickly extinguish it.

The other side was shooting, but only managed to put some holes through the fire extinguisher's plastic funnel. Preston called out to Barry, "How long before the next patrol comes through?"

Barry responded, "I believe they'll be here tomorrow. They might come looking for me tonight, when they discover I haven't returned."

Preston shouted over the noise, "Let's hope so. How is your wound, Barry?"

"It hurts like hell, but I'm okay to fight. What do you think they're going to do next?"

After a short pause to return fire, Preston said, "If they use standard SWAT team tactics, they are going to wait for darkness. They probably have 12-gauge breaching loads and will sneak up to shoot off the hinges of the door, kick it in and do a mad rush en masse." He continued, "Who knows, they might have tear gas or even flash bang grenades, but we thought of those possibilities when we built this place. See those L brackets on the door?" Preston walked over and picked up a 2 x 6, placing it across the door and into the brackets, securing the door from being pushed in. He continued, "The shutters on this cabin are built to keep bears out. I think we can hold them off until the patrol comes."

The shooting stopped and it was quiet. Preston thought that either they were running low on ammunition, or were strategizing their next move.

He turned to Amy and asked, "Amy, did you hit the guy you shot at?"

She responded, “I think so. I saw him flinch.”

“I sure hope you did, because that means we’re evening the odds up pretty quickly. Five against four now. That means we 6 have a real good chance of surviving this.” He then added, “unless, of course, he has more reinforcements coming, as he said, but I do believe that was just a bluff.”

Amy asked, “How did they find us?”

Preston replied, “They must’ve followed us. I bet they had a patrol out and just followed us straight back here.”

Amy, with a worried look on her face, said, “But how did they know I was in here?”

“I’m sure that was just a guess. They probably figured we headed in this direction when we escaped. Now they’re guessing that we’re the same people. They really never got a good look at any of us, but you.”

He turned to Michael, “How good are you at crawling?”

Michael replied, “Good, I guess. Why?”

“Well, if he’s down to five men, chances are he can’t surround this place. Even if he tried, a small boy crawling at night would be almost impossible to see. You know these woods well enough, so you could sneak past them, go down about a quarter of a mile in the woods, then sneak out to the road, making sure it’s safe, and run like heck to the next place down. Then, the others could get the word out quickly. If we can get reinforcements, this will be over fast.”

Michael was excited to prove himself and said, “Okay. That sounds good. I can do it.”

Amy protested, “No, you’re not.” Turning to Preston she said, “You’re not sending a child out to do this. I’ll go.”

Preston shook his head. “Amy, think for a minute. They’re here for you. So, if you get caught, they can just take off and we won’t know anything until morning. No, you’re staying right here.”

Michael looked at Amy with a hurt look. “You don’t think I’m good enough to do this, do you?”

Amy walked over and gave him a hug. “No,” she whispered, “I just don’t want to put you in any danger.”

Barry walked into the room and said quietly, “I agree with Preston. I say the boy goes. It’s only logical we send the smallest. I’m injured and we need Preston here to help defend, plus Amy is the prize for them. We shouldn't deliver her to them on a silver platter."

Amy hugged Michael tighter as she whispered, "You be quiet and move slowly. Don't take any chances. Okay?"

Michael brightened up, pulled back and looked up at her. "I will. Please stop worrying so much; you're not my mother."

Amy reeled back, hurt by the comment, but she let it go. She looked over at Preston and said, "Okay. How can we get him outside without being seen?"

Preston said, "In the root cellar there's a crawl space, all the way to the back of the house, where there's a small door. I think it's like 24" x 18. When he gets to that point, I'll shoot a couple of shots off so he can open the door. I'll keep shooting until they start shooting back. Their concentration and firepower will be up here, on the front. Michael can then go back a good 100 yards into the woods, then slowly and quietly work his way around them to the road."

He directed his words to Michael "Don't get in a rush. It's dark out and you don't want to be tripping on or breaking branches, making all kinds of noise. There's no rush. If it takes you an hour to get around them, who cares? You see what I mean?"

"Yes, I understand. I'm not a greenhorn anymore. I can do this."

"Good. I'll take you down and show you where the door is and then, in about an hour, it should be dark enough for you to leave. We have some face camouflage and light Camouflage gloves. With all your Camouflage on, you should be able to crawl right through without being seen."

Preston took him down to the root cellar. Shining his flashlight to the back of the crawl space, he showed him where the door was.

"Let me show you how you crawl with a rifle." He lay down on the dirt floor and, with his arms out in front of him, he placed the rifle across his elbows. "Stay low and use your forearms to keep the rifle close to your elbows. Once you get the hang of it, it's really easy. You crawl out until you reach the trees and then you can do what is called a low crawl. That's where you just bend over at the waist, staying low, moving through the brush. Once you're back into the woods about 100 yards, you should be able to stand up and carefully walk around them and out to the road. Once you hit the road, don't stop running until you reach somebody."

"Okay, I got it. I'm not dumb you know."

"Listen Michael, I'm treating you like I would any other soldier. Accept that and knock off the remarks. Got it?"

Michael smiled. "I'm a real soldier now?"

Preston chuckled. "You sure are."

They waited for full darkness. Amy followed Michael into the root cellar. Amy was going to be the relay. Once Michael reached the door, Amy was to let Preston know.

Preston was watching the cellar door and saw Amy's hand stick up with the thumb up, indicating he could start firing now.

He quickly fired a few shots towards where he had last seen somebody. He waited for muzzle flash or some type of target, so he could do some aimed shots in reply. He saw three muzzle flashes and heard the bullets hitting the wood above his head. He quickly fired off 9 more rounds, three shots for each target, then he ducked down.

Amy's job now was to crawl over and lock the door behind Michael. Barry was trying to watch out the back, but it was so dark, he couldn't tell where Michael was.

Preston called out, "Hey, Mr. SWAT team guy, how's it going out there? Where are all those reinforcements you were bragging about?"

He was met with silence. He heard something hit the door and fall to the porch and then he saw the flash. He heard the explosion and tear gas started coming in through his shooting port. He quickly picked up the board and sealed the shooting port. He heard the footsteps running up and a shotgun blast where the hinges should be, before there was a solid kick to the door, which shook the little cabin. The door held fast and he fired several shots, right through the wall, guessing where they should be standing.

He was lying on the floor as they started shooting above his head at waist level, tearing up the walls.

He heard one scream out in pain and then he heard scraping and the sound of boots as someone ran away.

By then, Amy had crawled back out of the root cellar and over to him, asking if he was hit.

He smiled, "Nope, but another one of them was."

She whispered, "I saw Michael make it to the woods. I think he's fine."

He whispered back, "Good. Now if we can hold out for a few more hours, then help should arrive."

Staying low, she crawled on her hands and knees, back to where Barry was. He was straining his eyes, trying to see movement in the dark. She whispered to him, "I saw him make it to the woods. Could you see him after that?"

Barry shook his head and whispered back, "I didn't even see him make it that far. The plan looks like it's working, so far."

"How's your arm? Do you need anything?"

She could see the pain in his face as he said, "Some water and the strongest pain medication that you have."

Amy nodded and crawled off, returning with his requested items.

Barry took them from her and swallowed the pills, saying, "Thank you."

"My pleasure," she replied, adding, "I'm sorry that you got hurt helping us."

"It wasn't your fault. I was just getting ready to head home. You didn't do anything."

"You know what I mean," Amy replied. "If we had never come here, this wouldn't be happening now."

"You don't know that. They could have been coming up here to do raids. They might've been trying to grab my wife. The way I look at it, this was a fight coming one way or the other."

Amy squeezed his good arm. "Thank you for saying that. You're a really great guy. I'm going back up to my post now, but if you need anything, just call out, okay?"

He nodded and said, "Sounds good."

An hour later they tried their next breach. This time they had two guys climb on the roof and start shooting down as they walked across the top. At the same time, two more again tried to breach the door with the shotgun.

They had already walked past where Barry was sitting. He could hear them walking up there and saw the bullets coming through, tearing up the bed. Using the SKS rifle he was given, he started shooting up where he thought they were. He continued shooting back and forth between where he guessed each of the men were.

His breach locked open and he fumbled in the dark, trying to find the stripper clips he had been given.

They were still shooting down and it was obvious that he hadn't hit anybody. He heard a magazine bounce off the metal roof as he shoved the 10 rounds into the SKS. He tossed the stripper clip and yanked back on the bolt, letting it fly, loading a fresh round in the chamber.

Amy was also firing up into the ceiling with her .22 250. The muzzle flash and high-intensity sound of each shot was killing her eardrums. The smell of cordite was thick in the little cabin. She could still hear Preston's AR singing out the front.

The men trying to breach the front door shot two more shells where they thought the hinges were and started kicking on the door again. One of the shells hit a hinge and it shattered off, but the other one held tight, having been missed by an inch. The 2x6 was not allowing them any access, no matter what they tried.

Preston had fired close to 10 rounds at where they should have been standing. When the two at the door ran off, the two on the roof were firing down into the cabin and working their way to the back. Preston got up, walking along and shooting upwards, guessing where they should be. Amy and Barry were also firing and then there was silence, as everybody paused to reload.

If their hearing hadn't been impaired from all the inside shooting, they would have heard the two guys jump off the roof. After that, they all reloaded their rifles and they waited, still pointing at the ceiling.

Amy started yelling, due to her temporary deafness, "Did we get any?"

Preston replied, "I don't know. Let's get back in positions everybody, they will be coming back."

They both replied in the affirmative. They had lit one small kerosene lantern, which gave them just enough light to see without tripping over things.

Preston turned back toward the front and there was gun smoke and pieces of insulation floating in the air. With the glow of the lamp, it had a surreal feel to it.

They waited while Preston inspected the door. They had managed to shoot off the handle and one of the hinges. Only one hinge and the 2 x 6 kept the door in place. One more attempt like that, and they would be in. He was worried about Michael, hoping he had made it. They desperately needed reinforcements.

Michael had no problem sneaking around them. Once he hit the dirt road, he took off running. After about a half mile he slowed down to catch his breath. He was almost to the main road when he heard a horse. He quickly hid in the woods. Alone in the starlight, the figure looked familiar. He took a chance and called out. "Scott?"

The horse stopped and he heard somebody bringing a rifle up. It had to be Scott, Michael thought. He took a chance. "Scott, it's me, Michael."

"Michael. Is that really you?"

Michael breathed a sigh of relief and stepped up to the horse. "It's me. Quick, we have to go get reinforcements. Amy, Preston, and Barry are in trouble. There are some SWAT team guys that have the house surrounded.

Scott stuck out his hand and said, "Come here and I'll give you a ride. Get on behind me."

Scott quickly pulled Michael up to the back of the horse. He turned the horse around and galloped off to get the men.

Preston thought, "This is it. The door is not going to take another assault. Once they breach the door and toss in the tear gas grenades, it's going to be over."

He crawled over to Amy. Their ears were still ringing. He tried to say it as quietly as he could, "We have to leave. We'll crawl out the same way Michael did. I'll cover you two, so go grab Barry and tell him the plan. I'll give you a few minutes to crawl over and get out. I'll give you some cover fire up front and then I'll be right behind you."

She nodded and crawled over to Barry to tell him what they were going to do.

Barry and Amy went into the root cellar and had crawled over and were waiting by the door. They heard Preston start shooting, so they opened the hatch and started crawling for the woods. Once they safely reached the woods, they took cover behind a tree, turning around and ready to give Preston covering fire, if needed.

Preston was almost to the open hatch when he heard the assault. He heard the 12-gauge blast, the door being kicked open and the tear gas grenades going off inside. He could see the light flash through the cracks of the floor and he heard footsteps as men came running in. Multiple shots were fired all around the cabin.

Chapter 20

Asked to Leave

"A warrior is only welcome until the end of the war."
~Unknown

Within an hour the wagons were pulling into the yard to finish loading up the supplies at the millionaire's house.

Philip walked down the hallway and, seeing the safe door open, quickly ran over. Looking inside, he screamed, "Yahoo! You did it! You did it!" His eyes got as big as silver dollars as he looked in the armory. "Wow, this was worth it. What a gold mine!"

Joe laughed, "Well, you can thank Mrs. Brainiac here," pointing to Jane, "she figured it out."

"Really? Jane, tell me how you figured it out. What was the secret?"

Jane laughed and said, "This girl never tells secrets, but I will tell you this, we tried everything, working late into the night without any luck. Then I woke up early and the solution hit me. So we came down and tried it and it worked."

Philip walked over and picked up one of the ARs, saying, "It really doesn't matter how you did it, it's the fact that we're in. That's all that counts. So what's the plan? How do we distribute the guns and to whom?"

Joe said, "I'm not sure, but one thing is certain. We should hold some training and teach the people that are going to have them how to clean, maintain and fire them. I would suggest that we take five guns, with ammo and magazines, and bury them as a backup cache, but that's totally up to you people. All I want for sure is two of these space-age shotguns and one more AR-15, along with some magazines and ammo."

More people were gathering and walking into the room. People started grabbing rifles and handguns.

Philip was almost shouting as he said, "Now hold on. Everybody get out. Put the guns down and leave everything. We're going to fairly distribute these among everybody. We'll have a meeting at my house tonight where we can all decide. Until then, all of you stay out of here."

There was some grumbling and complaining, but the guns were put back in place and the people left.

Philip looked at Jane, "You have the combo, right? Then we can lock this up and you can open it tomorrow." Jane nodded yes and Philip closed the vault door, turning the handle up to lock it.

That evening, a couple of hours before dark, Philip's house looked like rush hour as well over 100 people, not counting all the children playing around in the yard, were there.

As the group began to discuss the weapons, the arguing and bickering was getting out of control. It was getting too intense and Joe walked outside for some fresh air.

The women were setting up an outdoor table, doing a large barbecue. The children were racing around and playing. It almost looked like a normal life at a large family gathering.

Joe walked out to the road to think. He was never very good as a politician and these people had to figure out how they wanted to run their community on their own. They could hammer out the details among themselves. He told them his only request and, since Jane was the one who figured out how to open the safe, it was only fair that they should get their request.

He heard a horse galloping and saw a lone man coming quickly down the road. He thought nothing of it, thinking it must be somebody that got a late start getting to the meeting.

Joe turned and started walking back into the yard, thinking, "Great, one more voice to be squabbling and bickering over the booty." He was on the long driveway, about 50 feet from the road, when he heard the horse start galloping down the driveway.

He turned to look and see who it was, just as the man raised his rifle up and started firing. Joe dove for the ground and rolled, bringing up his rifle. He tried to get the man in the sights as he raced past, but he was moving too fast.

The man was screaming, "You killed my brother. You're all going to die."

It dawned on Joe that it was the man that got away, the night they took out those four other mercs at the millionaire's house.

The man raced toward the women and children, firing away. Joe fired at him as two of the children were cut down, screaming for their moms. One woman was hit while racing to pick up her child. The place erupted in chaos and men poured out of the house.

It was pure pandemonium. Shots were being fired, women and children running and all of them were screaming, trying to find cover.

The man was knocked off the horse by a shotgun blast to his stomach. He lay on the ground screaming as Joe, seething with anger, ran up to him and emptied the magazine into him, from his belly to his head. When he hit the man's head with three shots at that range, brain matter, pieces of skull and blood splattered all around the area.

A crowd gathered around him and the man who lost his daughter, the one Joe had punched in the face, stepped out in front of the crowd. His nose was still bandaged and his eyes blackened. He pointed his finger at Joe and yelled to the crowd, "These people are too brutal for us. They're nothing but brutal savages and I don't want them around my family. I don't care what they've done for us. I don't want this man teaching our children how to be savages." He then pointed down to the man who had caused the chaos and said, "Take a good look at what's left of this body. The man was dead after a few shots." He lifted his accusing finger back up, pointing right at Joe. "That's not normal behavior. This man—he's a psychopath and will kill us all if we don't get rid of him right now."

Joe was stunned by the man's words. Granted, he did let his anger get the best of him and he had lost control. He clearly had overreacted but, my God, this guy was shooting women and children. Any normal man protecting his family would've done the same thing.

Joe looked around at the other faces to see how the man's reaction and words were being taken. He saw what he was afraid of - fear and loathing. Not in all of them, but enough that he knew their time here was over.

Philip stepped up and cleared his throat saying, "Listen here, folks. Joe and his wife Jane have helped us immensely. We are now free of the warlord, thanks to their efforts, and this is how you want to repay them? Ban them? Throw them away like trash, because we no longer need them? And if it wasn't for Jane's help, we would have never gotten into that safe. Because of her, we have arms and ammunition to protect our community from now on. I, for one, will not stand for this; they have earned their right to be part of our community and I say they stay."

A few of the men nodded their heads in agreement, but, before Philip could say another word, the man interrupted. "This is not just up to you. This is up to all of us and I and my wife vote that these two be banned from our community forever."

Philip started to say something, but Joe pushed the magazine release on his rifle and pulled the empty magazine out. Placing it in his pouch, he grabbed a loaded one and smacked it in place, hit the release lever to load a fresh round and then placed the safety on with a loud click. He then slung the rifle over his shoulder.

A hush fell over the crowd and Joe looked at all of them. Deep in his heart he knew that, no matter how it turned out, there would always be problems if they stayed here. It was time for him and Jane to move on. Who knew, maybe Preston, Amy and Michael were already waiting for them at the hunting camp?

Joe looked around and said, "Thank you, Philip, but we will not be staying where we're not welcome."

Jane had come running up to him. Joe continued, "If it's all right with you people, all we ask for is somebody with the wagon and horses to help carry the supplies that we earned and take us up to the camp we're traveling to. It's right around a hundred miles, maybe a little more, from here. Either way, Jane and I are going back to camp, so you folks decide." He added, "We'll come talk to Philip about it in the morning." With that, Jane and Joe walked over to the barn, picked up their bikes and rode off.

Philip was totally disgusted with the crowd and let his anger be known. "You people are disgusting," he said, "if it wasn't for Joe, we'd still be slaves to a warlord and shaking in fear every time they rode into our yards. He came here and taught us how to stand up and fight. He warned you people, right from the beginning, that freedom comes at a cost and you knew people could die. Remember that, each and every one of you. Now get off my property, go home and think about it."

One of the men asked about the weapons and Philip said, "We'll figure out how to distribute the guns and ammunition later. I'm in no mood to hear anything else from anybody tonight. Now LEAVE."

He turned his back on the crowd and stormed off to his house. The remaining people helped collect their dead and left. Nobody touched the body of the shot-up merc.

After everyone was gone, Philip and Jacob went outside and collected the body. Using the wheelbarrow, they hauled it back to a brush pile and set it ablaze. Philip pulled out a flask, took a shot and then handed it Jacob. "Good medicine for calming your nerves."

Jacob took a shot. "What are we going to do, Dad?" He asked as he handed the flask back.

"I don't know, son. I've never been so embarrassed, angry, disgusted and fed up with our neighbors as I am right now. Part of me says you and I should hitch up the wagon in the morning and take Joe and Jane over to the house, loading everything that's in the safe. Load the whole damn thing up on the wagon and then escort them to where they're going and to hell with these people. They wouldn't have any of those things if it weren't for Joe and Jane. But I know that's just my anger talking. After we sleep on it, I'm sure I'll calm down."

He looked at his dad, a long silent look, and then he finally asked the question he had been thinking about. "Why don't we just pack up and go with them?"

"Don't tempt me. If it wasn't for your mother and sisters, you and I would be packing right now and be leaving with them in the morning, but this is your mother's home. This is our farm and our community. For better or worse, it's best that we stay. But you're old enough to decide for yourself if you want to stay or go. I won't hold it against you if you choose to leave. I would prefer you stay, but I understand if you wish to move on with your life."

Jacob thought for a moment and said, "I don't know, Dad. That's a big decision. Something I don't want to make in haste or anger. If I had to decide right now, I would leave, but that wouldn't be fair to you or Mom."

After a long period of silence, Jacob asked, "Dad, do you think I should go, or should I stay here and help you work and protect the farm?"

Philip smiled, "Son, that's your decision. Of course I'd prefer you to stay. You know how to work the farm and you know how to keep things in working order. If anything happens to me, the more men we have around, the easier it will be to defend and hold this property. Don't make a decision in haste right now. Sleep on it. I'm sure that we'll use our wagon and horses to take Joe and Jane where they want to go. I know that it will be a long five-day ride, giving you plenty of time to make your decision."

They left it at that and, once the fire had died down, they called it a night.

The next morning, when Joe and Jane arrived, there was a big breakfast spread of homemade sourdough pancakes and fresh bacon. They all sat down and ate.

Philip kept apologizing and trying to talk them into staying. Jane smiled and said, "We thank you, Philip. You are an honorable man, but it's just not wise to stay. The whole community will be watching us, waiting for another excuse to get rid of us outsiders. If it wasn't this, it would be something else. This is going to fester in that man's mind, so the longer we're here, the more he can blame us for his daughter's death. When we go, he can be at peace, mourn and accept his loss."

Philip said, "I was afraid that's what you were going to say, that you're leaving no matter what. Jacob and I will hitch up the wagon and help you load up what you've chosen to take and then we'll take you where you're going."

After they finished their breakfast, the men walked outside while Jane and the Misses said their goodbyes.

They all rode down to the millionaire's house and, once inside, Jane unlocked the safe again. They took one AR-15, 10 magazines, some stripper clips, 2,000 rounds of ammo, two of the space-age shotguns along with 500 rounds of buckshot and slugs. They also loaded up six months' worth of food, the good #10 cans of the Mountain House food and 20 pounds of the good coffee.

Joe said, "If I were you, Philip, I would stash the sniper rifle, three AR-15s, two of those space-age shotguns and lots of ammo for each in a hidden cache in the woods, but that's up to you. Jane gave you the combo to the safe, so it will be up to you what happens with the rest of the stuff."

Philip nodded and told Joe thanks for the suggestion. He planned to do just that.

After gathering and loading all of the items, they headed out. Joe and Jane rode their bikes, with Philip and Jacob in the wagon.

As they rode off, Jane thought, *Is this our new life, helping people but never really being welcome? God, how I hope Preston, Amy and Michael are alive and waiting for us when we get there. Oh, it would be so good to see Amy again. I sure miss our chats.*

The miles clicked by and, before they knew it, darkness was setting in. They stopped and made camp, found a pond for the horses to drink from and allowed them to graze the grass along the road. They shared one of the cans of Mountain House Beef Stroganoff with Noodles and Jane brewed a pot of coffee.

They took turns standing watch, each of them taking a two-hour watch. The only thing that happened that night was a pack of coyotes howling and yipping in the distance.

In the morning, Jane cooked breakfast over a fire. Well, she really just boiled water and poured in the Mountain House freeze-dried breakfast mix, but it tasted good and there was plenty to satisfy everyone. She made a second pot of coffee to put in the thermos to take with them.

On the fourth day, they ran into 2 men pushing a shopping cart. They chatted back and forth, trading news. They were warned not to go north because there were men patrolling the area that did not allow outsiders in their territory.

Over dinner that night, they talked about what the men had told them.

"Ten men on horseback?" Jacob began looking at Joe and said, "Sounds like you're jumping out of the frying pan and right into the fire. Maybe another warlord for you to clean out?"

"I don't know, but I do believe, once we're within a few hours of the place the men told us about, we should stash the wagon and you two stay with it to guard the food and weapons. Jane and I will go forward on the bikes and scout the area. It's the only safe way to do this."

Phillip said, "That sounds like a smart idea. We'll get out of sight and protect the supplies while you check out what's going on."

Jane said, "I sure hope Preston, Amy and Michael are there and everybody's okay and safe."

Joe said, "Well, we'll find out tomorrow."

Jacob asked the question he'd wanted to ask for the past 4 days now. "I've been trying to decide if I should stay with you guys, that is, if you want me to?"

Joe looked at him and smiled, "Of course we'd love for you to join us, but that's not practical for several reasons, the main one being your family. It's the only thing you have right now and you should stay with them to protect your folks' homestead. Unfortunately, we no longer have that luxury. We would have never left our homestead if we had not been forced to. The best decision you can make is to stay with your family."

Jacob sighed and said, "That's what I've been leaning towards. I believe that the old man," looking at his dad, "needs my help."

Philip laughed and said, "I may be old, but I can still whip your young ass."

They all laughed and called it a night, taking the same watch as they had on previous nights.

The next day, around one o'clock in the afternoon, they reached the spot that was roughly 10 miles from the camp. Jacob and Philip took the wagon down a dirt road a couple of miles and waited for their return.

Joe and Jane rode right through the area without seeing a soul. They rode down the dirt road and right up to the hunting camp. They had smelled the burning long before they reached the camp. A little smoke still whispered up from the smoldering timbers of what was once their deer camp.

They got off their bikes and Joe called out. "Preston, Amy, Michael. Is anyone here?" He was met with silence, except a few chickadees that flew through, chattering back and forth.

Jane broke down with tears streaming down her face. "Is this our new world? All of our property burned to the ground; all our friends dead? Are we doomed to wander the earth as gypsies, trying to survive? I can't take any more of this. I'm sick of the dying, sick of the burning, sick of watching children die and for what? Stupid people that can't shut up and get along, working together as a community?"

Joe walked up and put his arms around her. "We don't know that they're dead. We don't even know if they made it here. All we know is that the camp was burned down. They might have moved to a different house. We just don't know what's going on, so don't jump to conclusions."

"You don't understand. I'm sick of this. I hate this new world. I want to talk to Amy. I want to hug Michael. I even want to hug Preston. I want to be with friends, people we can trust. Don't you understand?"

He could see that she was at the end of her rope and ready to melt down. He said, "I know, I want to see all of them too. We can stay here for a couple of days and then go out searching for them. Maybe we can find this patrol we were told about and they might know what's going on. Let's not give up right now. Okay, honey?"

Jane got her emotions under control and they rode back to where Jacob and Philip were waiting. They gave them the news and told them that they were going to wait until morning to make a decision.

Philip said, "Maybe we should find you some vacant house so you can stash your supplies, because we have to get back to the farm. We have our own family. I hope you understand."

Joe said, "Of course we do and we really appreciate all you've done for us. We'll look for a place in the morning and then you and Jacob can head back home."

Chapter 21

Burnt Out Again

> "Hope rises like a phoenix from the ashes of shattered dreams."
>
> ~S.A. Sachs

After the hunting cabin's front door had been breached, one of the tear gas grenades caught the couch on fire. This quickly spread to the drapes and up the interior wall. The Raiders quickly searched the cabin and left as the fire spread. They circled around the back, looking for survivors, but found none.

Preston had made it to where Amy and Barry had hidden. They retreated farther into the thick brush of the woods. They were a good 300 yards back in when Preston called a halt. They each took up defensive positions and waited. He was betting that they wouldn't dare search for them in the woods.

Within 10 minutes they saw the glow of the fire. Amy whispered, "I thought the place was fireproof?"

Preston had a stupid grin on his face and said, "The whole outside was painted with fire retardant, which is good for preventing fires, but we never painted the inside. They must have started the fire from the inside. Once the fire has been burning for so long, the fire retardant will burn off and the whole thing will burn to the ground." He added, "But this is our chance to sneak up and use the light of the fire to shoot them down. If they're dumb enough to still be there, that is."

They sneaked up to the back of the camp and flames were quickly eating through the roof. With the bright glow of the fire, they could now see all around the camp, but nobody was on the backside that they could see. Before they could do anything else, they heard horses coming. They heard shooting and saw 5 men running behind the cabin for cover. They let them get really close and, when they were sure that they were the bad guys, they cut them down.

Holding their position, they waited. When Preston saw men flanking him on both sides, sneaking along, he recognized one of them. He called out, "Scott. Is this the patrol?" Everyone froze in position. Preston called out again, "Scott, it's Preston. Who's out there?"

A voice called out from the darkness, "Preston, is that you?"

Preston replied, "Yes it is. We have one injured. Did you bring a medic?"

Scott walked out into the open and towards Preston's voice. "Yes, we did."

They walked out to meet Scott and Preston stuck his hand out to thank him for coming. They shook hands and Scott said, "What's going on? Michael said they were SWAT team guys?"

"The guy in charge said he was a retired police officer and used to be in charge of a SWAT team.

Scott said, "That's too bad. I'm sure there are many fine police officers still out there and, even though some are retired, they're still protecting and serving."

Preston said, "Yes, I'm sure there are, but it only takes a few bad apples to give them all a bad name. Well, the good news is this little band of corruption is now stopped for good. I'm sure there's good and bad in any group and I'm not going to judge anybody, or any group, based on these clowns. I had a friend that, after serving in the Army, became a lieutenant in the Seattle Police Department and I would trust my life to him any day."

Scott said, "Well, I think that house I showed you is your new place to live now, right?"

Preston, looking at the camp as it was burning to the ground, said, "Kind of looks that way, doesn't it?"

They collected all of the weapons and supplies, tossed the dead bodies into the burning cabin so they would burn with it and then they rode off to spend the night at Scott's place. Little did they know that Joe and Jane would be looking at the burnt-out camp the next morning.

The next day, Preston, Amy and Michael moved into the new house. They had to haul water until they could figure out how to get a generator working. They spent the day cleaning and organizing the house. Amy asked what they were going to do for food? Scott and his family had given them a few days' worth, to get started, but they would need much more.

Preston said, "If we're lucky, the fire didn't burn down into the root cellar and maybe some of the food and supplies can be saved. The fire should be cooled down enough by tomorrow, so Michael and I will go and see if we can salvage anything."

The next day Michael and Preston rode down to the camp. They stood there, looking at the burnt-out structure. "What do we do now?" Michael asked.

"Well, we carefully work our way along the floor and see if we can get down to the root cellar."

They heard a voice call out from the woods, "Oh my God! Is it really you Preston? Michael?"

They both turned to the woods where the voice had come from and were shocked to see Joe and Jane come running out. Preston, with a shocked look on his face, said, "What? How can you two be alive?"

Jane ran up and gave Michael a big hug, saying, "We found you. Where's Amy? Is she okay?" She was crying and laughing at the same time.

Joe and Preston shook hands and gave each other a hug. Preston said, "Damn good to see you, brother. I would have never left if I knew you were still there. I'm so sorry; I had no idea. How in the world did you survive?"

"Well, there was one thing I never told or showed you. I built a fallout shelter in the basement. We dove in there just as the first round hit. The only problem was that one of the main beams fell across the door, blocking it, and I had one hell of a time getting us out."

Jane walked over and gave Preston a big hug. "Take me to Amy. Where is she? How far away is it?"

Preston laughed, returning her hug, and said, "It's good to see you too, Jane. Amy's fine and she can fill you in on all of the details."

Preston looked at Joe and said, "What took you so long? I had given up on ever seeing you again."

"Well, first of all, I had to get us out of there and, thank God, we had the Last Chance camp built. We stayed back there until Jane healed up and I traded for a couple of bikes. We headed out and spent a couple of weeks helping a small community get rid of a warlord. Afterwards, they didn't want us around anymore, so we left." He added, "It was well worth the wait. Just wait until you see the supplies we have. By the way, what happened to the camp?"

"We had a little trouble, but that's taken care of now. Come on, let's go see Amy."

They rode off to the new house. When they arrived, Preston walked in first, blocking the door and, as Amy was getting wheat sprouts growing, she looked up at Preston. "All burned up? Nothing worth saving?"

Preston had to keep a straight face as he said, "I don't know. We got interrupted by some people."

Amy looked up with worried look on her face. "More of the bad guys?" she asked.

He stepped to one side and Jane came running in. The shocked look on Amy's face was priceless. Her jaw dropped open and she stuttered, "What? That can't be...is it really you, Jane?"

They hugged each other and were both babbling at the same time and crying. Nobody could understand a thing.

Preston showed Joe around, "It has an electric water pump. They have a Mr. Brainiac here and he's trying to make a wood gasifier to run generators for everybody."

Joe said, "That sounds wonderful. By the way, we have some supplies stashed. Some really good supplies, but we need to go and get them right now. The friends that helped us bring it all up in a wagon had to leave. When we saw the camp burned to the ground, we stashed the stuff in a house a few miles from here." Joe asked, "Do you have some friends with a wagon that could help us haul it all here?"

Preston said, "Yes we do. We can send Michael to go get some help and a wagon. It shouldn't be a problem and you and I can go protect the supplies, but first we need to show Michael where it is."

They got on their bikes and headed off. It was a little more than a couple of miles. A couple of miles means different things to different people and it was more like 5 miles. They showed Michael where to bring the wagon and help, and then he headed to Scott's place.

Joe and Preston went and looked at the booty, with Preston ogling all of it. He looked at the Kel-Tec KSG shotguns. "Wow, I've never seen a shotgun like this. What does that thing hold, 20 rounds?"

Joe said, "It holds 14 in the duel tubes, seven in each one, and one in the chamber, so you have 15 shots. We have 500 rounds of buckshot and slugs to go with it."

Joe picked it up and started explaining the space-age-looking high-tech shotgun. "What's great about it is . . . look at this..." Holding the firearm, Joe worked the action. "See? It's like a normal pump action shotgun, right? The difference being that you grab it here," he said, showing him the handle. "Pull down and a handle drops down."

Preston responded, "That's awesome and it gives you a better hold for quicker action on the pump."

Joe continued, "You empty one tube, flip this little lever and the other tube is ready to go. If you're using three-inch Magnum's, you can only fit six in each tube."

Preston reached out and Joe handed him the shotgun. "Kind of heavy." he whipped it up to his shoulder, "Wow. What great balance it has." He worked the action. "Smooth, but I love that drop-down handle. How do you get it to go back up?"

"You push in on the stop button here," Joe showed him, "and then it will fold back up. It also ejects out the bottom. Here, let me show you how to load it."

Preston handed the shotgun back to Joe, who opened an ammo box full of buckshot. "You load it here," he said, showing him the loading and ejection port on the bottom, "pushing each shell in just like a normal shotgun, but here's the cool part. You see the slots on each side? You can quickly look and see how much ammo you have left in each tube."

Changing the subject, Preston asked, "How you doing on food?"

Joe told him that they had about 6 months' worth for two people, a little over 2 months for all of them. He asked Preston, "How's the stash at the camp?"

"I don't know. I got interrupted when you showed up and wasn't able to find out if it survived the fire or not. After we take care of this stuff, we'll go check it tomorrow. How does that sound?"

"Great. It's just so good to be here and know you guys made it. We really missed you guys."

A couple of hours later, the wagon pulled in with Scott, a friend and Michael. Preston made the introductions and they got to work. They loaded all of it into the wagon and took it to the new house.

Once they unloaded everything, Preston asked Scott if they could borrow the wagon and team, so they could go see if any of the supplies at the cabin survived.

Scott said, "Sure. Just make sure you take care of the horses. Give them plenty of food and water and you can bring them back tomorrow night. Will that work for you?"

Preston said, "That's great."

Scott asked, "But how are we going to get home?"

"You can borrow our bikes of course."

Scott nodded his approval and he and his friend headed for home on the bikes.

As Preston continued to show Joe around his new place, he said, "We can take that rain barrel," pointing to one at the corner of the house, "and take it down to the lake and fill it with water. We can use it to put a bucket full of water in the toilet tank and then we'll be able to use the toilet like normal."

Michael said, "What about toilet paper?"

"I give you a working toilet and you want toilet paper, too. Picky, picky, picky."

Joe and Preston both laughed and then Preston said, "That's your other job. Go forth and find us phone books and old newspapers. We'll find some scissors and just cut the newspaper to toilet paper size. Not the best, but it will have to do."

"What will we do for showers?" Joe asked, as they were riding down to the lake in the wagon.

"For right now, we can just use solar energy. Did you see that TV series of the survivalist experiment called Colony? They took a big black tank and put it up on the roof and then gravity fed a hose down to the shower with a shut off valve. We can do something similar. We can take "Navy" showers: soak ourselves, shut off the water, soap up and then rinse off. If we do it right and can find a 30 or 50 gallon tank, we can fill it once a day and have enough water to take our showers at night."

Joe looked at Preston. "And you didn't think to buy me that TV series as a Christmas present?"

Preston responded, "What? Why didn't you buy it for me? Oh, that's right, you didn't know about it. I guess we both have secrets, like you not telling me about your little fallout shelter. You know I would have dug it all out by hand to find you two."

"Oh, for Christ sake, don't bring that up. I had to listen to Jane for days about how stupid I was, so don't you start in on it." He quickly added, "I'm sorry. You're right, but please drop it."

Preston laughed heartily and said, "I bet in that small space you heard quite a bit about it?"

"Yes and I will never *not* tell you everything from now on."

They reached the lake and filled up the barrel, hauling it back to the house. They managed to get it off the wagon, without spilling too much, and put it close to the back door, which was nearest to the bathroom.

They had a great time that night and it felt so good to be back together.

The next day, Joe, Michael and Preston went to the cabin to see what they could salvage. Using rakes and shovels, they cleared a path in the debris to the door going down into the root cellar. Parts of the floor were burnt-out, but other parts of it were still together and holding strong.

They sent Michael down the stairs because he was lightest. He called up that some of the buckets on top were burned and melted, but it looked like the rest were okay. He asked, "What do you want me to do?"

Joe told him, "Carefully, try to move the top burned ones off and start hauling the good ones up."

Of the 46 5-gallon buckets stored in the root cellar, they had only lost eight. "At least we have food. Now we just need to add deer and maybe a bear and we'll be in good shape," Joe said.

Preston said, "Maybe even a cow, if we get lucky. We saw some feral ones running around a couple of weeks ago. Wouldn't that be awesome if we could eat some rib eye steaks come January? If Brett, the genius, works out this wood gas thing, we could be driving around in a truck, have electricity, a working freezer and a real water pump.

Life will be good. If he can rig up a tractor to run on it, we should be able to get the whole community going pretty easily and start rebuilding civilization, one wood gas generator at a time."

Joe smiled. "It would be great. Now all we have to do is clean up the vermin. We still have a score to settle with those Rainbow Warriors."

"You bet we do. But first, we need to take care of the necessities of life. Let's get our community going. Let's get our crops in and our cattle, pigs and chickens can start producing milk, real butter, cheese and, of course, bacon and eggs. If everyone on the outside will leave us alone, we've got a real good chance of making it here."

"What about the Rainbow Warriors?" Joe asked.

Preston said, "Well, according to Scott, they were stopped about 50 miles east of here. If we can join all the survivors together, under a mutual agreement, I'm sure we can clean them all the way out. We just have to find out what they're up to in this state."

Joe nodded and said, "Okay then, let's go meet this genius and get these gas generators and vehicles going."

As they were riding back to the house with the supplies, Michael asked, "Can I go bear hunting?"

Both men laughed and Preston said, "Not with your .22, but I think you're big and strong enough to use the 12-gauge with slugs. You need some serious fire power to knock a bear down."

Michael said, "Good. I always wanted a bearskin rug."

Joe laughed. "That will definitely impress the girls. They'll be fighting over you, Michael."

"Girls? Huh? What the heck do they have to do with the bearskin rug? Besides, I don't even like girls."

Preston laughed. "In a few more years you will and then you'll spend your lifetime trying to figure them out. I'll give you a hint, don't even try."

Both men laughed, but Michael just had a quizzical look on his face.

They made it back to the house and unloaded all of the supplies, and then Joe and Preston left to return the wagon and horses.

When they arrived and thanked Scott, he mentioned that they should go see Brett tomorrow and see how the plans are coming for the wood gas.

Joe said, "It would be great if we get some vehicles running. We can do real patrols and clean out this area, keeping the vermin out. Then we'll have a nice community."

Joe asked, "By the way, how many people are there in the community?"

Scott said, "Well, we're looking at about 300 people in the community, but we used to have 4500 in the whole county. Almost a 95% reduction. And I really couldn't tell you how many we lost due to murder, disease and starvation, or they just packed up and headed out."

Preston said, "My figure was that 90% of the population would be gone the first year. I say this fall we take care of this county and then expand south. Joe already knows some of the people down there. We do that county next year. We keep training teams, sharing knowledge and expanding, then we should be able to handle two counties the following year."

"It will be a long, slow process and we need to figure out some type of monetary system. We can branch out through the whole Upper Peninsula of Michigan and even into Minnesota. We can write a Constitution and keep the damn lawyers out. Who knows, in two hundred years America might be a really nice place to live. We're going to have set it up better this time—term limits for elected offices and no government bureaucracy—just hire the minimal number of people the government needs to operate, with firm limits on everything and the things they are allowed to do, and with an honest money system based on silver and gold. I think we should ban lawyers altogether. The whole corrupt justice system needs to be canned and reworked, so all laws are written for the common man and anyone can defend themselves when disputes arise. We get rid of this whole 'judge-deciding-what-the-jury-can-and-can't-hear'. No special justice language. No special "good old boys" club of lawyers deciding everything."

When Joe finally finished, Scott looked at him and said, "Sounds like paradise. How do we do it?"

"Well, my idea is that we will have to build in restraints to hold the government accountable to the people, with grand juries of common men and women being convened to oversee all government officials. The second the officials step out of line and break a law, they'd be immediately tossed in prison; of course, after being given a fair trial."

"We go back to "knock first" search warrants, no more SWAT teams, no more flash-bang grenades and breaking down the door. We can do this right, but the only way is with grand juries to review government officials. Term limits, prison time and accountability; that's the only way I see it working."

Preston said, "Aren't you getting a little ahead of yourself? Don't you think we need to take care of surviving first?"

Scott laughed, "Okay gentlemen, have a good night. Let's plan on meeting here in the morning and we'll go talk to Brett. Let's take care of the immediate problems first and worry about the rest later. But I do like what you're saying, Joe, and by the way, welcome to our community. You're a fine asset."

Joe smiled and shook his hand. "Scott, I like you already and I'm looking forward to hammering out a new civilization with you."

Preston and Joe rode the bikes back to the house and called it a night.

Chapter 22

Scavenging

> "One man's trash is another man's treasure, what he doesn't appreciate the next man will."
>
> ~Unknown

That morning, Joe and Preston were at Scott's house and they rode over to meet Brett and see what he had come up with. They warned Joe about Brett being a little eccentric.

Arriving at Brett's house, they knocked on the door and Brett once again opened the door and stood there staring at them, lost in his own world of thought.

Scott said, "Brett, did you find the gasifier book you were looking for?"

Brett looked at him like he had just asked the dumbest question ever and said, "Of course I found it. You guys can handle this; I'm going to fix them windmills." He motioned for them to come in and continued, "You see, what Americans have done wrong is, instead of having lots of devices to do things, they should have made one unit to take care of everything in their house. Instead of having an electric or propane cooking stove, a furnace for heat, and a separate hot water heater, they should have made it an all-in-one unit to take care of all the household needs."

He led them into the kitchen and explained, "You are going to have a wood stove going in the winter to heat your house, right?" Not waiting for an answer he continued, "So all you have to do is have a wood burning stove to heat the house and cook on, plus plumb the stove with tubing to heat water. Having the water tank near the stove, you can let thermo siphoning move the hot water to the tank for storage. As the water heats, it naturally rises in the tank, displacing the cold water. Placing a boiler tank by your wood stove, you can run a loop of pipe inside the wood stove and then to the tank. As the stove heats the water, it rises into the tank, circulating the cold water into the stove to be heated, thus eliminating the need for a hot water heater.

Constructing it this way, you wouldn't have to worry about adding a circulating pump to move the water. Let nature do it for you using a thermo-siphon system."

Joe and Preston looked at each other and then to Scott, who had a quizzical look too.

Brett went through some papers on the counter and pulled out a single piece of paper. He held it up, showing it to them and said, "Here gentlemen, I wrote it all out for you. It's all of the principles you need to understand. First, let's look at the hot water heater part. There are a few technical details you need to know before you can just run off and do this. You want to use galvanized three-quarter-inch pipe and preferably stainless steel pipes, if you can find them. You make one simple horseshoe loop inside the top of your wood box and run it out the back. Now, in order to get nature to work for you, your cold-water return has to be a certain height above the wood stove. Here's a simple rule that you must follow in order for it to work." Brett pointed to the drawing and said, "For every two horizontal feet away from the stove your storage tank is, you must have 1-foot of vertical drop; so if your wood stove is 5 feet away from the hot water heater, you need to be two and a half feet above the wood stove. It's fairly simple. Are you following me?"

Scott looked at the drawing and said, "It sounds fairly simple. I think I can work it out from the information you have here."

Brett continued rattling off information. "Also, try to avoid 90 degree elbows because it interrupts the flow of the water, so 45s are preferred. Only thing you have to be careful about is making sure the pressure relief valve on top of the hot water tank is operating properly and is piped safely outside. If you're getting the water too hot, you don't want your water spraying inside the house. It's kind of a delicate act to get this all just right, but once it's set up and finished, it's well worth the time."

He continued, only pausing long enough for a breath, "This would be your fall and winter hot water source. In the summer, when you may only have a fire in the stove for a meal, I suggest that you guys build a simple solar tank and install it on the roof. Paint it black and let the sun heat the water for you, while gravity provides the water pressure. Doing this would give you hot water year-round and eliminate the need for a propane or electrical water heater."

Preston was getting a little frustrated, as they just came to get the information on the wood gasifier. He said, "Thank you very much for all the technical information. Now, the most important question is how do we get our generators running on wood gas?"

Brett picked up a black binder and said, "I have that information right here. The most important thing is finding enough barrels and fittings to produce them for all of the residents."

He quickly added, "Like I said before, I think people should use batteries to run lights and small electrical devices, keeping them charged with the gasified generator. When you really think about personal comfort, you only need hot water, which we just solved, a refrigerator with a freezer to keep food from spoiling, and it would also be nice if the washing machine worked. Clothes could be hung to dry. Hang them outside in the warmer months and inside by the stove in the winter and colder months. Drying the clothes indoors in the winter would also help the humidity."

Brett's mind was working faster than his mouth and, barely taking a breath, he said, "To run the electrical appliances, you would run the generator. You could run it a couple of hours a day to provide electricity for those. Limiting the opening of the refrigerator and freezer, it would stay cold enough throughout the day."

"Now, with generators, you have to keep the oil changed to keep them running, so you need to find a source for that. I think most gas generators are only rated for about 1000 hours. So, let me see." He closed his eyes and did some math in his head. "If they ran up 2 hours a day for 365 days, that's 730 hours. That leaves us with about 135 days, so they should last about 16 months per generator. That is, of course, if the people maintained them." He managed another breath and continued, "The air filters must be cleaned regularly and have the oil changed on time. And, let me see, those calculations were if we started with new generators. If we have used generators, it would, of course, change the length of time they would last. But it would definitely give us some time to get other things in operation, like my wind generators. That's why I'm still working on them. And if we could find a couple of large industrial diesel generators, like the hospitals use, we could provide electricity to whole neighborhoods."

The 3 men could only listen as Brett gave them all of this information. They politely nodded every once in a while, letting him go on.

Brett continued, "As for getting some cars and trucks running on wood gas, we would have to find some of the older models that were still working before the EMP and then we could adapt the gasifiers to fuel them too. They did it in Europe during the war, so there is no reason we can't do it now."

Scott took Brett's brief pause to say, "Right now, we should probably focus on getting everyone generators, batteries and wood gasifiers, then each household could have and manage their own power."

"Yes, yes, of course, gentlemen," Brett interjected, "but that just puts a temporary patch, a band-aid if you will, on the problem. We need to think bigger. Plus, the word will spread quickly around the different areas, which will mean more people coming here for the good life. Have you thought about how you're going to deal with that? More people generally equals more problems. Anyway, I think for the long-term we need to get the wind generators fixed and use the existing electrical grid. I'm not quite sure how to fix the transformers, so I haven't figured out how to put out the high-voltage. We need at least 10,000 volts to even run a mini-electrical grid and then we have to step it down with a transformer to 110 volts going to each house. With all the transformers blown, I haven't figured out how to do that yet. Maybe the wood generator is the best way to go, for now."

Pausing to think, he continued, "But even with little generators, you will need at least a 5,000 watt output to operate each home. It is still just a band-aid fix. And then there's the other option of going with gas or diesel engine out of vehicles to power a 10 to 20 KW generator, providing power to several houses at a time. But again, we come back to a temporary solution."

Preston smiled, "You did a great job, Brett, and we really want to thank you. We'll get the band-aid going and you can continue to work on your long-term project. If we get the bigger engines, the 3 or 4 cylinder types, we might even get lucky and get 4 years out of them."

"Yes, yes, of course, gentlemen, but it's still a band-aid fix. I have a book here somewhere that shows how a big power plant works. We could even make a steam plant, or something along those lines, but I must get back to work." And, without a pause, he said, "Good day, gentlemen." With that, Brett turned and left the room. The men took their cue and left the house.

Scott smiled, "Yes, he's a little eccentric, but you'll get used to him after a while."

Joe said, "A little? I'd say a lot. Okay, where to now?"

Scott suggested, "Let's go see the guy in charge of the salvage team. His name is Bob Shoenrock. He owns a junkyard and is a master at turning junk into treasures."

They rode the horses Scott had provided for about an hour and pulled into a big salvage yard. Bob was out in the garage clearing an area, so they had space to work on the gasifier. Scott made the introductions and asked for an update.

Bob started, "Well, finding enough generators can be a problem. We have 75 homes that need them and, so far, we've only been able to find 12 generators. So what I think we should do is start looking for 5 to 10 horsepower size engines." Pointing out into the junkyard he said, "We can rig up alternators from the cars to run DC lighting, using 12-volt automobile lights, but we'd still need inverters to power the AC items like water pumps, freezers and clothes washers."

Scott handed Bob the plans for the gasifier and asked if Bob could build one of them. Bob looked it over and said, "Sure, but 75? I doubt it. We'll be doing good to get 20 of these up and running before winter, heck, it may be only 10 of them. I say we get a couple of trucks running first; that way, we'll be able to travel farther and salvage more. Plus, we can definitely use them for patrols. We can rig up a couple of 4 x 4s with a trailer and we should be able to haul in a lot of stuff."

Scott said, "Patrols out of a real vehicle? Tell me I'm not dreaming."

They all laughed and Preston said, "This wood gasifier was for a fixed system, so how can you adapt it to work for a moving vehicle?"

Bob said, "For the short run, I can find enough old oil and cooking grease to run diesel engines without having to adapt them. For running other engines on wood gas, you let me worry about that. Now, if I were you guys, I would get out salvaging. Even if you can only find generators with blown engines, it doesn't matter; we can replace them with a good engine. We just need the generators."

The 3 men rode out, heading back to Scott's place. They discussed how they would go about finding the generators. Where would they look? What would be most likely place to find some?

Joe said, "We're not fussy. A 5000-watt generator is all we need. Heck, we'd even settle for 3500-watt, if that's all we could find."

Preston offered, "If we can get a water pump, clothes washer and a freezer going, we would be in great shape."

Back at Scott's place, he took them over to a map and pointed to a spot. "All right, here's the section the salvage teams have already searched. Generators are first come first serve. Whoever finds them, keeps the first one for themselves. It's only fair, since they're the ones doing the work. After that, they add them to the pile. You guys are going to have figure out who gets what. You let me worry about making them work. Two of the guys that used to work for me are on the salvage team, so you two need to relieve them because I need them here. You will also need to take over being in charge of the salvage team, because George needs to get back to work on the farm."

"Okay then, we'll get out of your hair." Joe said.

Scott turned to Joe and Preston, and said, "I'll see you two in the morning."

Scott took their horses and they got their bikes, said their goodbyes and headed home.

When they got home, they had a new problem. They needed water and, without the horses and wagon, they had no way to haul it. Using two bikes, they strapped two-by-six pieces of wood across the frames, making essentially a four-wheeled cart. They strapped eight of the 5-gallon buckets onto the wood and walked it down to the lake.

They filled each bucket, secured it back on the platform and took these back to the house. They almost filled the 55-gallon drum. They repeated this, filling the barrel the rest of the way. While doing this, they discussed how Michael might be able to do this by himself. They both concluded that he would have to carry fewer buckets and make more trips, but it was doable.

Joe said, "We have got to get a generator up and running so we can run the water pump. This hauling water is for the birds."

Preston laughed. "Maybe we should just pick the house up and move it closer to the lake. Sure would be easier."

Joe chuckled, "Okay, Superman, let me know when you get it done. Maybe we should look for a better location. Something closer to water this time."

"Well, after talking to Brett and Bob, it may be a month or more before we get something up and running, so we should seriously think about finding another place."

"Well, we could let Amy, Michael and Jane search the area for another house. We could tell them the things to look for and, if they found something, we could look at it."

"We should leave somebody here with the supplies. We have way too much to lose if everyone's gone and someone stumbles across this place. I say we leave Jane behind and let Amy and Michael go out searching."

Joe said, "That sounds like a plan." He then asked, "Do you know how a ram pump works?"

Preston shook his head no and Joe continued, "Basically it uses the flow of the stream and you can actually pump water uphill, as much as 300 meters. If we could find a house or a big camp near a fast flowing stream, we could rig up a ram pump. That could take some serious work, but it sure would be worth it."

Over dinner that night they talked about their plan. Michael said, "That's a great idea, plus I can go fishing every day and I'll bet you I can find where to go bear hunting."

Jane looked at Michael with raised eyebrows, saying, "Bear hunting? You're not going bear hunting. You're too young."

Amy added, "That's right. You have to wait until you get older."

Michael smiled and said, "Too late. Preston and Joe already said I could go. I'm going to use one of those new fancy 12-gauge shotguns. A 12-gauge slug would knock over an elephant, so there's nothing to worry about."

Before either of them could protest, Preston quickly added, "That's right, he's old enough now and he's definitely big enough. Besides, Joe or myself will be with him at all times, so there's nothing to worry about. He's got to grow up sometime."

Jane looked at Joe, "Next time you two make such a decision, I think we should all talk about it before giving or denying anything."

Amy jumped in, "They say bear lard is fantastic for bread grease. I think it would add to our baking and I'm sure we can figure out how to make it taste good. Shouldn't have to use very much and we could definitely use it. I just think we should wait until it cools off, like the beginning of October. The bears should be nice and fat, looking for a place to hibernate." She turned back to Michael and said, "Looks like you're going bear hunting, Michael."

Michael was beaming from ear to ear. "Cool. I'll get a great big one and have a great big bear rug to keep me warm at night."

The next morning they met Scott at his house, left their bikes there, got on the wagon with seven other men and headed off in search of generators.

Some of the summer homes were powered with off-the-grid solar panels, which charged battery packs and had generators for backup. These were the places they were looking for first. The men on horses rode ahead and 3 men would check each house, doing a quick search for the materials that they needed. Any and all pipe fittings, pipe wrenches, barrels and inverters were collected and brought back to the wagon. If there was a generator, they would direct the wagon to the house so it could be disconnected and loaded. One man always stayed out on the road to watch for trouble.

It was the most efficient way to get the job done. That way the wagon wasn't wasting time traveling down each road or driveway to an individual house. They were also looking for any survivors.

By two o'clock that afternoon, the wagon was overflowing. They had found one more generator and some boxes of different pipe fittings, but what filled up the wagon were all the different size barrels they'd found. They decided to call it a day and head back to the junkyard.

It was already August and they needed to hurry up before fall brought rainy weather. They also had to find a couple of wood chippers to make fuel for the gasifiers. At least they were working together as a community and everyone was pitching in to help. Tomorrow they would repeat the process.

The next day was pretty much the same thing, but, as they were heading back at around three in the afternoon, they spotted a man near a house. He was wearing all camouflage and sitting on a horse, holding the reins of six other horses.

They stopped and Preston pulled out his AR-15 from the wagon. Joe pulled out his new high-tech shotgun and the rest of the men spread out around the driveway.

Once the men were in place, Scott called out, "Who are you and what are you doing here?"

The man called into the house. "We've got company." He then looked at the back of the open wagon and saw the barrels and generators. He called out, "We're doing the same thing you're doing. Salvaging what we need to survive."

Scott hollered back, "Sorry, but this area is protected and you will have to move on, preferably peacefully. If not, we can handle that too."

By then most the other men had come out of the house and mounted their horses. They rode right up to Scott and the wagon and, seeing that they were covered, they drew no weapons. The one that had been talking continued, "So where would you like us to go and, by the way, who the hell are you to tell us where we can and can't go?"

Scott responded, "The County here has duly elected us as the Wisconsin Militia, to patrol and protect this area. It is our duty to keep the community safe. We are not going to have any trouble in our community and we decide who stays and who goes. Any more questions?"

Scott could tell that these men were battle hardened; you could see it in their eyes, and he felt the tension mounting. They all had rifles slung over their backs and none of them wanted to get into a shooting match right now.

Scott tried to ease the tension and asked them, "Where are you boys coming from?" He was hoping to defuse the situation and hoped the men would choose to move on without violence.

He could tell that these men were unafraid and, rather than answer Scott's question, the man said, "So what happens if we decide to stay?"

Preston interrupted. "If you want to make this difficult, you'll have one hell of a fight on your hands. We tried being nice about it. To put it bluntly, you can ride out of here peaceably or we can bury you here. It doesn't matter to us if you want to fight. So what's it going to be, boys?"

The spokesman for the group looked around at the men and their weapons and then said, "We're leaving. How far south do we have to travel to get out of your county?"

Scott interrupted, "We'll be happy to escort you out of the county. This is your friendly one-time pass and we advise you not to come back, or we will have a fight on our hands.

The man said, "Not a very friendly bunch are you? We're leaving and we won't be back."

Scott smiled, "That's good, because we have a heck of a lot more men than what you're seeing and it would not be good for you if you returned." They backed their horses out of the driveway and Scott pointed in the direction for them to go. "We'll be right behind you, just in case you get lost."

After they rode past the group, Scott stopped at the wagon and told them, "You two go ahead and take this stuff back. I'll swing by your house later tonight and let you know what happened."

Preston and Joe talked back and forth as they drove the wagon. Preston said, "Kind of reminds you of the Wild West, doesn't it?"

Joe gave him a half smile and said, "I guess in a lot of ways that is what we are now. Think about it. There's no real law enforcement. No jails, no judges, or courts." He continued, "Once they ride out, they start all over and each community they go to will have to deal with them. It's not like we can call the Sheriff in the next county and let them know what's going on. And there's no TV news reporting on what they've done, so I guess you're right, it is the new Wild West."

Preston asked, "What do you think—five years, ten years, before we get everything settled down again?"

Joe laughed, "I hope it won't take that long. Look where we are already. People are going to have to learn to work together to survive.

Sure, there are some bad asses and tough guys that want to play Wild West, but I think, within a couple years, we can have this community up and running and have a fairly good life here. The cold, harsh winter is going to be our best friend, keeping the riffraff out."

They took the wagon to the junkyard, dropping off the stuff, and then returned the wagon to the Scott's house. They unhitched the wagon and removed the gear from the horses, releasing them into the corral. They then jumped on their bikes and headed for home.

Scott stopped by on his way home that evening, just to let them know that the men left the county without any problems.

Chapter 23

Crop Planning

"Farming is a profession of hope"

~Brian Brett

Jane and Amy began working on a nutritional chart, something to give people a rough idea of what they needed for food. They were going off the Mormon basic of just dry goods; meat was up to the person to trade, barter, or hunt for.

They came up with a list of needs. A family of four would require: wheat - 600 pounds, 100 pounds of oats, 200 pounds of rice, 240 pounds of beans, 100 pounds of white flour, 100 pounds of cornmeal, about 200 pounds of honey or maple syrup as a sugar substitute, 200 pounds of lard, 50 pounds of assorted dried fruit and about 300 pounds of meat. And that was just the bare bones. Milk and water would be essential liquids, along with fresh fruits and vegetables, especially if the family had young children.

They just had to get a tractor going so they would be able to plant more food. The wild rice in the area would help, of course. They figured an average yield of 22 bushels of wheat per acre, or 968 pounds, without using pesticides. Plus, they would have to save the seed stock for the next year's planting, too. They figured there were about 75 households and the amount of food needed would vary, depending on how many people were living in the house. Sixty households would need the above amount of food. They roughly figured 44 pounds to a bushel, so they were going to need 50 acres in just wheat. They concluded that they would have to grow at least 100 acres, so they would have enough extra for seed stock, plus extra to save for bad years. They had no clue how much they needed for white flour, unless someone had put up white wheat berries. For corn, they figured 25 bushels an acre, with no pesticides, and around 40 pounds per bushel, or 1,000 pounds per acre. They'd need 15 acres, again saving seed stock, plus saving for bad years. They had Great Northern white beans and figured about 20 bushels an acre, at 45 pounds a bushel, 900 pounds per acre, call it 30 acres with seed stock, plus saving for bad years. They could supplement the corn to cover more acres as a backup, for the possibility of a bad wheat crop.

Jane said, “Having running tractors is a must. Of course, each family can grow their own gardens to have potatoes, tomatoes, squash, etc. Organizing this on a countywide cooperative is going to take some hammering out.”

After they finished the list, they went over it again and then Jane said, “Let’s not forget about the acres we’ll need to feed the livestock.”

Amy said, “Oh sure, throw a monkey wrench into our plans. I completely forgot about that. How much feed do we need for the chickens?”

Jane said, “I don’t know. I guess we can talk to the chicken farmers and find out how much food they say we’ll need. I know for cows they figure 10 acres per cow/calf pair; that’s 5 acres for pasture and 5 acres put up in hay.”

Amy said, “This is getting really complicated, isn’t it?”

Jane nodded and then continued, “According to what we’ve figured, we need to butcher about 50 cows each year. So, we need 500 acres just for the cows. I don’t know what the pigs need. We are going to have to learn all this the hard way and keep good records for future years. This is all just math, so we need to talk with the ranchers and find out how much they really need for the herds that they have.”

Amy said, “From what I can tell, we have to get everybody on a timetable for producing the food. The luxury of going to the grocery store to pick up things is over. We are going to have to dedicate a lot of hours each day in the field, just to make sure this works. Food is a number one priority.”

Jane was flipping through an old Countryside magazine and found an article on raising pigs, with a breakdown for the cost of raising a single piglet until it was 200 pounds. The feed alone was 1,350 pounds of grain. She told Amy, “You can supplement their feed with acorns and let them root around for food on their own, but at least 1,350 pounds of feed is needed.”

Amy just shook her head and wondered how they would be able to do everything that was needed for all of their survival. It was a daunting task they had ahead of them.

Jane added, "You also have to feed the stock that produced the piglet and, because they are larger, more mature animals, they require food for the full year. Therefore, figuring 60 pigs to fill our needs, we would require 12 females, with one male to service them. That would entail 2,400 pounds of feed for each of them and, figuring roughly 990 pounds per acre for grain, that would take another 116 acres of feed just for the pigs."

The next day, Amy and Jane rode over to the chicken farmer to gather real data and he told them that a medium-weight laying hen would eat about a pound of feed per day when she is producing.

Jane, using her paper and pencil, said, "So, two hundred chickens, at 50 pounds per day," doing some more math, "would be 18,250 pounds a year. That means we will need 405 bushels for chicken feed. Figure about 20 acres of the 781 acres in food production."

Amy said, "That seems like an incredible amount of land. How did we feed all of the people before this?"

Jane smiled. "We had modern food production with pesticides and optimal yields. A farmer in Iowa, for instance, was getting 200 bushels of corn per acre and, of course, this was field corn used to feed animals. In North Dakota, the wheat farmers were getting 45 to 55 bushels an acre for wheat. I'm just estimating as we don't know what we're going to need until we see the harvest reports and figure out how much per acre we're getting for yield."

Amy said, "Well, I know what little bit of experience I have in my garden, you have to kill the heck out of the weeds and the more weeds you kill, the more nutrition that goes to your plants, equaling a higher yield."

Jane smiled, "Yes, people had to dedicate a lot of time working these farms. The only thing I'm really worried about Is what happens if we have a bad crop year? A drought hits, a late frost comes, or not enough rain and there are a thousand other things that could go wrong. If we don't have a backup, there's no going to the next state, or country for that matter, getting the food we would need."

"We'll just have to do a lot of praying, a lot of hard work, and hope for the best. You do realize that with the plan we have, we can't take in any new people to the community. We'll have to be coldhearted and turn them away for our own survival," Amy said.

Jane nodded and added, "I know. That's why I don't want to be with the ones on patrol, as they are the ones that will have to turn women and children away, but I know we can't take in everybody. It's a hard, cold new world we're living in."

Shaking her head, Amy said, "From what I've seen of the crops around here, I know we don't have enough for this year. Let's hope the guys can get some tractors working and we can plant and work the heck out of these fields next year. We're in good shape for this year, with the supplies you guys brought in and the ones that were saved from the fire. But next year we have to have all this land and food production, or we are going to be toast."

They took all of their findings and went over to talk to Fred, leaving Michael behind to guard the camp and supplies.

Fred invited them into his house and said, "Welcome ladies. Nice of you to stop by." He gestured for them to sit down in the living room, saying, "The Mrs. is over working at the cattle farm, getting milk and butter for us to have tonight."

Jane looked at Amy. "Oh, we forgot the milk cows." Turning back to Fred, "We worked out a nutritional chart and it is based on some rough estimates, but we figured that for 300 people in the community here, we would need 781 acres planted for food production."

Fred laughed, "That's not counting the dairy cows, right?"

Jane and Amy laughed and Jane's face turned a little red. Amy jumped in and said, "Do you know what's going on with the gasifiers? If we can get these hooked up to run some tractors, putting the land into production shouldn't be that difficult."

Fred said, "Hang on a second ladies and let me grab the county map of the area." He walked into the other room and returned with the map, spreading it out on the coffee table. "Most of us are concentrated in this one third of the county. This is where we can easily patrol and keep an eye on things, watching out for one another. Now, if we expand just a few miles all the way around, I think we can have roughly 4,500 acres of farmland."

Jane and Amy smiled and nodded their heads, happy to hear that news.

Fred went on, "If we get that all into food crops, we're sure to have surplus and, using the storage bins in the area, we should even be able to put some food away for emergencies or bad years. I want to thank you both for breaking it down so we now have a rough idea of how to set up the plantings."

He added, "This year we barely had 200 acres planted, which we thought was quite good, and because you guys already have food you'll need less of a share. We can make sure everybody has food to get through this winter and hopefully all of the way to next harvest. It's not easy thinking in these terms, I know, and making decisions on who can come in and those we have to reject has kept me awake many a night."

Jane said, "Yes, we know we can't accept any new people in. We do want to thank you for allowing us to be part of this community and we will do our fair share of work." She added, "I don't know if Joe told you, but I'm also a qualified nurse. Are there any doctors in the area?"

Fred thought for a moment and then said, "I don't think so, but we do have a veterinarian; he doesn't have a nurse working with him and I'm quite sure he could use your help." Looking at Amy he said, "Do you have any special skills, my dear?"

Amy smiled at him and said, "Who, little old me? I'm a hard worker and not afraid to get my hands dirty, with no special skills, but we're all battle proven and I ain't a half bad shot, if I do say so myself."

Jane laughed and said, "Yes Fred, you don't want to be in front of her sights in a battle."

He smiled and said, "Ladies, it all sounds great and I thank you for your skills. Now, if you have the time, we can take a ride over and I can introduce you to the vet. Jane, you can start working for him and Amy you can pick which farmer you're going to help."

They rode over to the vet's place and were in awe of what a beautiful house he had. It was a totally restored two-story farmhouse and even had the white picket fence around the front. There was a nice big front porch and it even had a swing on it. Amy thought it was right out of a movie setting; it was so perfect. There was a very well kept red barn with a huge corral that had different animals running all over the place. There were goats, sheep, cows, horses and even chickens. The ladies weren't sure if they were patients, or belonged to the vet.

They walked up to the barn and the door was open. They saw the vet was walking toward them with a bucket.

Jane spoke first, "Are we interrupting you? Are you attending a sick animal?"

The man appeared to be in his fifties, with gray hair and farmer's coveralls. Jane's question caused him to laugh out loud. "Nope. I'm just collecting milk from the goats. Would you care for a glass?"

He then asked, "Fred, who are these lovely young ladies you brought to me?"

Fred made the introductions and the vet said, "Name's Tyler, but everybody calls me Ty."

Fred said, "Jane here is a registered nurse and I thought she might be able to give you a hand attending the sick people. I'm sure she'd be mighty handy for tending animals, too."

He looked Jane up and down, sizing her up. "Is that so? Well, why don't you come up to the house for a spell?" Looking at Amy, he said, "Are you a nurse, too?"

"No," Amy laughed, "I'm her friend. We travel together. Our husbands are out on the salvage team right now." She didn't want to mislead the good doctor into thinking they were single, just in case he was looking for a mate.

"Husbands? And here I was hoping you were single. It gets quite lonely out here, since my wife passed away. It would be nice to have a nurse to help me. Please come up to the house."

They walked up to the house and, once inside, they were surprised to see his house was very well kept and clean. He had beautiful antique furniture and the room felt warm and cozy. They walked down a hallway and into the kitchen, which had a long wooden table that appeared to be made out of oak. There were six tall-backed chairs around the table and he said, "Have a seat." He grabbed four glasses and poured everybody some fresh goat's milk.

Ty sat down and said, "I have an operating room that we've converted to treat people. We no longer take animals inside for treatment; we treat them out in the field, or in the barn." He continued, "I stored powdered bleach, like they use for swimming pools and we mix up batches to use for cleaning and sterilizing things. Like all hospitals, cleanliness is very important." He paused and then said, "Where are you living now, Jane, and how fast can you get here?"

She looked at Fred as she said, "Well, I think it's about a three-hour ride from here." Fred nodded, indicating that was about right.

Ty shook his head and said, "Three hours? That's not going to do. You're going to have move closer. If there were an emergency, I would need you to be within an hour. Is there a problem with moving?"

Jane laughed, saying, "We just got here. We were looking for another place as, at the place we're living in right now, we have to haul water in 55-gallon drums and 5-gallon buckets. Do you know of a place close by that has water close to the house? A stream, creek, or river would be good."

Ty's face lit up and he said, "Of course I do." He looked up at Fred and said, "Why didn't you show them the Berg's summer place?" Looking at Amy and Jane, he continued, "Some rich folks have a second home not far from here and it has a stream flowing about 50 yards from the house. On horseback, it's only about a half an hour away. So, the first step is for you guys to move over there—that's, of course, if your husbands agree."

Amy and she both laughed and Jane said, "If it's got water that close, don't worry, they'll agree."

Amy said, "And I'm looking for a farm to work. Where's the closest one around here?"

Ty said, "Well, if you don't mind working at a chicken farm, there's one about a 45-minute horse ride from here."

Changing the subject, he asked, "Do you guys have any children?"

Jane said, "None of our own, but we do have a twelve-year-old orphan that we've adopted. His name is Michael."

Ty smiled, "Good. We need a young lad around here to help keep the barn clean. He's not afraid of work is he?"

Amy spoke up, "If you let him ride horses, he'll work for hours for you. He does love riding horses and fishing too. We don't have horses and ride our bikes everywhere."

Ty finished off his glass of milk and said, "Fred, show these lovely ladies to their new house. I would expect it will probably take a week or so to get moved in and settled. After that, depending on the work-load, of course," looking at Jane, "you and Michael can plan to come by Mondays, Wednesdays and Fridays, if that's okay? And, of course, you'll be on call for any emergencies. Is that something you're willing to do?"

Jane answered, "Of course. I've been a nurse for a lot of years and that schedule would be almost routine, so that won't be a problem."

Fred interrupted, "Okay ladies, let's go look at your new house." They said their goodbyes and rode down the paved road, taking a left onto a dirt road.

When they arrived at the place, Jane and Amy couldn't believe their eyes. It was a beautiful two-story log home with a green metal roof and was right on a nice looking trout stream. It was a dream house. They walked into the house and in the center was a massive old-style river stone fireplace, with a high efficiency stove built in. The rustic wooden furniture fit the cabin perfectly and above the fireplace was a huge mounted elk head. The living area was open all the way to the roof and the other half had a log staircase going up to what they assumed were the bedrooms. There was a bedroom down-stairs, just off the pantry, and a door to a basement. There was a full bathroom and short hallway that led to the kitchen. It had a washer and dryer in the mudroom and led to the back door and a three-car garage.

Neither Jane nor Amy could believe their eyes. Amy asked, "How come somebody else hasn't taken this place already? What is it, haunted or something?" she laughed.

Fred chuckled, "No. No ghosts that I know of. Believe it or not, the remaining folks wanted to stay in their own homes, so it's wide open and you're more than welcome to move in. We have no idea what happened to the owners, but it's been almost a year and nobody has shown up."

Jane and Amy were so excited and could hardly wait to tell the boys about this incredible find. The girls were sure that the guys would jump at this perfect place.

Over dinner that night, they explained the events of the day and described the house so fast that the men couldn't get a word in edgewise. They all agreed that it sounded perfect and they would check it out in the morning.

There was no debate about moving and the next week was spent taking everything over to the new location. Joe had borrowed the horses and wagon to haul their belongings and supplies to the new house.

Everybody was extremely happy with the new place. Jane was especially happy to find a stainless steel Berkey water filter system, with the charcoal filters, in the kitchen. That was a lucky break for them, because the ceramic ones tend to crack and split in the cold weather.

The first thing Michael did was explore every single room, including the garage and basement. He reported that the garage had a small workshop set up and the basement had a water pump and a heater, plus cupboards and lots of storage.

He asked if he could have an upstairs bedroom and they told him they would discuss it at dinner. It took three trips to get all of the supplies to the new house, then Preston and Joe returned the horses and wagon.

They all agreed to let Michael have a bedroom upstairs, discovering that there were three bedrooms. Joe and Jane would take the one with the master bathroom and Preston and Amy could have the downstairs bedroom and bathroom.

Later that week, over at the junkyard, Bob had built his prototype of the gasifier and had it up and running. It was working like a champ and, when loaded up with small pieces of wood, it would run for about 2 hours. He had it hooked up to a generator and it was putting out power. He was almost as excited as the other men, knowing it meant more could be built and would help provide power to other homes.

Having the generator providing power, he was able to use the power tools he needed to start mass-producing more of these gasifiers and hopefully enough for everybody.

The following week, the wheat harvest began and the majority of the people were out in the fields with anything that would cut the stems. They had sickles, machetes, grass cutters and even kitchen knives. One man had the job to keep all of the tools sharpened. He had rigged up a foot-pedal grinding wheel and was able to sharpen all the tools.

It was a real community effort; as the people cut the tops off, they were collected and put in bushel baskets. Others hauled them to the cleaning area. This was where the wheat kernel, called the wheat berry, was rubbed off onto a sheet. Once the pile was big enough, it was then used to toss the wheat into the air to winnow the outer husk, or chaff, and clean the wheat berries. The idea behind this was that the wheat berries were heavy and the chaff, once broken free, would be taken away with a light breeze. The trick, of course, was to have the correct amount of wind and not toss it too high. Maybe, if they were lucky, they could have a combine running for next year's harvest. That would make all their lives so much easier. The modern combine was truly one of man's better inventions. Not only did it cut the stocks, but it also broke the outer husk off, throwing it out the back and leaving nothing but the clean wheat berries.

Even with those long hours of hard work, everybody worked together because they understood how important having their daily bread was.

The wheat harvest took five full days. After they were done, the cattle were put in the field to fatten up on any of the grain that was missed and clean the field. Their by-product, of course, would help fertilize it with their own special piles.

In roughly 2 weeks, the sweet corn would be done and another massive harvest would be needed. The corn, of course, was eaten fresh, but most of it had to be stripped off the cob. Again the teamwork was amazing. While some of the people were harvesting the corn, filling up bushels, others hauled it up to the cleaning stations. The job of those people would be to strip off the outer layer and then, using a homemade tool, strip the kennels off the cob. Massive drying racks were set up using window screens; their purpose was to have dried, cracked corn for grinding up into cornmeal.

Some of the stripped cobs were fed to the pigs and most ate the entire thing, while some was dried out and ground as fodder for the cows. Several acres of corn were left to dry on the stocks and would be harvested and hand-shelled later for use as animal feed.

The last big harvest was Great Northern white beans. Again, these were collected and put in baskets, hauled up to a cleaning station where the husks were broken off and the beans were put out to dry. There was no loafing around. Your share was being determined by the amount of hours you worked.

Once the final harvest was done, they had a big Harvest Festival. Aside from great food and music, they planned weddings at the same time. The local Deacon from one of the churches served as the minister for those couples that wanted to get married. Of course, the women were making a huge deal out of this. Amy and a local nineteen-year-old girl named Barb were getting married at the same time. Wedding dresses were located, clothing, accessories and shoes for the wedding parties were found, and wildflowers and roses for decorations and bouquets were collected. The brides were going to be beautiful for their special day. Everyone pitched in and helped to make this day of celebration special for everyone.

The whole town went on a hunt for nice dressy clothes and shoes. Jane and Amy convinced the women to go and find beautiful clothes, shoes, make up and everything they could think of. A hair dresser was located.

Jane and Amy asked for help from all the women and really wanted the whole town involved with the celebration. This would be the first day since the world had ended that they would celebrate life and love. All the people here needed that. They needed to remember that life could be good and fun too. Life was not just hard work, hungry bellies and living in fear. They needed the feeling of hope, happiness and a bright future in their hearts, even if it was just for one day.

A feast fit for kings was prepared to be served after the ceremony. They even had a local country-western band playing live music for the occasion. This was the biggest event the community had gathered for since the lights went out. Everyone was looking forward to it and everyone did their part to make it the best festival ever.

Preston, with the help of junkyard Bob, had melted down a gold coin and made it into rings. He used sandpaper and lapping compound to polish them out.

Amy and Jane were running around like chickens with their heads cut off. The big day was finally here. Preston borrowed a suit and tie, but still wore his combat boots. He strapped on his .45, because the world was still a dangerous place. Almost every person carried a gun wherever they went, just in case something came up.

Joe came up to Preston laughing, "Are you sure you know what you're doing? You're going to be stuck with her forever." He handed Preston a Mason jar that had clear liquid in it. "Here, take a drink to stop your hands from shaking."

Preston took a smell and it made his eyes water. "Where in the heck did you find moonshine?" He took a drink and put it down. "Wow. That's some strong stuff." He took another drink and handed it back to Joe. "You have the rings ready, right?"

Joe looked confused, "Rings? I thought you had them."

Preston scowled at Joe and said, "Don't give me that nonsense. You'd better have them on you. Do you know how many hours of work it took me to make them?"

Joe let out a big laugh and said, "Of course I have them. By the way, who's giving Amy away?"

Preston was struggling with his tie and said, "Ty said he would do it, since it's his place that we're having this festival at."

A local church had brought over a small organ and they could hear it begin to play. Preston looked at Joe with a panicked look. "Oh no. I think that's my cue. Let me get one more shot."

Joe laughed, "Nope, my friend." He reached up and straightened Joe's tie, patted him on the shoulder and said, "You're ready as is. Stop making excuses and get your butt out there. If you don't get out there right now, Amy will shoot you and yell at me for days about what a lousy best man I was. If you think I'm going to listen to that, just because you chickened out, you don't know me very well. Now get out there."

They walked outside where benches were set up on each side of the aisle. A platform had been built for the Deacon and they walked up with the other bridegroom and his best man.

Preston thought, *If he looked more scared than me, I'd feel better.* The organ began playing, "Here Comes the Bride." A cute little boy and girl that looked about five walked in front of the brides, sprinkling wildflowers along the path. When they made it to the end, they kissed, turned and walked away. The little boy wiped his mouth on his sleeve and said, "Yuck!" and everyone laughed. The two brides came walking down the aisle, with Amy wearing a beautiful white wedding dress, which was lent to her by one of the women. Next to her was Barb, also in a beautiful white dress. Both brides looked radiant and beautiful.

Preston thought, "Oh my God. She is so beautiful." She had a wild rose in her hair and the dress was flowing behind her. They reached the platform in front and, just then, the moonshine started to hit Preston.

All he heard was, "Dearly beloved, we are gathered here..." and then, after a few minutes, there was silence. Everybody was staring at him and the minister was nodding his head toward Amy. She was holding his hand and whispered, "You need to say 'I do'."

Preston felt like he was in a dream. He smiled and said, "Of course I do." The next thing that registered in Preston's mind was, "You may now kiss the bride." Amy wasn't waiting for him to make the first move; she leapt into his arms, kissing him.

The rest of the wedding was a blur of food and wine, the typical speeches and then the farewells. Before he knew it, they were loaded up in a buggy and headed off for their wedding night. They were going to take four days for the honeymoon and stay at the house they had just moved from. There, they could have some privacy and be alone.

On the third day, Joe came racing over to the first house and beat on the door. "You two get decent." He yelled.

Preston looked at Amy and said, "What the heck?" Preston threw on some clothes and stepped on the porch as Amy got dressed.

Almost out of breath, Joe said, "We've got trouble—the Rainbow Warriors. Some Colonel has declared himself governor of the whole state of Wisconsin. He is demanding that all firearms be turned in. Whoever gives up their firearms voluntarily is given food." Joe paused to take a breath, “He took over some major shipping outlet in Green Bay and now controls hundreds of tons of food.”

Preston said, “Can’t even enjoy 4 days of a honeymoon.”

Chapter 24

Planning for Battle

"Tomorrow's battle is won during today's practice."
~Samurai maxim

Preston and Amy returned to the cabin as quickly as possible. Joe briefed both of them on what was going on.

Joe told them that because this man elected himself as Governor of Wisconsin, he was going to be sending an army across the land to enforce his policies. As it stood right now, his so called administration and army were the most powerful forces in the state. Unless they and their community wanted to conform to his laws, they would have to fight.

Joe said, "A Northern Alliance was forming, so Fred and Scott were sent to represent our group. The doc was working on setting up a field hospital so the wounded can be carried in the back of the wagon and Jane will be the operating nurse. Amy will be security at the field hospital."

Preston interrupted, saying, "Wait a minute. Do we have intel on how big the force is and when they might be coming to our area?"

Joe said, "Scott selected a few men to travel east and see what they could learn, so we should have some additional information when they get back. But, until then, we need to plan and get ready for a fight."

Up to this point, having a field hospital set up and supplies available was about all they could do. Now they needed to have several different battle plans worked out so that, when they knew for sure what the situation was, they could adopt one of the plans and move on it quickly.

That evening, Joe and Preston were sitting around talking, and Michael asked, "Do you think it's possible that 16 guys could turn around an Army of a thousand men?"

Joe looked at Preston and then at Michael. He was about to say something when Preston said, "I don't know if it's true or not, but military history is full of incredible documentation of small units stopping superior forces."

Joe nodded in agreement and Preston continued, "I've studied the history of war and will tell you of a few battles that might answer your question. The first one dates back to ancient Greece, with the Spartans. The 300 Spartans, as they came to be known, stomped the Persian army and killed over 20,000 of their men. Now granted, there were up to a thousand other Greeks that stood by their side, but still, 1,300 men with primitive weapons killed 20,000 Persians. Now that's the stuff legends are made of. In the end, the Persians finally wiped them out down to the last man, but they paid a heavy price."

Michael wanted to know about the battle so, between Preston and Joe, they explained how the 300 managed to kill so many of the enemy. Preston drew a simple map on some paper, showing how they used a natural canyon to funnel the army through a narrow passage, allowing the Greeks to have a superior position over their enemy.

Joe said, "I know of a better one than that. Have you ever heard the story of the Battle of Longewala in 1971?" Both Preston and Michael shook their heads, so he continued, "It was the war between Pakistan and India. They made a movie about it called "Border." The 1997 film caught my interest so I researched it and the true story is even more amazing than the movie was. Imagine this: you are a major in the Indian Army, sent to protect the border. You only have 120 men. The Pakistani army is advancing on your border and the only thing stopping them is a three-strand barbed wire fence, like ones you would put up to keep cattle in. Now, you have one 81mm mortar, four medium machine guns, one 106mm antitank weapon mounted on a Jeep, two antitank recoilless rifles, which you probably know as bazookas and a handful of landmines that can take out tanks."

"Wow, that sounds pretty good." Michael said.

Joe continued, "Ah, but you don't know what they're facing yet. On the other side of that fence wait 65 tanks, 2,000 infantry and one mobile infantry brigade. The India defenders also had four aircraft, but they could only fly during the day. Remember, this was 1971 and the night vision technology hadn't caught up all around the world." He continued, "The Pakistanis attacked at night. A patrol of 20 men called the major and told him of the large number of tanks heading his way. Headquarters gave the major the choice to do a tactical retreat, or stay and hold through the night. Reinforcements and air support were 6 hours away. Okay Michael, you're the Major and you have no vehicles to transport your men, but it's nighttime and your men would have a good chance of retreating unseen. Those are your options. What would you do?"

Michael said, "Stay and fight, of course."

Preston chimed in, "Remember, you are responsible for 120 men, most of whom are married and have children. Now think about this: if you survive, you have to tell all those wives and children why their husbands and fathers died. That's a heavy responsibility."

Joe continued, "That is what the major decided. He thought the best chance of survival for his men was to stay and fight in a fortified position. This was desert terrain and if they were caught in the open, they would quickly be cut to ribbons from the tanks."

"The battle started roughly at 12:30 a.m. The Pakistani artillery opened fire on the post, killing 5 of the 10 camels that were used for patrols. As the 65 tanks approached, the Indian defenders started planting antitank landmines. One infantry man was shot and killed while planting a mine."

He continued with the story. "The Indian defenders were waiting in the dark. Their Jeep, with the mounted 106, took out the first two tanks of the battle and one Indian defender was killed. When their infantry hit the barbed wire fence, they immediately thought it was a minefield for the tanks, so they stopped the tank advance. The tanks had been outfitted with additional external fuel tanks and, almost immediately after the first few shots, one exploded, lighting the area up and giving the defenders ample light to shoot them down."

"The Pakistanis sent their minesweepers in and, after 2 hours, they finally reported there were no mines. It was a full moon and the Pakistanis could not advance across the open terrain due to the heavy small arms fire and mortar rounds coming from the defenders. This emboldened the Major and he made the decision to stay in their fortified position. This situation totally frustrated the Pakistani commanders."

"There was an Indian artillery support unit a few miles away and the major used their assets to direct firepower on the Pakistani position."

By now, the girls had come in from the kitchen and sat down to listen to the story. Michael was spellbound and waited for every word.

Joe continued the story. "At first light, infantry was ordered to attack. At the same time, the tanks had positioned themselves on two sides of the outpost. Because of poor planning on the Commander's part, the tanks were ordered off the road. This was desert sand and a lot of the heavy tanks become bogged down and stuck in the sand."

Joe paused and took a drink of his coffee. Michael said, "Go on, tell us the rest."

He said, "Well, at first light the four jet fighters arrived. They were loaded with missiles and 30mm cannons. They attacked freely because the Pakistanis had no air cover. The aircraft rolled in and quickly started taking out tanks and troops. Twelve of the tanks had been taken out by the post defenders and 22 tanks were taken out by the Air Force, plus many abandoned their armored vehicles. Nobody knows for sure how many men they lost, but two hundred men is the best estimate."

"The Indian defenders were greatly outnumbered and sure to have been slaughtered to the last man if you just look at the numbers. With all of the tanks they were facing, incredibly, they only lost two men."

Michael's eyes were as big as saucers. "Really? Only two men? Did they make that major a general and put him in charge of all Indian troops?"

"Not that I know of," Joe continued, "but they did award the major the second-highest medal his country had to offer. For losing the battle, the Pakistani officer was dismissed from service. Nobody knows what happened to him afterwards."

"Think about that, Michael," Preston said, "Now that is an officer and a gentleman. So, is it possible that a 16-man force could turn around an army of 1,000? I don't know for sure, but I do know that throughout military history, incredible men have faced and defeated an enemy when all common sense said they didn't stand a chance."

Joe continued, "And don't forget the Alamo. Right here in America 189 men held off Santa Anna's army of 1600 for, how many days?

Thirteen days. Like the 300 Spartans, all 189 men perished, but they took out 600 of the enemy. Military history should never be ignored."

Michael hesitated and then said, "What about the people that come through and say it's impossible for so few men to do that? They think they must have had more troops sniping them and that's why they killed so many."

Preston said, "We will never know for sure, unless we meet the men that were there, and remember, he didn't defeat them, he just stopped the forward advancement and they retreated."

"And don't forget Tombstone. Wyatt Earp, Doc Holliday and three other deputies took on over 100 cowboys, not all at once, but over the course of their lifetimes. Numbers are just that, numbers. It's the general in charge and the spirit of the warriors that decide the outcome of the battle."

Joe said, "This is what we used to tell our units in the Army. We are the warrior class, a special breed that few can follow. We stand in front of the gates of hell, sworn to uphold our sacred honor that freedom is never free. It must be paid in blood, sweat and tears. We ask for nothing but the chance to fight, to prove that, yet today, we are still the warriors willing to shed the blood of our enemy. May they shake in fear before us."

A few days later, Scott and Fred returned and called together the men that they planned to put in charge of each ten-man fighting unit. Scott, Joe and Preston, would be in one unit. They were going to be the forward recon and harassment team.

Fred did the briefing, pulled out a map and shared what intelligence they had on the Green Bay Rainbow Warriors. He said, "They are trying to establish a supply route across the top of the state and hook up with the Minnesota Rainbow Warriors. Our job is to stop this from happening. The easiest way would be to blow out the bridges. The only problem with that is, once we win, we won't have that route opened for trade."

He continued, "They are trying the northern route, using Highway 8, which runs straight across the state and hooks up with Interstate 35, just above Minneapolis. Minneapolis is reported to be one of their strongholds." Looking at Preston and Joe he said, "They can tell us what they have in the way of weapons and forces. Our job is to first gather intel and then break the supply route, even if we have to take out one main bridge. Our area of operation is from the intersection of Highway 51 and Highway 8 to Highway 13, which is 30 miles to the west. We must find every back road, ATV dirt trail, snowmobile trail and anything else going through the area."

Joe said, "All we can tell you about the Minnesota Rainbow Warriors is that they have a very skilled 105mm cannon team. They are definitely battle proven. We should keep them out of the state at all cost."

Fred said, "We agree. But right now our priority is to keep their forces divided and stop them from establishing the supply route. There are some bridges crossing the lakes down there, which we could easily take out. It would stop any forward advancement."

Preston asked, "You're not telling us something. Why all of the sudden urgency? The way I understand it, this Green Bay Army was turned back the last time they tried to come through here. What do you know that's causing us to go into action now?"

"The Rainbow Warriors had a lieutenant who defected and he filled us in on the plans. Green Bay has tons of extra food, I should say hundreds of tons, and they want to clear out all of the people within 10 miles on either side of Highway 8. This will be a no-man's zone. Then they can supply Minnesota with food, getting their cooperation and reinforcements before winter. Our job is to make sure neither gets any support from the other."

Joe interrupted, "Do we know what are they're sending to clear out this area?"

Fred said, "From what we've heard, it could be an army of 500, but they're only taking one of the 105's."

"What are the others of the Northern Alliance doing?" Preston asked.

Fred responded, "We met the man that stopped them before. His name is Clint Bolan. He's training an army and we're sending him 80 men. Not counting recon teams, we have a little over 300 men and, if we can trap them out in the open, we should be able to win."

Joe inquired, "Do we know what their numbers are exactly?"

Fred continued, "Our estimate of troop strength is 900. In Minnesota there are 2,500 or more."

Preston asked, "When do we plan on moving out? How much time do we have?"

"They're moving in 4 days." Scott said. "It's going to take us a day to get down there and we estimate they'll be in our AO 3 days later. It doesn't give us much time, so we're leaving first thing in the morning. We have homemade MRE'S, nothing fancy, but it will get us through. Have your pack gear, rifles, ammo and everything you need to survive for 7 days. We are bringing one wagon with us and that will be left in the rear to resupply. Two men will stay with it to guard the supplies. That leaves eight of us on the front." He looked at two guys, "Sam and Chris, make sure you bring your crossbows. Bring 500 rounds of ammunition. We'll carry 180 rounds on us and leave the rest in the supply wagon."

That night the tension was thick in the cabin. Amy pulled Preston into their bedroom and started in on him. "We just got married and you volunteer to run off and get your dumb ass killed. You're not going and that's final, or I'm going with you."

Preston looked her square in the eye and said, "If you want to raise a family and have our own children, then we have to have an area that is safe. The only way that can happen is to stop this here and now. You have already been assigned security detail for the field hospital. You may not like it, hell, I don't like it, but I'm going. We will only survive as a community if we fight together to keep it free."

She walked up to him and put her arms around his neck, "We just got married. We should still be on our honeymoon. It's not fair. Somebody else can go. You don't have to be on the recon team."

"You know I'm going; I have the experience. Do you really want to send some kid that used to work at a sawmill and has no military experience, so he can die while I stay home and survive?"

She hugged him close to her and said, "I know what you're saying and yes, I agree, but it doesn't mean I have to like it. If you get yourself killed, Mister, I'll hunt you down and kill you again."

Preston laughed, "I'll make sure I don't die. I would hate to be killed twice." He scooped her up and took her to bed.

Jane and Joe had been through this before in the many years of his combat career and she didn't like it, but she knew better than to interfere with Joe's decision. The best thing they could do was to spend the night together like it might be their last time ever.

At daybreak they took off. Michael, of course, wanted to go, but his job was to stay and guard the camp and get the firewood in.

That first night they made camp off the road, about 10 miles north of the highway. Two men were assigned to guard the wagon. In the morning they'd send two scouts out to find the location of the army. In the meantime, the rest of them were to scout the entire area.

The next morning they spent the day going down the highway, following all the roads and trails that extended from it. They needed to have escape routes figured out. Two other men went forward, looking for a bridge they could take out, or something small that wouldn't take too much gunpowder to destroy. Taking a bridge out isn't as easy as it sounds. They are built on solid steel I-beams with reinforced concrete on top. The trick was to find a weak spot to break and use the weight of the concrete to cause the bridge to fall.

That night they returned to camp and the six of them compared notes. A map showing the different routes they could take and places to set up ambush spots was crudely drawn.

About 20 miles down the highway, they found the bridge they were looking for. It was about 50 feet long and crossed over a lake. There was no easy route for the enemy to bypass the bridge and go around, especially with the 105 and heavy supply wagons.

Now they had to figure out how to collapse the bridge. They had 16 pounds of gunpowder, but they couldn't just put it on the steel I-beams because an explosion will always take the path of least resistance. It would just go outward and maybe crack the I-beam, but not take it out completely. If they could bolt on some type of steel box with the explosives in it, it just might work. The weakest spot was right in the middle of the bridge. It had 8 telephone pole size supports and, if they had to, they could soak them in oil and set them on fire. The problem was that it would take a long time to weaken them and would put up one heck of a lot of black smoke.

It was decided that tomorrow they would continue scouting. The scouts should be back sometime in the afternoon and then they could figure out how much time they had before the army would be there.

The next day the scouts left before sunrise. They returned late at night and said that, at the rate the army was going, they had at least 4 days before they would get there. They also ran into the other recon team and they would be joining them tomorrow. The scouts told them where to meet.

Preston and Joe talked it over with Scott and decided that they would burn the bridge support pillars tomorrow, just to be safe. And if the bridge didn't fall, they would have to look for something heavy to put in the middle to see if they could make it fall.

Scott said, "Sounds good to me. I'll meet the other team and you burn all of the support pillars."

The next day, they took two other men and spent the day collecting oil out of vehicles along the highway. They filled buckets they had found in neighboring houses. They then climbed out along the beams of the bridge and, using rags, they painted them with oil. Once all of the support pillars were painted, they mixed up some oil and gas and painted about 4 feet from the top of each beam. They then used one of the crossbows and shot flaming arrows into the support pillars.

It didn't work as well as they had hoped. The pillars burned and smoldered, but didn't burn all of the way through. In fact, it only burned about 2 inches into the wood of a 12-inch beam.

They laughed, "It's pretty bad when you're a failure as an arsonist," Preston said.

Chris laughed, "I'll get some gloves and we can collect and reuse all eight of the aluminum bolts. Look at the bright side; we're not wasting crossbow bolts. The target tips should be fairly easy to pry out and the fire should've cleared most of the wood that the bolts stuck into."

Joe said, "Then, while you guys are doing that, I'm going to find us a wood bit and brace. Hopefully, with a half-inch, or three-quarter-inch wood bit, we can drill holes down at angles, all the way around the pillars from about 4 feet below the top, to 4 feet up from the water line. Four holes evenly spaced all the way around will help weaken the supports."

Ken said, "I think we should chip away what's already burned with our axes. That way we're not wasting time trying to re-burn the same area."

The others agreed and they spent the rest of the day getting it done, returning to camp around six o'clock.

They reported on the day's activities and Scott introduced them to John, the guy in charge of the other recon unit.

John was a former recon Marine and was a no-nonsense kind of guy. He told them, "So gentlemen, this is what I want to do. Once the bridge is out, we harass them all the way back to Green Bay, which means hit-and-run."

He asked Scott, "You still got the gunpowder and cannon fuses? We can use those in different homemade weapons."

Scott nodded and John continued, "I say we rob them of their sleep and, since we've got two teams, we will piggyback off each other, with one team hitting them each night and then sleeping during the day. The other team can jump past the next ambush, ready to harass them and, if we can keep it up, we can chase them right back home."

"I got a better idea," Joe said. "Let's get their 105. Why don't we do a joint operation and capture the 105. Fire off a round and destroy as much in their camp as we can. Hook up horses to it and race off into the dark."

John looked at Joe and said, "I like how you're thinking, but how will our horses hook up to it?"

Joe didn't even hesitate, saying, "Well, it's my understanding that it's already rigged to be pulled by horses. It may take quite a feat to do it, but I know we have some highly trained and skilled people among us. I'm sure we can adapt our harnesses so the cannon can be easily pulled." He continued, "Let's hit them as soon as they stop at the downed bridge. They'll be confused and disorganized. We rush in and steal their gun, take it to the high ground and then pound the hell out of them."

John looked up at Scott. "What you know about engineering and bridge construction? What I'm thinking is to find a way we can use it as a trap. Nothing I would like better than to give 100 of these as-sholes a nice cold bath."

Preston interrupted, "There's one problem with that. If we can't take it completely out and the damn thing holds, then all this time has been wasted and they could get away."

John smiled at Preston and said, "One of the guys that used to work for me had worked a former job blowing up rocks to clear the mountain passes in Montana. He told me how they would blow huge rocks off the mountainsides, closing the highways off. They had to clear large areas on the sides to prevent rockslides. They would mix ammonium nitrate fertilizer with diesel fuel. By itself it's pretty useless. You can even light it on fire and it won't do anything. What you need is an explosion to set it off and for that they used regular dynamite."

He continued, "The old-timers taught them how to use just black powder. Of course it was much more dangerous, but they would actually pack the drilled holes with black powder. They'd use a brass non-sparking rod to tamp the powder tightly and then plug the hole with a tapered piece of wood. The plug had a hole drilled through it to allow them to push a fuse through. Then they would light the fuse and run like hell."

Scott said, "Well that would be great, if we were in Montana and had mountains around the bridge. How is that going to help us here?"

John gave a low chuckle and said, "Simple. You say the bridge is made of concrete, right?" They nodded their heads. "We just drill holes in it at an angle. I'm thinking a 1/2-inch hole on the bottom side, widening the top to 4-5 inches, even if we have to use a chipping hammer. But if we can find a concrete bit, that would work really well. We drill through at an angle and make wooden plugs with a hole drilled through the center, then one person could light the fuses from underneath and escape. The top side we pack full of diesel-soaked ammonium nitrate fertilizer and seal it in with quick-dry cement loaded with gravel."

"We would have to do the same on the pillars and then plan escape routes for the men lighting the fuses. You said you already have the holes drilled in the pillars, right? All we have to do is pack them full of gunpowder and diesel-soaked ammonium nitrate fertilizer and make plugs for them. We will have to work out the fuse timing, so they explode when we want them to."

The men listened to John's idea and were thinking, when he said, "The guys under the bridge would blow their charges, causing the concrete to turn into pieces of small rocks like a grenade at the same time as the pillars blow, sending all of the troops trapped on the bridge into the water."

"I know we don't have a lot of time, but I think we can do it. Who do we have that could figure out the fuse timing and how to connect the holes together?"

Joe said, "The only problem I see is that the pilings are only in the middle of the bridge. If we have explosives on the pilings, the only part that will blow up is the middle. I have no idea exactly how that would affect the rest of the bridge. It may take out the center, but that may allow the troops to retreat and escape.

Preston said. "If we do this correctly, the top of the bridge is going to kill or wound a lot of the troops."

John and the others liked that idea. They needed to have their fastest men light the fuses and escape. Ken and Chris volunteered and all agreed that they were the fastest and could do the job. The important thing was getting the timing of the fuses correct. If they went off too soon, the army would simply stop and prepare for battle. If they went off too late, the troops would be able to escape.

Scott found 2 men that had worked with explosives before and put them to work on the timing of the fuses. They also needed to tell them where to place the charges on top, so it would give them the desired outcome. They only had 390 feet of slow-burn fuse, so the planning had to be precise; 54 seconds a foot burn time.

The 2 men chose the spots for the charges and men started chipping away, making the holes for the black powder. One cement drill was found and they shared it with the others to drill the holes deeper.

Black powder was packed and tamped into the holes. Next came the wooden plugs, with the fuses in place. These were pounded into place on the bottom side. The black power was stored in plastic bags to prevent moisture. The fertilizer soaked with diesel fuel filled the rest of the hole. A mixture of cement and gravel was used as a cap for the top. The hole on the top side was about 4 inches round and tapered down to ½-inch at the bottom side. After the cement had dried, a 10-pound rock was placed over it. Rubble in the street was nothing unusual to be seen.

John looked over at Joe and said, "I understand you're pretty good at training people. I'm putting you in charge of training the two fuse lighters. You need to figure out how they are going to light the fuses and make their getaway. They should have preplanned places to hide before the charges go off."

Joe accepted the responsibility and sat down to think out a plan of action.

Chapter 25

Blowing the Bridge

> "Ten soldiers wisely led will beat a hundred without a head."
>
> ~Euripides

The four scouts were to constantly keep an eye on the progress of the Army and report back. Everyone else was either gathering supplies, drilling holes, or finding tools they needed to make the plan work. They were all constantly working on something.

Joe started training Chris and Ken. "All right, between the two of you, we are going to have a contest. It will be to see who can safely climb up and down the pilings quickly. See these crossbeams," he pointed up to them, "I'm thinking we could build a ladder in the center, or strap a ladder to the top, allowing a guy to quickly climb down. If we can find a long aluminum ladder, we will have to wrap cloth and rags around it to make sure it isn't banging and rattling, making a lot of noise."

Joe told the guys looking for tools to find a 20-foot ladder, preferably a wooden one, but an aluminum one would work.

They picked the side of the lakeshore that had the most brush and Joe said, "Okay, I know this can be a pain, but we have to find out how far you both can swim underwater. We have to clear a spot underneath the brush where you can pop up, breathe and then swim another distance. The second spot, we will take driftwood and make you a well camouflaged hide."

"The man on top is going to have the hardest job. He will have to light the fuses and then climb down the ladder without making too much noise. And then, about 10 seconds apart, you are going to swim to the first breathing hole, get a breath, and then swim to the hide. Once we get a ladder, we can time it and figure out how much fuse time we have."

"You two are going to be totally on your own. The whole plan depends on you getting these fuses lit. You will have no cover and no backup. The only chance of surviving is to train and don't make any mistakes. Are you sure you guys want to do this?"

That afternoon, they had been given a wooden ladder, so they attached it to the crossbar. Joe timed them going up and down. Chris was a little bit younger and a little bit faster, so he was going to be the top man. Ken was just going to have to hide on a platform they had built and covered with brush. All he had to do was light the bottom fuses. They had 2 minutes, from the time the fuses were lit, to reach their safe spot.

The bombs were placed in the holes, with the fuses sticking out the bottom, under the bridge. After 2 days of cleaning up the area, everyone left, with Chris and Ken staying behind. They would sleep under the bridge until it was time to blow it.

They knew from the scout reports that there was a 10-man patrol out in front of the main force, about an hour ahead of them. It was reported that they had scouts in the fields on both sides of the road, sweeping the area to make sure it was clear. They were being very cautious. The cannon was at the end of the troop column and a wagon with the shells followed it.

John ordered the men to fall back, not really wanting to engage the enemy with so few men. Joe and Preston were hidden across the lake with their eyes on the bridge, watching with binoculars.

Ken and Chris had been hiding since first light, ready at the moment the troops began crossing the bridge. Chris was carrying a Light My Fire Mora knife. He simply needed to turn the top of the handle, pull out Swedish fire steel, use the back of a knife to scrape it along the blade and a shower of sparks would ignite his mini torch. He would have to open the can of lighter fluid and soak the rag wrapped on a stick and then hit it with the sparks. Ken was using a Zippo lighter to light his fuses, 8 poles with 4 fuses tied together. From the time he lit the first one he had 54 seconds to get the rest of the fuses lit.

He was timed pretending to light fuses, walking to the next pillar and so on, until he could get them all lit in about 45 seconds. The fuses were then timed for him walking along the beams, 3 seconds to light each pillar.

As daybreak came, there was fog lying over the water and a light mist in the air. Waiting was the worst part. Minutes seemed like hours and hours seemed like days. They were committed now and there was nothing they could do but wait.

A slight breeze from the north was giving them a morning chill. A few pigeons flew under the bridge and landed on the crossbeams. They cooed back and forth. Ken watched them with interest.

About nine o'clock, they heard the patrol ride over. They were surprised how well they could hear from underneath the bridge. The shoed horses were easily heard and this brought their anxiety levels even higher. Still, the minutes slowly clicked by. As the day warmed up, the fog seemed to intensify under the bridge.

Ken guessed it must be because the cooler waters under the bridge were hitting the warmer air radiating from the bridge, but it gave the fog a thick, hollow, oppressive feeling, like he was in a dream state, and this was not really happening. He thought he would soon wake up and his mission would be uncompleted. *Knock it off,* he told himself, *it's just fog*.

The fog was thick on the topside too and Chris was having his own doubts and anxieties. He stared at the pigeons and saw one turn into a Raven right before his eyes. He thought, wasn't a Raven the sign of death for one of the Native American tribes? He blinked his eyes and it changed back to a pigeon. His mind was playing tricks on him. Just relax, he told himself. Joe said nothing in the whole world matters, but to just do my job and don't think, just react. Do as I've been trained.

They heard the army coming long before they made it to the bridge. The sounds of 500 men on horseback echoed off the shores and through the bridge. There was no doubt that the time of action was coming soon.

Chris peeked under a beam and looked at Ken. He was staring off into the lake. Each man was lost in his own thoughts.

When they got closer, Chris sat up on his knees, pulled out his knife and had his striker ready. His hands were shaking badly as he heard the first of the Army enter onto the bridge. He opened the can of lighter fluid, sprayed the fluid onto the rag and then he waited until they were at the halfway point. They were directly above him. He tried to scrape the fire starter with the back of the knife blade, but his hands were shaking too badly. He pressed the fire starter firmly down onto the rag, pushing it firmly onto the beam. Both hands were still shaking, but, taking a deep breath, he waited until he calmed down and then he firmly scraped it down as hard as he could. A shower of sparks lit the rag. He locked the flint back into the handle and using two hands he carefully put it into his sheath.

He picked up his mini torch and waved it down. That was the signal for Ken to light the fuses. He peeked down and saw that Ken's torch was burning brightly. The sound above him was deafening and the clacking of that many horses on the cement reverberated to his very bones. He stood up and started lighting fuses. With the fog and light mist, the fuses didn't take off right away. He had to hold the fire on them for a couple of seconds before they took off. He did just as he trained, lighting each of the charges on the pillars. Last step—the explosives in the bridge itself. When the last one was lit, he dropped the burning torch straight into the water. He looked down at Ken and saw that he was already waiting for him in the water.

In his haste, he stepped too quickly and tried to jump on the ladder. The wooden rungs were slick from all the moisture, and his left foot slipped off, going straight down, while his right leg went into the inside of the rung. He couldn't get a firm hold on the wet rung and, losing his grip, over he went. His right leg straightened out and slammed into the rung above the one he had slipped off of, snapping his leg. He yelled out in pain, but luckily there was so much noise above that nobody heard him. He bit down on his tongue and forced himself not to cry out. He was hanging upside down like he was caught in a snare, in some bad B-grade movie.

Ken swam over to the ladder and quickly climbed up. Chris whispered, "Get the hell out of here. Those fuses are lit, it's going to blow any second."

Ken didn't say a word. He placed his shoulder to Chris's shoulder and climbed straight up, lifting Chris up until he could get a hold of the ladder. Climbing down, he whispered up, "Quit screwing around. We've got some swimming to do."

Chris, using two hands to hold on a rung and leaving his right leg straight, hopped down, one rung at a time. He looked up at the fuses and thought, "How much time? Got to move faster." He staggered his hands between two rungs and let himself drop. Reaching the water, Ken whispered, "Can you swim?"

He responded, "Not fast, but I can manage." He didn't feel the pain as much, due to the cold water, and was trying to ignore it, knowing his survival was on the line.

They swam up to the edge, took a deep breath and dove under. They were almost to the first breathing hole when they heard the explosions go off.

Ken made it to the first breathing hole and popped his head up into the brush, took a breath and quickly stuck his head back underwater, looking for his friend. He saw Chris and then a large black shadow racing toward him. Like a monster out of a nightmare, one you could not escape, one of the support beams came down directly on top of Chris, just as he was coming up for air. The beam smashed his head wide open. Blood and brain matter shot out in the water around his body.

Ken stood up, as if having his head above water would somehow be different. Just then, as the bridge hit the water, a wave hit him, knocking him back under water and against the shore.

He came up again and was spitting out water, shaking his head and wiping his eyes clear. He saw horses and men in the water, swimming around in shock. He saw the bodies, the water turning blood red from the men and horses floating everywhere. He didn't feel happy or excited that the plan had worked so well. He felt revulsion, sick to his stomach and in shock. His eyes were glazed over as he looked at the destruction he had caused.

Like coming out of a dream, he noticed men running towards the shore to help their fellow wounded comrades. The screams of pain penetrated his thinking, but he knew he had to get out of there before they got organized. He took three quick breaths and swam off. Crawling into the hide, he shivered in the wind and thought, "All I can do now is wait...wait for darkness."

He tried to get comfortable as he thought about Chris and all of the years they had known each other, all of the fun times that they'd had together. He would have to tell Chris's parents what had happened and how he had failed to save him. Would they ever forgive him? Would God forgive him for what he'd done against these men? He had no beef with those men. He felt so miserable, he just laid his head down and closed his eyes. He silently prayed that Chris would be welcomed into heaven. He prayed for forgiveness and he prayed for the men he had killed.

Joe and Preston were watching through binoculars when they heard the explosion and saw the flames, but the fog had been too thick for them to see what had happened to Ken and Chris, nor could they tell what had happened to the troops on the bridge, but they could clearly hear the screams of pain echoing across the lake.

Joe smiled and said out loud, "That's for my farmhouse, you bastards."

Preston asked, "How many do you think we got? 20 or 30?"

Joe said, "I was hoping for a hundred. Who knows the count? It really depends how many were on the bridge when it blew. Maybe 50 or 60 would be my guess and, if we got really lucky, 70 or 80."

The charges blew 10 huge 3-foot-diameter holes in the concrete, showering the Rainbow Warriors with high velocity concrete shrapnel.

The major in charge of the Rainbow Warriors was a man of action. Unlike other officers, he led his men from the front and that was the only reason he was still alive. He and 50 men had made it across the bridge before the explosion took out the bridge. The ensuing chaos from the shockwave had knocked them off of their horses. The major stood up, covered in gray cement dust, and looked back toward the bridge. There was an empty space where the bridge once stood. On the other side of the bridge there were men knocked off of their horses too. He ran up, looked down into the water and started barking orders. "Get those men out of the water." Some of the men woke up from the shock and ran down to help. He wondered, *How many men did we lose and why didn't the patrol check under this bridge?*

The bridge didn't fall straight down into the water, but broke in the middle, each side collapsing into the water. The men just entering the bridge were violently thrown down into a melee.

Somebody is going pay dearly for this, he thought. He found one of his sergeants and told him to get 10 men and collect the horses. Some of his men were pulling people out of the water and to the bank. He called down for them to take the wounded to the other side. "Swim over with them if you have to. The medics are on that side, in the rear, I think."

He saw one of his lieutenants standing on the other side. "Lieutenant," he called out. When the man looked up at him, he barked orders for him to get all of the wounded to the medics right away, adding, "Then I want an accounting of how many men we've lost and how many are wounded. I also want to know how many horses we lost."

Whoever they were up against wasn't playing games. That was okay. He wasn't about to let his men be picked off by a bunch of stupid rednecks, like that incompetent general who lost almost half his men.

He finally collected all his men and they swam their horses across to the other side, becoming one force again. He had sent 2 men to bring back the forward patrol. He was going to give a lesson in discipline to men who failed to follow orders.

When they returned, he took the sergeant-in-charge in front of everybody and made him stand at attention. He asked him why he had allowed 52 men to die and 26 to be wounded. Why did he not do his job and thoroughly check under the bridge?

The man said, "I'm sorry sir, my bad. It won't happen again."

The major flew into a rage. "You're damn right it won't happen again, because you are now a private. Your punishment is 10 lashes. Guards, tie him to that tree and remove his shirt."

They ripped his shirt off and the major called out to a gorilla of a man, Boris, "Ten lashes from the whip."

The whip whistled through the air, cracking on the man's back. The man yelled out in pain. Some of the men flinched each time the whip cracked, breaking the flesh and leaving a bloody mark.

After eight lashes, the man passed out from pain and slumped down against his ropes. The major called a halt to it and called out to all the men. "The next man who ever uses the phrase 'my bad' will get 10 lashes automatically. You are all given a job to do and I expect you to follow my orders to the letter. Sloppy patrol work cost us 78 men, dead or wounded. I will not allow this to happen. The supply route is broken and we have to find a detour around this. I will shoot the next man in a patrol that allows us to walk into an ambush. Is that understood?"

A few men mumbled, "Yes sir."

He yelled out, "I can't hear you. What was that?"

All of them yelled, "Yes sir!"

"That's better. I'm sending out two patrols and one of them had better come up with a route around this mess. Now let's get to work."

The fog had burned off and it had turned into a beautiful day. Preston and Joe had worked their way around to the opposite side of where the army was. They waited there to pick up Ken and Chris. About 1:30 p.m. they saw the Army pull away. Backtracking, they worked their way closer.

Preston said, "Why don't you stay here, old man. I'll go get them two and be back in a flash."

Joe smiled, "Old man? Just for that, you can stay here and I'll go get them."

Preston laughed, "We are both of equal rank, so I'll flip you for it."

"No. You go right ahead and I'll cover you. I'm the better shot."

With that, Preston started sneaking up to the hide. It took him about 20 minutes and he was about 20 yards away when he called out, "Come on guys. Let's go."

He was met by an eerie silence. They had not heard any gunshots after the bridge came down, so he called out a little louder, "Guys. Let's go." But there was nothing but silence. He crawled up to the keep and looked inside. He could only see one person. He tapped him on the shoulder, "It's me. Are you okay? Are you hit?"

Ken looked up at him with The Thousand Yard Stare. He said, "Chris is dead. I killed him. I couldn't save him. I tried, but I couldn't save him. He broke his leg and I should have helped him more. He's dead. One of the beams hit him in the head and crushed his skull. It's all my fault he's dead. How am I going face his parents?" His eyes wouldn't focus. It was like he was looking through Preston.

Preston shook him, "Snap out of it. We've got to get moving."

Ken didn't move. "Did you see all of them dead bodies? Did you see all the blood? This is hell. We killed so many. It was horrible. I can't stop seeing all the dead bodies."

Preston tightened his grip on the man's collar. "Look at me. We are leaving. You survived and this is war. It's not pretty; it's ugly and nasty, the most insane thing you can do to another human being, but we don't have time for this right now. Come on soldier, move."

The man stood all the way up, uncaring if he was being exposed. Preston was sneaking forward at a crouch in front of him. He turned around and, seeing the man walking without a care in the world, Preston went back and yanked him down. "Snap out of it. If you want to die, that's fine, but don't get me killed because you don't give a shit right now."

Ken snapped out of it. "I'm sorry, this is my first battle. I wasn't ready for this."

"Okay, just follow me and let's get out of here." Ken started moving right after that.

They made it back to Joe's position and Preston shook his head, saying, "Let's go."

Joe knew his friend well enough that there would be time for talking later. About nine o'clock that night, they made it to camp. They reported to Scott and John. They informed them of what they thought had happened. They said that about 60 to 70 men on the other side were dead or wounded. They had lost Chris and Ken was shell-shocked.

John asked, "How bad is he? Do you think he will snap out of it and be fit for duty?"

Preston said, "I don't think so. I think we should send him home. He wasn't ready for this type of carnage and his mind overloaded. I think, for all of our safety, we should send him home."

Scott asked, "What you think Joe? Will he be fine in a couple of days?"

Joe said, "I don't think so. He's gone. Every time we stopped, he just kept babbling about all the dead bodies, blood and how he didn't save Chris. That kind of trauma takes some time to heal. For all our safety, he needs to go home."

John said, "You two take him back and, before you object, I want people to move in pairs and you guys are already a team." He pulled out the map. "I figure it's going to take you 3 days to take him back and then return." He pointed to the map, "We'll meet you here at this cross-section. If we're not there, I'll have 2 men waiting there for you."

Preston said, "And what fun are you guys going to be having while we're gone?"

"No need for you to know that right now, just in case, by some odd turn of events, you are captured. We don't need you spilling the beans. Head out in the morning and we'll see you in 3 days."

Chapter 26

Make it Back on Foot

"When people don't believe in you, you have to believe in yourself."

~Pierce Brosnan

The next morning they headed out after a quick breakfast. Ken insisted that he could make it back by himself, but Preston convinced him they were going back to see their wives.

They rode right through the night and arrived at about two in the morning. They dropped Ken off at his house and took his horse with them. They rode on to their house, crawled into bed with their wives and immediately fell asleep, sleeping like the dead.

The next morning they had the dreaded job of telling Chris's parents the bad news. Jane and Amy had to work at the vet's, so they said their goodbyes and left. Joe and Preston rode over to Chris's parents' house to give them the bad news.

Chris was only twenty-two at the time of his death, way too young to die. His body was at the bottom of the lake, stuck under the beam that killed him, so they couldn't return it to them. They calmly and respectfully told them what happened. The Mrs. broke down crying, screaming and yelling. She told them they had no right sending him out there to do a man's job. She said, "You were the ones that were trained; you should've done it. My son is dead because you two were cowards." The father tried to calm her down.

Joe said, in a calm, even tone, "We did offer to do it, but they insisted that they were ready to handle the responsibility. The only way to make soldiers is to put them in the combat. It's a cold hard fact. If we want freedom, we need soldiers. We're so sorry for your loss. He was a fine young man and can be considered a hero for his part in stopping that army."

They politely nodded to each of them and got on their horses and headed back to the front lines.

Preston said, "Maybe you and I should've done it."

Joe responded, "Maybe, should have, would have, could have is not going to bring him back. And you, of all people, should understand that. Unfortunately, this new world is not fair or just. Sacrifices have to be made. Young inexperienced men are going to die. It's the facts of war. We'll never turn them into warriors if we do everything, keeping them in the rear for their own safety, and we can't second guess our decisions."

Preston acknowledged what Joe had said and added, "I know, but a few days of training means nothing. We need more time to train these men."

"That's what we're doing. We're buying Clint the time he needs to train the men he has. Come on, we need to cover a lot of ground."

They made camp, still having about 20 miles to go. Little did they know that on the front line John and a team of 10 men planned on stealing the 105 that night.

John had the men cover the horses' hoofs with rags so they could quietly move them into place. The plan was to use knives and cross-bows to take out the sentries as quietly as possible. They would then hook the horses up to the cannon and pull it out, hopefully disappearing into the night before anyone knew it was gone.

The major was on edge and he had placed an extra patrol of 10 men, 5 on each side, to silently sneak up and down the lines around their camp. After the bridge incident, he expected a possible night attack and wanted to have advance warning.

The next day, Joe and Preston reached the meeting place at ten a.m. There were 2 men waiting for them. One of the men said, "We have to take your horses. Your orders are to work your way back up to your house. You're on your own."

"Why? What's going on?" Joe asked.

The other man said, "We tried to steal the 105 last night. It went bad and we lost all but three of the 10 men that went in. Those three managed to steal the 105, but not the ammunition wagon. John wants to use the extra horses in relays, changing out the ones hauling the 105."

Joe said, "Doesn't he need us to help?"

The reply was, "I don't think so, as his orders were pretty explicit. I think he doesn't want to jeopardize any more men."

The other man added, "To say that the other side is pissed is an understatement. They split up and have ten patrols out searching for the 105, with 40 men in a patrol. You have to stay off the roads and work your way back through the brush."

They got off their horses and pulled out their supplies. "What are we going to do for food?" Preston asked.

He threw them 2 MRE's. "Sorry, that's all we have. We really don't have time to tell you anymore. We have to get these horses back where they are desperately needed, or the patrol may find them and we'll lose the 105. Good luck." With that, they raced off with the horses.

Preston said, "Well, back to the good old days of walking everywhere. I say we walk just off the road. We should be able to cover about 10 miles and then lay low until night. Once it's dark, we can hit the road and cover as much ground as we can."

Joe agreed and said, "I hope so. Either way, we need to get out of sight."

They left the road and moved into the brush. They were back about 50 yards from the road, just enough so they could still see any activity on the road but were still concealed. A couple of hours later, a patrol went by at a fast pace; they were looking for that 105. They took cover and watched them go by, counting the men.

Joe whispered, "I counted 38, which is way too many for us to take on by ourselves."

Preston said, "If there were supposed to be 40 men in the patrol, we'd better keep a sharp eye, just in case they have two bringing up the rear. I guess they don't have a sense of humor. Now that they lost their big toy, they want it back."

They stayed there until dark and neither the patrol, nor anyone else, came back through, which was worse because all they knew was that they were somewhere in front of them. To stay low, they walked in the low part of the ditch, which was smoother, easier walking than trying to travel in the brush at night.

They traveled about 15 miles that night and, when the predawn light was coming up, they got off the road. They buried themselves in a pile of leaves and went to sleep. Around noon, they were up and whispered back and forth. Joe asked, "What do you think?"

Preston said, "I think we should find the patrol and steal a couple of horses tonight."

Joe grinned and said, "You're never a boring date, are you? Come on, let's quit goofing around and start covering ground."

They headed off and kept listening for any sharp noises, like horses hoofs on the pavement. About six that night, they came up to a small stream. There was still plenty of daylight out, so finding a log fallen across the stream, almost reaching the other side, they used it to cross over.

Joe went first and made it to the other side without a problem. When Preston was halfway across, they both heard the patrol coming. The sound of the stream had covered up the sounds until they were almost right on top of them. Preston crouched down on the log, holding onto a branch. The patrol was on the nearby bridge and stopped.

Preston's leg started cramping. Did they see him? He saw 6 men on the bridge. He looked over and the others were leading the horses down to drink. Preston thought, *Oh, what are the chances?* He was just a big still blob and, as long as he didn't move to attract attention, he would be fine. His rifle was slung over his back, so he slowly turned his head and saw Joe had his rifle at the ready, covering him. His leg started twitching, and he had to shift his body weight. Holding onto the branch, he leaned back and started slowly to straighten out his leg, when the branch cracked with a loud snap and he fell into the stream.

The little stream was deeper than he expected and he went completely underwater. As he popped up, bullets started whistling by his head. Joe was returning fire, so he dove under and swam toward Joe. He popped up next to shore and scrambled up. The men by the stream were rushing forward. He crawled over to Joe and said, "Let's go."

Using the brush for cover, they ran as fast as they could. They heard the pursuers coming and weren't going to hang around to find out how many.

They had been shooting at them and thought they had gotten lucky so far. They ran back along the stream for a quarter of a mile when Preston felt the sting in his leg. It was like a bee sting on both sides. He felt the wetness running down his leg.

Catching up with Joe, he said, "We need to find cover quick." He pointed down to his leg and Joe saw the torn pants and the blood.

"You got hit? No time. Let's find a thick pine and climb up."

Lucky for them, this was northern Wisconsin, with plenty of pines, cedars and spruce trees. Joe said, "I'll lure them away and you get up a tree."

They could hear the men chasing them, but they were still a good 200 yards behind them. Preston found a hemlock about 30 feet tall and he climbed about 20 feet up and sat down on a branch. He was fairly well concealed by the branches, so he pulled out his first aid kit and quickly put a battle dressing on the wound to control the bleeding. The bullet had gone cleanly through, missing bones and any main arteries.

Joe went 50 yards off to one side and, when he started seeing brush moving about 75 yards behind him, he fired off three quick rounds. He then took off running for all he was worth, leading them away from Preston's position. The pursuers quickly changed directions and went after Joe, except for one man, who was sneaking along the edge of the stream. Preston thought he was there to prevent them from circling back. He watched the man carefully as he moved through the brush, quietly and with purpose. When he was about 20 yards away from the tree Preston was in, he stopped, cocked his head to one side and looked in the direction that Joe had run. He was listening to the others chasing Joe. The man started sneaking along again and Preston watched him until he was out of sight.

Sitting on a thin branch is anything but comfortable. As your legs start going numb, you have to slowly and quietly move so your legs don't cramp or fall asleep. Preston was worried that his wound would stiffen his leg and he would have trouble climbing down.

It was starting to get dark now, as the sun faded. He could smell the pines and hear the stream below. This would be a perfect setting if people were not trying to kill him. All of a sudden, he saw movement but thought it was too early for Joe to be coming back. It was the lone man sneaking back along the edge. He passed within 10 feet of the tree Preston was in and was soon out of sight, heading back for the road.

After dark, around one p.m., Preston climbed out of the tree. His leg was stiffening, but he knew he had to get walking on it. He had to wait for Joe and would give him a couple more hours, or until midnight, and, if he wasn't back by then, they were both on their own. He found a small sapling spruce tree. Pulling his knife, he cleared the branches out so he could lean against it, but it would still give him plenty of cover. He sat down and waited for Joe. Before sitting down, he scraped all the branches and leaves out of the way with his boot, so he could move quietly if he had to.

Joe had taken the men on a wild goose chase. He ran for about 2 miles and then circled back to the road. He found a low spot, a dip in the road, and, not seeing anybody, he crouched low and ran to the other side. He got in the brush and waited. If they had a really good tracker, he would know before dark. How much time would they waste on only 2 guys on foot? He waited until darkness and then worked his way back towards the stream. He watched the troops mount up and leave.

He waited for an hour after dark, directly across from where they had charged in. He watched for movement or any telltale signs of somebody left behind. He listened and smelled the air, but there was nothing he could detect.

It looked like they had cleared out, so he slowly started working his way back to Preston. It took him over an hour and a half to reach Preston's location and, when he did, Preston said, "You're getting old. It took you long enough."

Joe chuckled, "If you weren't such a clumsy ox, getting yourself shot, we'd already be miles away. How's the leg?"

"Just peachy. A little stiff, but the bleeding stopped, so let's get moving."

He got to his feet and they headed back to the road. Just before they reached the road, they heard men on horseback riding by. It was too dark to tell who or what they were. Joe whispered, "They're kind of serious types, aren't they."

Preston whispered back, "What's the plan, boss? I say we stay low in the ditch, travel until we find a farm field, or something open, and then we can get off the road." Joe nodded in agreement.

Preston's leg limbered up and still caused him some pain, but it didn't slow him down. They had traveled about 5 miles when they saw a field off to the right. Staying close to the edge of the woods, they worked their way back a half mile and ran into an abandoned farmhouse. They checked the inside for any food or needed supplies. Finding none, they decided to spend the night there.

They didn't think it was good idea to stay in the house, as that would be a prime place for the troops to look for them, so they stayed off in the woods, burying themselves in the leaves. They both slept and, a couple of hours after daylight, Joe got up and did a quick recon of the area. They needed food. Going up to some collapsed buildings, he saw a groundhog run underneath some boards. As nice as some meat might be, they couldn't risk the noise of a shot. He looked for an old hand-pump well, hoping for water, but he knew he was dreaming.

Joe returned and Preston asked, "See anything?"

Joe replied, "Just a groundhog, but we can't risk taking a shot right now."

Preston said, "Well, Amy packed me some of her professional grade self-locking snares. It's real simple; all you do is close down the loop, feed it around a tree and through the swivel and that will anchor it there. Get yourself a stick, about 2 inches thick, sharpen one end and jam that into the ground. Split the top about 3 inches down and jam the snare in there. Then make about a 6-inch loop, positioning it about 2 inches off the ground, right in front of his hole."

Joe said, "That sounds easy enough, but Amy is the expert. Can you make it work?"

"Yeah, it's pretty simple. You just have to make sure the only thing that moves is the loop closing. None of the cable behind the stick can move. It has to be solid."

Joe looked at him, still a bit confused. "I've never done this before, so why don't you hobble over and help me?"

"Quit being a baby. I'm going to clean my wound out. Now go get us some protein."

Joe said, "What if I screw up and spook him? Then we'll both go hungry."

"That's the beauty of snares. The worst that happens is they knock the loop over. They just think it's some stick and don't know any better. Then you just open the loop up until you get it right. Even a bonehead like you can handle this."

Joe took the snare and headed to the place he had seen the groundhog. Preston dropped his pants and pulled out his first aid kit. He used alcohol pads to clean up all the blood around his wound. It looked pretty nasty. Using a fresh pad, he cleaned out all the debris and dirt that was in the wound. Then he poured activated charcoal right into the wound. The doc, or he should say vet, was a firm believer in using activated charcoal. He said it would absorb any infection in the wound. It hurt like hell, but it was the best thing they had.

The doc told him he was supposed to leave that in for a couple of hours and then clean it out, fill it up again and bandage it shut. As he finished, Joe was returning with a smile on his face. "Okay, it's set. Now what?"

"Well, I would think you need to go find a spring or a pond, someplace with some water to clean the ground hog after you butcher it. But first, did you see any old coffee cans we can make a hobo stove out of?"

"Hobo stove? What the heck is that?"

Preston shook his head. "Kids nowadays don't know anything. Go get me a 3 pound coffee can and I'll teach you something."

Joe returned a short while later and handed him an old Hills Brothers coffee can. "It had some rusty nails in it. Does that matter?"

Preston laughed, "Nope. You go find some water while I make the stove. The wind has been coming out of the Northwest all day, so I doubt if anyone can smell a fire this far off the road, especially with the wind in our favor."

Using his K-bar knife, he cut a small door in the side of the can near the top, then he punched a lot of holes on the bottom side of the can, so the fire could vent out. Flipping the can over and placing it over the fire would concentrate the heat on the flat bottom and it would be used like a griddle for cooking the food. It's a very simple and quick way to cook something. He gathered a large pile of small sticks and broke them into about 4-inch- long pieces.

Joe returned saying, "That's about the goofiest thing I've ever seen."

"Don't you worry about what I am doing. Did you find some water?"

"Yeah, I've found an old spring. I'll fill up our canteens and then I'll go check the snare."

He quickly returned with the canteens filled and then went off to check the snare. As he approached it, he couldn't believe his eyes. There sat a big fat groundhog, all wrapped around the tree he had anchored the snare to.

The groundhog was staring right at him. He picked up a piece of wood and gave it two quick smacks to the head, putting the animal out of its misery.

"Fresh meat," he mumbled as he unwrapped the snare from around the tree. It was all kinked up, but it had served its purpose and given them the food they needed. He carried the groundhog over to the spring and quickly cleaned it. He left the skull on and, using a piece of string, he tied it off to a branch so he could skin it.

Preston got a small fire going and, once it was burning well, he placed the can over it and used the door to feed in small branches. Joe cut pieces of meat straight off the groundhog, with no bones so it would cook faster. None of the pieces were thicker than an inch.

Preston said, "Give me a piece of that fat while I'm waiting for you." Joe handed him a piece of fat. He had already whittled a turning fork and, using that, he placed the fat on the lid. It hissed and sizzled, turning to liquid grease.

He said, "Hurry up, would you? We need to get some meat cooking while the stove is hot." Joe handed him a small handful of meat and Preston spread it across the lid. Using a couple of wild raspberry leaves for flavor, he placed them on the meat. The meat sizzled and popped as it cooked. He turned it quickly and within a few minutes it was done.

He used his carved fork to put the meat on a piece of wood he had split and said, "Joe, come take your food and hand me some more to cook."

Joe took the cooked meat and, taking a bite, said, "This is really good. You're going to make Amy a fine wife."

"Don't tell her I know how to do this. Tell her I burnt it horribly and you were barely able to choke it down."

"Don't worry; your secret is safe with me. I'll tell her you are the worst damn cook I've ever seen in my life and the only reason I didn't leave you behind was that I was afraid the bears would get sick and choke on you. Don't want to be cruel to the animals, you know?"

After they finished eating, Preston cleaned out the wound again, refilled it with the charcoal and bandaged it tightly so he could walk that night.

Chapter 27

Stumbling in the Dark

"Enjoy when you can, and endure when you must."
~Johann Wolfgang von Goethe

"How is your wound?" Joe asked.

Preston said, "Look, it's no big deal. I'm ready to travel. Are you ready to keep up?"

It was about an hour before dark and they worked their way up to the edge of the road. They had only seen one patrol go by the whole day. At dark, they started walking along the ditch. They traveled for a couple of hours, maybe 5 miles, when they approached an intersection. Something didn't feel right. Everything looked normal, but something just wasn't right with the area. Joe didn't know what was going on, but he gave hand signals for Preston to be careful.

Preston worked his way up to Joe and whispered, "What's the matter?"

Joe whispered back, "I don't know, but something doesn't feel right. Humor me and let's stay right on the edge of the woods."

"Slowly, quietly, let's work our way up to the intersection. We're going to stop and watch it."

When they were about 50 yards from the edge of the intersection, they stepped off into the woods. Joe whispered, "You stay here. I'm crawling up to see what's going on."

Preston waited on high alert, his rifle at the ready. He had been with Joe long enough to trust his instincts.

Joe slowly crawled up, being careful not to break any branches or make sudden movements. He was about 20 yards from the intersection now and his mind was screaming to get out of there, it's a trap, but he still couldn't see anything. It took all of his willpower not to take off running, as he could feel something was dreadfully wrong. He sat there for five minutes, watching and listening, when he heard a guy cough. He couldn't have been more than 10 feet in front of him.

He was right, it was a trap. Even more cautiously, he crept back to Preston.

He whispered, using one hand over Preston's ear, "We've got company. I don't know how many, but there's one guy for sure watching the intersection. I'm guessing there's a whole lot more. I say we back up another quarter of a mile, then head in for a mile, maybe two, and then head out to the other road and cross there."

Preston agreed and they slowly started working their way into the brush. The problem was that it was a really dark night, with no moon, and with the tree canopy being so thick it was pitch black. They were moving at a snail's pace, not only due to the darkness, but also to keep their noise down, not to mention the new hazard of getting slapped in the face with branches they couldn't see.

It took them almost 2 hours to travel a mile, it was that dark. It took another hour to work their way up to the other road. They looked for a low spot to cross. Finding a dip in the road, they crossed safely to the other side. After another two hours of walking through the dense forest, they turned to head back to the road. It was like two blind men walking in the forest without the aid of a walking stick, having to take short half-steps. Using their hands, they had to feel which way to quietly go around branches and it was excruciatingly slow. About 4:15 that morning they made it back to the road. With a little luck they should be able to travel 5 more miles before it was daybreak.

At daybreak they stopped and got off the road, buried themselves with leaves again and slept. At this rate it would take them 10 days to get back.

Meanwhile, John, Scott and the remaining men returned with the 105 that morning. They had lost eight men and had two unaccounted for. Two more were wounded, so they were down over half of their force. Without stopping for sleep, they made the rounds and told the widows what had happened to their husbands. Unlike a regular war, where somebody else back home would have the duty of telling the people of the lost loved ones, these officers did it themselves. Some of those lost were friends, some were family, but everybody knew everybody, which made it that much more difficult. The last place they stopped was the hospital, but Amy and Jane had already heard from the wounded they were tending.

Amy asked in an accusatory voice, "Who made the decision to leave our husbands on foot?"

John admitted, "I did and I'd do it again. That 105 is too important. Both your husbands are trained and, of the men I had with me, they stood the best chance to return alive. Depriving the enemy of that 105 might very well have saved hundreds, if not thousands of lives. I hope you can understand."

Amy, in a less than understanding voice, said, "Show me on the map where you deserted them."

Scott looked at her. "Why? What are you thinking?"

"Jane and I are going to ride down there and pick up our men. What do you think?"

John said, "Sorry, but you're not going. You both have duties and are needed here." Looking at Jane he said, "You are a very needed nurse." Turning to Amy, "And you have the responsibility of security for this hospital. You are both staying. Is that clear?"

"We can do our duties here during the day, and ride down there at night," Jane said.

"Absolutely not," Scott said, almost shouting. "Use your head, Jane. You, of all women, should understand this. Both of you could ride down and right into a trap, or compromise their position and get them both killed. The best thing to do is to wait here for them to return."

Amy jumped in, "Okay, we'll give them two more days and, if they're not back then, we quit your militia and we're going looking for them. Is *that* clear?"

John took a deep breath. "If you do that, you will not be provided with any assistance. That means no horses, no wagon and no support from us whatsoever. And if you do find them, by some miracle, what assistance could you possibly offer them?"

Scott jumped in and said, "Give me your word you'll wait two days and then we'll talk about it." Both women nodded their head in agreement. With that, the 2 men left.

Jane looked at Amy, "You know they are going to be okay, don't you?"

"Damn it. I hate this shit. I just got married and my dumbass fool of a husband is going out, trying to get himself killed. And those two dumbasses volunteered for this."

Jane said, "They are dumbasses, careless and reckless, but we need to find out where they were left behind."

Amy said, "Let's question everyone that comes in for the next two days, until we find out where they left them."

They did just that and, once they found out, they made a plan. Using a map to pinpoint the location where they thought Preston and Joe were, they talked it over with Scott that evening.

Scott said, "You know I can't let you go, or assist you in any way, so this conversation never happened, but let's just say, maybe right at 10:00 tonight, two ladies noticed that the stable guard was sound asleep and they borrowed four horses, well then it would be on those two ladies' shoulders, wouldn't it?"

They simply smiled and nodded, offering him a bottle of Scotch they had found at the cabin. He poured them each a shot. "Here," showing them the map, "See this secondary road? This is the planned escape route. They are supposed to wait here," pointing at an intersection 20 miles south from where they are. "This is where they are supposed to wait for pickup from the patrol." He went on, "They were last seen down here," pointing on the map, "about 70 miles south of us. The Rainbow warriors are not coming this far north and we don't know why, but this is the farthest north we saw them, 40 miles from here," pointing to a spot on the map.

"If I were giving you orders, I would say don't go any farther south than where the Rainbow Warrior patrols were last seen. Chances are that Joe and Preston don't know this information, so they're going to be traveling at night. Your best bet is to wait for them at the pickup spot. Then, during the night, walk this section trying to find them. Just don't get shot or shoot them. It's dangerous for you both; you know that, don't you?"

Jane said, "They are our husbands. We are both trained and we understand how they think and move. We stand the best chance of finding them out of anyone."

Amy was almost in tears. "I hate this waiting and not knowing is driving me insane. We have to do something."

Scott patted her arm and said, "I figured you two would be going, so I already warned the patrol to be on the lookout for you. Don't forget you have friendlies out there patrolling too."

"It's 8:30, so why don't you just take the horses now and go. Just remember the plan; you stole the horses."

They grabbed the horses, which were already saddled and packed with food and a first aid kit, and headed out, stopping by the house for some more ammo and to tell Michael the plan. He, of course, wanted to come along, but they explained they needed him there to guard the house and supplies. If anyone asked, he didn't know where they were.

There was kind of a no-man's-land in between the two territories: parts controlled by the Rainbow Warriors, then 20 miles of a buffer zone and then the territory of the Wisconsin Northern Militia. Not that they knew it at the time, but the Rainbow Warriors were ordered to stop at a certain intersection, going no farther north, and one thing the major did believe in was following orders. He thought it was bad enough that he would have to go back and explain to the Colonel how he lost the cannon, plus almost 100 men dead or wounded. He didn't want to give him another reason for punishment by disobeying a direct order.

All they were able to torture out of the one wounded man they had captured was that they were up against an army of 300, with no artillery and no other support in the area. The man died before they could get any more information out of him.

The major split up his men into 10 groups of 40 men each, to patrol and try to cut off the men that stole the 105. Every road heading north was being patrolled.

They set up a night watch at all major intersections, hoping to ambush them if they came through. So far, after two days, the only report was of 2 men on foot and it was hardly worth the time to chase them. He wasn't sure how in the world they disappeared so fast, having to pull that cannon, and without a trace. They must have had several teams of horses to switch out and must have stayed on the paved road, never stopping once they had it.

The major was frustrated beyond belief, unable to complete his mission. In two days, he was supposed to be in Minneapolis to report that the supply route was open and secure. He lost his only artillery piece and had now spent almost three days trying to get it back. The only good news was that the raiders didn't get the ammo supply wagon for the 105. Neither side had a working weapon. Now the big question was, did they know about the supply route, or was that just an ambush to thin their numbers out? They'd found an alternate route heading south: traveling 15 miles south, then 10 miles west and 15 miles back, to Highway 8. He was going to be able to complete his mission, so he sent word for all the patrols to come in.

The major thought that if he could get reinforcements from Minneapolis, they could quickly crush this little uprising from the peasants.

Jane and Amy had only been gone a few hours when they ran into their patrol. They were surrounded, but luckily the patrol had been warned that they might be coming through. They were told not to go any farther than the intersection and wait there.

They made it there by about 2:30 in the morning. There was a corral at an old farmhouse, so they let the horses go and put the saddles in the barn. They walked the edge of the road all of the way to the intersection and found a spot in the woods where they could see in all four directions. Amy cleared a path where she could pace back and forth without making a lot of noise. Every time she walked up to Jane, she would whisper in her ear, "Anything?"

Jane whispered back, "You're making me nervous. Would you please stop pacing?"

"They should be here already," Amy whispered back. "We should walk down and go look for them."

Jane took a deep breath and let it out. "No, we're staying here. We don't know which of the three directions they are going to be coming from. With our luck we'd pick the wrong one and they would come through the other way and we'd miss them."

Amy whispered back, "I know you're right, but what if they are there and in a firefight, needing backup right now?"

Jane shook her head, "If they were in a firefight, don't you think we would hear it? I hear nothing and that's a good sign. Here, you take watch for a while and let me pace."

Jane whispered, “Don’t stare at one spot for too long or you’ll start seeing shapes and your mind will play tricks on you. It’s easy to convince yourself somebody’s coming, so you must constantly keep scanning and looking for movement.”

Jane crept back about 20 feet and sat down with her back against a tree, closing her eyes. “Jesus, Joe, where the hell are you?” She was so tired but prayed he was okay. She just wanted to close her eyelids and rest for a few minutes. The next thing she knew, Amy was shaking her and it was daybreak. Amy whispered right into her ear, “Two guys are sneaking along, coming up the road.”

With excitement in her eyes, she asked, “Is it them? Is it the two boneheads?”

Amy whispered back, “I don’t know. Come take a look.”

They both crept up to the watch position and saw the two guys crossing the road. One was limping. “Looks like them.” Jane took a chance and whistled. Both men froze, lifting their guns in the direction of the noise. Once the men were facing them, they recognized both of them. Jane called out, “Over here.”

Joe recognized her voice and couldn’t believe it. They both ran over to them. Joe said, “What in the hell are you doing here?”

Amy jumped into Preston’s arms, crying and talking at the same time.

“What’s wrong with your leg? Why are you limping? Are you hurt? Who shot you?

“Jesus, woman, take a breath. I’m fine. It’s just a little hole. No big deal. Let’s get out of here.” Preston said.

Amy was so happy that he was all right and told them that they had four horses just up the road. She said, “I’ll go get the horses.” And with that, she ran to the road and took off.

Jane came over and gave him a hug, “What took you so long?”

Preston smiled. “Your old man is getting old and slow. Besides, we had some people that were trying to kill us and had to hide from them. I guess some people were a little upset about losing their toy gun. By the way, did those guys make it back okay?”

Jane smiled. “Yup, but they lost 7 men taking it, eight counting Chris, and have two wounded; you’ll make that three. What’s wrong with your leg?”

Preston said, "It's just a small bullet hole. It's a long story and can wait. But hey, we made it back. It only slowed us down a little bit."

Amy came riding up with the horses and they mounted, riding straight to the vet to have Preston's wound checked out. Joe returned the horses, took all of their tack off and stored it properly in the barn. He then turned them out into the pasture and reported to Scott.

Scott welcomed him home and pulled out a map. He wanted to know all of the enemy positions that they knew about. Joe filled him in.

Looking at the map, Scott noticed that some of the locations went as far north as the last sightings reported, which were 10 miles to the east. He pointed to the map and showed Joe, saying, "They must have orders not to go past this line. That's good to know." Showing him on the map he said, "This is as far as we patrol. It's roughly a 20 mile buffer zone between us and them, a no-man's-land. So you're sure you didn't see anybody in those 20 miles? No patrols went past you? No recon scouts?"

Joe, confirming that, said, "No, that was the last place we encountered anybody. Where's John?"

"He's turning over the 105 to Clint and getting further orders. What do you think we should do?"

"Well, first thing we need to find out is where these troops are. Did they make it to Minneapolis, or did they turn back? If they made it to Minneapolis, we should hit them again on the return trip. I know a guy that has a .50 Cal sniper rifle. Give me a couple of days to rest up. I'll go talk to him and see if he wants to join us."

"Sounds good," Scott said. "You two got some good women there, but they stole the horses and went looking on their own, disobeying a direct order from John."

Joe laughed. "Yeah, I know, they filled us in. I won't say a word if you don't. John doesn't need to know everything."

"I agree. Now go home and get some rest. We'll meet back here in three days." Joe climbed on his bike and headed for home.

Upon returning home, Michael wanted all of the details. Joe said, "Sorry, but I'm too tired right now. I'm going to bed. You're on watch."

Chapter 28

The Sniper Rifle

"Do what you can, with what you have, where you are."
~Theodore Roosevelt

The Doc told Preston he was stay off the leg for 4 weeks, until it was totally healed, and to make sure no infection set in.

That morning, Amy began throwing up and thought it must be the flu. Jane asked her when was the last time she had her period and a panicked look came across Amy's face.

"Oh God, not that. No, I can't be." She looked at Jane. "It's been two months."

They told the doctor what was going on and he smiled, saying, "Good. I've been saving some prenatal vitamins and was wondering what I could use them for. Does Preston know?"

Amy started stuttering, "Ah, ah, ah, we don't know for sure and he's wounded, so I don't need to bother him with this right now."

Jane grabbed her by the shoulders, turned her around and marched her right into Preston's room. She pushed Amy in and, as she closed the door, she said, "Amy has something important to tell you."

Preston got up and started getting dressed. "The Doc cleared me to go home. What do you have to tell me?" He had his back to her as he was putting on his shirt.

Amy started, "I'm glad you're coming home and uh, uh," and then in a really fast voice, "I might be pregnant."

Preston turned around, "That's great. How far along are you?" looking down at her stomach.

She rubbed her stomach and said, "Two months."

Preston rushed to her and held her closely in his arms. "This is so great. Let's go tell everybody. Do you think it's boy or a girl? What's your intuition say?"

Amy put her arms around his neck, saying, "Are you sure you're happy about this, because I don't even know if I am, for sure."

Preston said, "Of course I am and you're going to make the best mother ever."

She said, "I have no idea if it's a boy or a girl. It's too early to know. Let's wait another month to be sure before we start telling everybody. What if it's just stress and I just missed two periods? Please, for me, let's just wait."

He smiled. "Okay, that's not a problem. Take me home so I can get outta here."

They walked out and Preston thanked the Doc, before checking in on the other two wounded men. One had been shot in the gut; the Doc was able to remove the bullet and sew up the wound. He needed a lot of bed time, but was going to make it. The other had a knee blown out. It was so badly shattered that they'd had to amputate just above the knee. Preston felt bad for wasting time lying in a hospital bed overnight when these brave men deserved all the care and attention.

When John returned, he called a meeting. When the men were gathered, he told them, "Our mission recon was to find out where these troops are and find possible ambush sites along Highway 8, ones that have high ground on the sides. Clint thinks we should harass them all the way back to Green Bay. Using small two-man teams, a spotter and sniper, they will snipe them all the way back until we get them into the trap."

Joe said, "What trap?"

John said, "That's on a need-to-know basis. We are not sharing that information in case any of you are captured."

Joe didn't like being left out of the loop, but understood. He said, "Okay, when do we leave?"

Scott said, "It's going to be myself and you as one sniper team. We're going to go visit your friend and see if we can borrow that .50 Cal sniper rifle. We'll leave in the morning."

That night Preston threw a fit saying, "The hell with that! I'm fit for duty. I'm going with you. There are real men in that hospital and I only had a little scratch. My leg is a little stiff, but I can keep up with you."

Amy jumped in, "You're staying right here, Mister."

He looked her straight in the eye and said, “Don’t even talk to me about following orders. We’re a team. Joe and I have been through a lot together and can work together as one.”

Joe said in a loud tone, “No, you’re staying, unless you’re trying to get me killed. You can’t even get up and run to the door right now. The Doc said 4 weeks. If this was your third week and your leg was feeling good and you could run, then we could talk about it. Even after it heals, it’s still going to take it 2 to 3 weeks to get your strength back. You know that. Let’s face it, you’re out of this for now.”

Everybody looked at Preston. He looked straight at Joe and said, “Okay, you guys win, but don’t get your dumb ass killed. I would never forgive myself.”

Michael said, “I can go and take Preston’s place.”

Preston said, “I’m sorry, but you’ve got to stay here and help me. I can’t do it alone, especially in my condition. You can help guard this place because I can only hobble over to the door to help you fight if something goes wrong. You have to be my eyes and ears, plus, who’s going to get the firewood?”

In the morning Joe and Scott headed out. Scott told him that Clint said he was going to fly the Black flag, with no quarter for the enemy.

Joe said, “Black flag? Like a pirate? What’s that all about?”

Scott added, “After he heard that they tortured our men for information, literally tortured them to death, he swore that he wouldn’t accept any surrender and no prisoners. They all die.”

“Kind of harsh, don’t you think?”

“Not at all. They are bringing the war to us and this is a cancer that must be wiped out. We’ve all heard of the rapes and killings, even children, just for eating meat. These people need to be stopped once and for all. Hitler and the Nazis used the same thinking. They made the troops think they were the superior race, evolved higher than other races, and wanted to allow animals equal rights with people. He planned on converting everyone to be vegan after the war. Without meat proteins the people would be more docile and less likely to try to overthrow him, too.”

Joe shook his head, “Makes perfect sense. I knew he registered all the guns and then collected them all before the war started.”

On the second day, they reached Philip's house. Philip was glad to see Joe. He said, "Things have really turned around here for the better and several people have asked, if by chance you ever returned, could I talk you into staying on as our Sheriff?"

Joe laughed and said, "That's quite a change of heart, but no, there is no way I feel that I could come back here."

After explaining why they needed it, they talked him into lending them the sniper rifle. Joe smiled, saying, "We have a new home now and a new threat — The Rainbow Warriors. You should have a meeting tonight and any men that can should go join Clint's army. Make sure you keep enough back here for support, just in case they swing this way."

"Can we get that rifle now?"

Phillip smiled and said, "After what you did for us, of course you can have it. I'll even lend you a horse to carry it. You know it weighs about 35 pounds, plus the extra ammo, so it would really slow you down. I can rig up a pack to secure it on a horse, then you should be free enough to move quickly."

He filled up a saddlebag with oats for the horses and had his wife pack them a lunch.

Joe shook his hand and said, "Thank you, Phillip. You have been a good friend. We'll have this back as soon as we can."

They mounted up and rode off, leading the packhorse. When they we're out of ear shot, Scott asked, "What happened when you were here? Why did you leave? Those people look like they genuinely care for you."

Joe said. "Not all of them. When we were trying to take out the warlord, some young teenage girls were killed. One of the fathers blamed me for getting his daughter killed. It was better for us to move on."

"I see," Scott said. "The life we have right now is not an easy one, but I feel that once we get our feet back on the ground, we can rebuild."

"I hope so, but right now we have to find out where these troops are and start picking them off. You ever shoot a .50 Cal before?"

"The .50 caliber machine-gun, yeah, but never the sniper rifle."

Joe said, "I have, a couple of times, but never enough. It was too pricey of a gun for me to buy. Either way, let's cover some ground."

Two days later, they were about 10 miles from Highway 8 when a man ran out in front of them. He held both hands up in the air.

Joe and Scott both pulled out their rifles and were ready for an ambush.

The man said, "Relax, I'm alone and unarmed. You the guys fighting that Army, right?"

Joe kept his eyes scanning around, "Maybe. Why do you want to know?"

"Because I have some information you need to know. They found a detour and kept going west."

"Who are you and why are you helping us?" Scott asked.

"The name is Neil and those bastards killed my family and burned my place to the ground. I was up north trading and when I came back my wife and son were killed; shot in the head and left out in the chicken pen. The place burned to the ground and I buried them both. I've been waiting for you guys to come back so I could join your forces and fight these animals."

Joe tried to size the man up and said, "How do we know you aren't a spy and trying to lead us into a trap?"

"I kind of figured that you might think that, so just tell me where to go join up and I'll walk all the way there, I don't care. But first let me give this map and some local information you might need to know. Is it okay if I pull my map out?"

"Yes, but do it slowly. No sudden moves," Joe said.

He pulled the map out and unfolded it. Pointing to a spot, he said, "See, this is where you blew the bridge up. They came up this way 6 miles and then took this road around and back down here. You cost them about a 20-mile detour. I used to be a logger and here on the map is something you need to know. This area right here," pointing to the map, "was logged off and you can gain access from this logging road, which comes off this road. It is logged within 100 feet of the highway. It's a great area to watch them from and you can do whatever you are supposed to do." He handed the map to Joe.

Scott said, "Okay. You know how to get to Rhinelander from here?" Neil nodded yes. "Well, you head there and make sure you come through in the daylight. A patrol is going to meet you there and they will direct you where to go to join up."

"Why don't I go with you guys? I know the area and can be very helpful."

Joe said, "I'm sure you could be, but we have to keep moving and you being on foot would slow us down. Besides, you need to go up north to get some training before you are ready to see combat."

Neil nodded his understanding and said, "Good luck. Please kill a couple of extra for my wife and son."

Riding off, Scott said, "We could have taken him on the pack horse. His local knowledge could save a lot of time and effort."

Joe smiled, "And what if he really was a spy? He could slice our throats and we wake up dead. I trust you, but I don't know him. I would never get a wink of sleep."

"Good point."

The man's information paid off and they could clearly see where the Army turned off the paved road and onto a dirt road.

They spent the next three days figuring out where to put the snipers' nests. They preferably wanted to hit them in the morning, when the sun was in their targets' eyes and at their own backs. They would have to be careful to avoid contact too late in the afternoon, or they would be at a disadvantage, with the sun in their eyes. The man's information was spot on, with the logged clearing being a perfect ambush spot. They could easily hide their horses and had a number of spots they could shoot from.

Joe figured they would start shooting at 1,000 yards, get three shots off and then move. The only thing he was worried about was the forward patrol. They would hear the shots and come racing back, but they would have to figure out which side of the road they were on before charging in and by then they would be long gone.

Over the rest of the week, they made three separate sniper hides. They built a small dugout with a roof and shooting port. They did two more, 10 miles apart. They met the recon patrol and passed on the intel they had gotten, saying they were ready and bored.

Joe was starting to wonder if their intel was bad. Were they setting up a new supply route, or just wasting their time? What in the hell was Clint's trap anyways? What if he spent all that time making the trap and they never showed up? Too many variables, but they were just going to have to wait for now.

Finally, on the ninth day, they were hiding in their sniper hole when they saw the forward patrol of 10 men go by.

Joe shook Scott and told him to wake up, it was show time. The patrol went by and they began timing to try and figure if the Army was still traveling an hour behind.

The minutes ticked by and the patrol was all they saw, no Army. Another 30 minutes had gone by when they heard them marching.

Joe said, "It's a good time to take out an officer."

He saw the leading troops nearing the 1,000 yard marker. They had marked it with small wind ribbons. Only a slight breeze was blowing and the sun wasn't perfect, but it was still in the troop's eyes.

Joe was looking through the Night Force 5.5-22x56 NXS Ill. scope, among the most advanced field tactical scopes ever produced, with the built-in lines from 200 yards to 1,000 yards. The .50 Cal also had the option to go all the way to 2,000 yards. Philip had just kept it sighted in from 200 to 1,000 yards. The rifle was perfectly balanced and, using the bipod along with some sand-filled socks, which were placed on the rear of the stock, it helped to level it out and hold the gun steady.

Joe was waiting for them to hit the yard mark. He asked Scott, "What is the cross wind?"

"I would guess about 5 mph, coming from the north."

He was looking through his scope and could not believe his eyes. The 3 men on horses in front of the troops were the officers. The one in the middle had something on his helmet which looked like a high-ranking officer's insignia, and the ones on both sides of him looked like officers, too.

Adjusting his windage, Joe said, "I'm taking the center one first and I'll then swing on the other officer, saving the last shot for the other man on horseback. Are you ready?"

"Ready," Scott reported, as he watched with binoculars.

When they hit the 1,000 yard mark, which was marked by a lone wheel from a car, Joe squeezed off the first shot. Then he quickly worked the bolt action to load a fresh round.

Scott called out, "Hit. There's more down behind him too."

Joe concentrated on the other officer. He hesitated a second and then squeezed off the second round and loaded another round into the chamber.

Scott said, "Oh man, you blew his arm off. Remember the wind."

Joe aimed back into the troops, 200 yards farther back. They weren't reacting to the shots yet, so he squeezed off the last round. "I just used the Davy Crockett height and windage."

"More down." Scott called out. "Good, now let's move."

They climbed out of the hole and ran for the horses. Carrying that heavy gun made it seem like it took them forever. They quickly strapped it in the case, jumped on their horses and raced across the logging road. They were in the open for a half mile to the other side and were expecting to hear shooting or yelling, or see some troops coming after them, but nothing.

They made it across the open area and kept on going. They didn't slow down for 5 miles. Finally, letting up on the horses, they slowed to a trot. Going another 4 miles, they turned off onto a 4-wheeler trail, which took them to their next hide.

They had pre-positioned 5-gallon buckets full of water for the horses and cut hay for them. They had walked the horses the last mile, letting them cool down. Tying the horses up with food and water, they grabbed the gun and climbed into the new hide.

Only then did they whisper back and forth. Scott said, "You nailed both of those officers. The first one is dead for sure and the second one, well, I saw his left arm go flying off in the air. The last shot I saw 4 men go down for sure. That was some great shooting. I would say maybe 12 men total were killed or hit, maybe more."

"Let's play it low ball, so I'm saying six hit for sure." Joe said. "That was the easy one. We might be able to do this one more time. That's why I insisted on the last hide off this highway being right on the road, using that old truck."

Scott asked, "What do you think they will do, now that their leader is dead?"

"I don't know. If we got all of the officers, maybe the sergeant will be able to lead them, but they could all just fall apart and run for home."

Their adrenaline was still pumping and it took some time for both of them to calm down.

They waited until dark, but nothing came by them.

Scott said, "We need to get the saddles off the horses and let them rest. I'll take care of that and then we should eat."

Their meals-ready-to-eat were parched corn and beef jerky with some cookies.

When Scott returned, he said, "I'll take first watch and you get some sleep." Scott let him sleep until midnight and then woke him and they switched. About 5 the next morning, Joe woke him up to get the horses saddled.

They ate breakfast and then Joe napped, wanting to be fresh for their next encounter.

At 7 a.m., Scott woke him up. "We have a patrol coming. They're spread out and moving slowly."

Joe got on the scope. "Damn, the easy stuff is over. I'm thinking we should hit these guys. It's time to make all of them really nervous."

"Okay. I agree," Scott whispered. Just then they heard a stick snap in the woods. From their hide, Scott looked out and, about 100 yards away in the woods, was a foot patrol.

"Joe, we got trouble. Come on let's move," he whispered.

Hearing the urgency in his voice, Joe pulled the gun in. They did a low crawl out of sight and then raced to the horses. They were 100 yards back farther off the highway, strapping the gun on, when they heard a voice call out, "Hey, I found something."

Climbing on their horses, they took off down the trail and away from danger. They hadn't gone 200 yards when a pack of wolves charged, attacking the horses. A pack of six raced out of the brush, trying to flank the horses.

Horses, at the sight and smell of wolves, go into a complete wild panic. Deep inside the horse's primitive mind, they instinctually know that wolves are the ultimate predator to fear.

Scott was in the lead, on the big blue dun, who was not having any of this nonsense and charged the lead wolf standing on the trail. The others were racing in between the packhorse and Joe's horse, trying to break off one or all of them. The growling and snapping was fierce. My God, they were as fast as greased lighting. Joe thought he couldn't draw a weapon, but he was doing all he could just to stay on the horse.

The big dun raced right over top of the lead wolf, knocking him clear of the path. The rest of the horses followed and they raced off. Joe was able to pull his pistol and fired off a few rounds at one that was closest to his right side, but missed. The noise of the gun made the pack back off. The men and horses had gotten away, but not unscathed. The packhorse had suffered a gash along its rear flank, about 12 inches long. The wolf had been trying to pull him down, but was kicked off.

When they reached the dirt road, they turned east. They had only gone about 400 yards and, as the horses were calming down, Joe glanced over his shoulder to see that the damn wolves were on the road, trailing behind them. The smell of fresh blood was a beacon and they must be starving. Damn, this was bad. They had to shake these wolves or kill them. They didn't want to have a running battle with the wolf pack, as the patrol was tracking them for sure.

They stayed at a gallop for another 5 miles and then stopped to inspect the horses. The horses were still a little spooked, but they got off and inspected each one. The gash on the packhorse wasn't really bad, but it was a beacon for the wolves. Looking back down the trail, there were three wolves at about 300 yards back. The other ones were most likely trying to flank them. Joe pulled his rifle and they scattered into the brush. *Rifle shy and smart, just great.* Joe thought.

Scott whispered, "What's the plan?"

"Let's mount up and then we'll take the next road north." They travelled a few more miles and turned north, but the damn wolves were still trailing behind them. He rode up next to Scott, saying, "We need to travel at least 10 miles and then find a barn to keep the horses safe. Then we can focus on killing these bastards."

Scott said, "I agree. Hell, even a two-car garage with good doors would work."

Traveling north, they turned off again onto a paved road and headed east. They came to a dirt road that might go to a farm and headed north again. Finding an abandoned house with an attached two-car garage at about 6 that night, they put the horses in and secured the doors. They had let them drink earlier at a pond. They fed them oats, thanks to the saddlebag full that Philip had given them. From inside, they couldn't see the wolves, but they knew they were there.

Chapter 29

Harassing the Troops

"Never fight fair with a stranger, boy. You'll never get out of the jungle that way."

~Arthur Miller

Clint and the men had moved down to the location and were busy constructing the trap. They were setting up all kinds of nasty surprises for the coming Army. Clint was worried. He still had no intel on whether the troops were coming back this way for sure.

Jane was at the hospital working. One man was injured during training and they had to set his broken leg. Because power was so important for the hospital, they received the second gasifier Bob had built and he gave them a battery bank and lights. One of Amy's jobs was to fill up the generator and run it every morning. She almost enjoyed coming to work, due to Preston being moody as all heck, like a caged lion. *Poor Michael*, she thought, but Preston did really like him and tried to make him feel good about all the work he was doing.

When she got home at night, she felt like she was being interrogated by Preston. "What's the news? Where is the Army? Any word on Joe yet? Where are the troops?"

Jane was worried about Joe and the strain was starting to show on her. She snapped at Preston, "Would you shut up already. He's fine. Stop worrying like an old woman."

Amy stopped what she was doing and her mouth hung open. She had never seen Jane lose it before. She was always the calm, rational one of the group. She asked, "Are you ok?"

Jane took a deep breath and finally said, "Yes. I'm fine. I'm just sick of hearing this every single night." She turned to Preston and said, "He's fine, Preston. There's nothing you can do about it either way. When we hear something, we're going to tell you." She walked over and picked up her coat. "I am going for a walk. Just leave me alone for a while."

There was an uneasy tension in the cabin. "Damn it, Preston. Get a hold of yourself. You're making her crazy." Amy said. "And you're driving me crazy, too."

He limped over to her. "I'm sorry, but I'm just sitting here in the dark, not knowing anything. I'm used to being on the front lines."

"Good. Now you know how we feel when you're gone."

Meanwhile, Joe and Scott were having their fair share of problems. While they holed up with the horses, the wolves waited outside. They waited until midnight and then attacked the door. Joe heard them howling. The wolves were scratching at the door and growling. The smell of fresh blood was driving the ravenous beasts to try and dig through the door. The horses, smelling them, were in a panic. They were neighing and kicking the door. Joe and Scott ran outside in the dark. It was an eerie feeling, seeing the shadow of the wolves, and you could feel the death in the air. They wanted those horses and were willing to risk it all to get to them.

Both men fired off a couple of rounds and the wolves disappeared, like ghosts in the night. Scott walked into the garage and calmed the horses down. Joe said, "We need to sit on the front porch and guard the garage doors. We should sit and wait, like a hunter, just not moving and wait for the shot."

Joe grabbed a lawn chair and positioned it on the porch, which had a wooden rail around it. He put his back against one end and sat down. He turned on the small LED light and scanned the area. Holding his rifle up, he could easily hit a wolf from this position.

Scott returned and it was decided that Joe would take the first watch. Part of his mind was hoping that just being out here would keep the wolves away. He heard them howling all around him. *Ah-woo-ooo-ooo*. He listened to the others answer and counted 5 for sure. That eerie, lonely and long wail was such a piercing and gut-wrenching cry, it raised the hairs on the back of his neck.

It was a dark night with no moon and he heard nothing for hours. A light breeze was hitting him in the face. It was cold enough to keep him awake, but not bone chilling. He leaned back and looked up at the stars. His eyes had adjusted to the darkness well enough that he could see the driveway in shadows.

Around 2:45 AM, they came in. A lone wolf came trotting up the driveway. Joe started to slowly lift his rifle, when suddenly he heard a growl off to his right. It was close, way too close. He slowly turned his head and the growling intensified. What a horrible feeling, knowing that a man-killing eating machine was only a few feet away. It could clearly see him, but he was unable to see the vicious beast.

He saw nothing in the blackness when suddenly he heard another growl in front of him. He whipped his head around and, in the starlight, he could just make out the first wolf standing at the bottom of the steps. And then another growl, this time it came from behind him.

He felt panic and was sweating. He was unnerved and his hands began shaking. He felt like he was trapped in a junkyard with three big Rottweilers surrounding him. The growling intensified his anxiety. They were working themselves up to the attack. His mind was racing. If the one behind him grabbed his neck, he would be ripped to shreds in seconds. It was hard to describe the feeling of your whole life being decided in the next few seconds.

He was frozen in panic and his mind was screaming to run into the house. Move, run, my God, but with three of them so close, it wasn't a good idea to run. His breathing was coming in short gasps, like he was swimming for his life. His mind screamed, "My God, shoot. For God sake, shoot."

The one in front of him charged with a growl and snap of the jaws. He flipped on his light, shooting at almost point blank range. The wolf was a mere 7 feet away and the shot caught it full in the chest. It spun around, howling and yipping, biting at the wound. Joe stood up quickly, which most likely saved his life, as the wolf behind him leaped over the railing. The 120 pounds of muscle and teeth knocked him flat to the porch. The wolf sank its teeth into his coat and started shaking him like a rag doll.

This is it, he thought, *killed and torn to shreds by wolves, never to see my loving wife again.* The wolf beside him would be tearing at his arm next, he thought. They were just like gangs of bullies; they work in a team to kill. The strength and power of the wolves' jaws was what shocked and terrified him. He would have to roll over to shoot as his rifle was pinned under his body. He forced himself to think, *Don't give up, or you're a dead man.*

Just then, he heard shots ring out and felt the wolf on him flinch in pain and then leap off. More shots were fired and another wolf yelped in surprise and pain. Scott shone the light around, looking for more targets. Joe was in shock and lay there, afraid to move until he was sure the shooting had stopped.

"Clear." Scott called out. "How bad are you hurt?"

Joe sat up, shaking like a leaf. "Are they dead?"

"I see two dead in the yard and I wounded another one in the back leg." Holding his rifle in one hand, he helped Joe up. "Come on, get inside and you can tell me what happened." Closing and locking the door behind them, Joe felt much safer.

"My God, those things are powerful. He knocked me over like I was nothing. It was like being hit by a freight train with all muscle and teeth."

"Are you hurt? Did any of them bite you? Are you bleeding?"

Joe shook his head, saying, "No. I don't think so. One of them had me by the coat, but his teeth didn't go through. Thank God you woke up in time. The third wolf would have joined in and I would be dead right now."

Scott told him, "Take off your coat and let me check your neck for wounds."

Joe took his coat off and Scott pushed the shirt down, examining his neck. "Wow, did you get lucky. Those razor sharp teeth just missed you. You'll have one hell of a story to tell, with the coat for proof."

Joe's hand was still shaking. "Screw the story. We need to find a way to wipe the rest of these bastards out. Damn, I'd be dead right now if you hadn't been here."

They spent the rest of the night uneasily inside. In the daylight, they saw that the other wolves had eaten the two dead wolves in the front yard. "Damn. That's sick. I didn't know they were cannibals," Scott said.

Joe said, "That explains a lot. They must be starving. All the game in the area must be wiped out. What's our plan for today?"

"We're supposed to meet the recon team today and pass off our intel. I think we can circle around, hopefully without running into a patrol or any more wolves."

It took them all day to work their way around to the meeting spot. They passed their intel on and were told to set up a new sniper hide, hit them again and then meet in a new spot in three days. Other teams had been hitting the Army at night, using crossbows and taking out one or two sentries, before leaving. The teams had done a few more sniper attacks, but none had matched what Joe and Scott had done in terms of damage.

John gave them new orders to hit them at the pond. They knew where they were going to stop and water their horses, so they poisoned the whole pond. When the horses started falling over dead, they were supposed to start shooting.

The whole idea was to demoralize the troops, taking away their mobility and making sure they never felt safe. They wanted to wear on them, physically and mentally. It was working great and their speed had been cut in half. They were traveling 25 miles a day before the attacks started and now they were doing good to make 10 miles a day.

How does an Army fight ghosts when they hit and run? There is no battle plan or strategy to stop it. They also started using silencers on .22s and the enemy had no idea what was going on. They would let the troops pass and then shoot the last guy in the head. The SRT "Comanche" is a user-serviceable silencer, about 1" in diameter and 6" long. It has slightly funneled baffles that fit loosely enough that they can be disassembled for cleaning. Mounted on an old Martini target rifle . . . the combination is VERY accurate, with a wide variety of ammo.

It is quietest with the sub-sonic ammo below 1,080 fps. The enemy only hears the phap. With all the troops moving, most of the time they never heard anything accept the body hitting the ground. Sometimes they didn't even hear that. The two-man sniper team would then disappear into the brush. Sometimes the other troops didn't notice for 200 or 300 yards. They would hit at all hours of the day and night, surprising them at every turn.

The troops were exhausted and the lieutenant in charge, after the major and his top sergeant were killed, was pulling his hair out. They had roving patrols, switching people around. He also had a constant Fast Response Team, or FRT, consisting of ten of his top men, ready to charge off and capture these snipers, but nothing he tried had worked.

The brush was too thick; they had better, faster horses. His men were on edge, weary and tired, dreading each day.

At the rate they were going, it would take them eight more days to reach Green Bay. *Thank God*, he thought, *sanctuary and a place to relax and rest up*.

Noon the next day, they stopped to water their horses at a small pond. It was the only water in the area that was easy to access. The patrol had swept all around the pond and gave the all clear. About half the horses had drunk and they were switching them out, when one of the horses stumbled, got a crazy look on its face, bucked once and fell over dead. Everyone just stared at the horse, thinking it must have been heart attack. Then another horse went down, then another and soon 45 horses lay dead. In the panic someone yelled out, “They’ve poisoned the water. Stop the horses from drinking.”

Joe, with the .50 Cal sniper rifle, had been watching the troops and took out 3 men sitting together in a row. The second shot nailed two that were running in line to the rear and the third shot took out a man barking orders. The patrol could not go after them because their horses were dead. Not taking any chances, they retreated as before. The trap was set before the next watering hole, which was 10 miles away.

What Joe and Scott hadn’t seen was the foot patrol that had stolen their horses. Unlike before, their new hide was the back of a broken-down RV on the side of the road. The foot patrol had been searching for a sniper spot that was dug in, as they were working their way back to the troops, and they were a good 800 yards away when the shooting started. Joe and Scott panicked and ran into the woods. Their best bet was to head off into the thick brush; the only problem was that the foot patrol were now on *their* horses and charging after them.

Joe was trying to run with the heavy rifle and called out to Scott to stand and fight. They took cover behind some trees. Joe propped up the .50 Cal on a strong limb and waited for a target.

He waited until they were 50 yards away and then cut the lead guy down. Scott dropped one too, but the third man dropped, rolled to the ground and started firing at them. The AK-47 was tearing up the brush all around them. He heard more men rushing up, so Joe had no choice but to abandon the .50 cal. He pushed the release button and yanked the bolt out, shoving it into his pocket. He called out to Scott, "Leap frog."

They might lose the sniper rifle but, without the bolt, it would be useless to the enemy.

He unslung his AR-15, his old friend, fired a couple rounds at the charging men and then ran back yelling out, "Go." He fired a few more rounds and Scott ran past him. They did that two more times and were out of sight of any enemy or their gunfire.

They took off at a dead run, through the oak forest and to a little opening, too open for their liking, but they had to cross over it to hit the swamp land. Two miles to go and Joe caught up to Scott. "Act like a deer."

Scott looked at him with a puzzled face, saying, "What?"

Joe was almost out of breath, but managed to say, "Men travel in straight lines, while deer head off at 45 degree angles. Once you're far enough ahead, the pursuers never see you. Trust me, I have tracked a lot of deer, plus it puts more trees between us and them, which is always a good idea."

"Lead the way," Scott said.

They ran for 2 more miles, finally coming to a hill going down into the swamp.

Joe said, "We'll stay here for a minute. Let's see if they're still chasing us."

They sat down to rest and watch with binoculars. After 10 minutes they saw what they were dreading, 50 men trotting up about 800 yards away. Scott said, "I guess they have no sense of humor."

Joe replied, "We're on foot, so they think they have a chance of catching us. Let's go into the swamp and lose them." They got up and moved, quickly and unseen, into the swamp.

Back at the Northern Alliance, Clint was ready with the trap, just waiting for their arrival. His Army had swelled in numbers to over 400 men and women and they were all ready to fight.

They were fresh, well fed, rested and ready to go. He picked a steep hill with high hills on each side of the road, so they controlled the high ground. They had made homemade mortar rounds and had ten teams, five on each side of the road, on the high ground. They also had round hay bales, those 1100 pounders, soaked in used motor oil, on top of the hill, ready to light and roll down on the enemy. Two machine gun posts, lined up with the ditches, were to wait until the mortar round scattered the troops into the ditches, then cut them down. One was an old Gatling gun and the other a WW II .30 Cal machine gun that fired .30-06 ammunition.

The rest of the men were scattered along the top of each end, to snipe them all. He had 20 men on horseback that he held in reserve to take out any that tried to flee.

Chapter 30

The Trap

> "Wars are won in the planning room, not on the battlefield."
>
> ~Gen. Dwight D. Eisenhower

Looking at all of the dead horses, the lieutenant in charge was beyond words. He could not believe the evil the other side was using against them. To poison the water supply and kill innocent horses was evil, sadistic and cruel. Should he waste time burning the dead horses, honoring them, or just push on? He decided that they should push on. In fact, his only thought was to not stop until they reached Green Bay. They were close and, if they went at a Quick March, increasing their speed to 4 miles an hour, they could make it in 2 days.

His top sergeant told him about the 50 men and the chase for the two snipers. He ordered 2 men to find them and tell them to return. Quick March was their only hope to get home before their food ran out. Their morale was in the dirt. They had no choice but to get back to Green Bay and resupply.

These stupid inbred rednecks thought they could beat us, but how can such low life meat eaters be winning? Then he smiled because he realized that they had not brought their army against his superior forces. They had just made small runs on them, hit and run actions.

They marched on, leaving the dead horses behind as a warning the pond was poisoned. He told his troops the plan; two days of Quick March and we will be home safe. This spurred them on with less bickering and faster movement. They were beginning to make good time and he felt they were in better spirits. They were going to make it home.

The highway was cleared 50 feet up the hill to the tree line on both sides and the Lieutenant saw the first hint of fall as the trees were changing colors. He began to think that maybe all they were facing was a small group of snipers. Maybe there really wasn't any army to face after all. They could wait for winter and, once the snow hit, they could track these sniper teams down and wipe them out.

They were traveling up a hill and he was in the middle of the troops as he watched the large cans come floating down from atop the hill. At first he thought it was a bird. He watched it hit and then explode. He looked up and saw eight more falling all around his troops.

These were number 10 size cans filled with shattered car glass or rocks and others had rusty nails. They had timed fuses on them and were taking out his men 20 at a time. One landed right behind him and he turned his horse to flee. Getting away from it was his last thought. The blast ripped him and his horse to shreds.

The troops had some training; Clint gave them credit for that. The ones that had survived on his side of the road charged up the hill. The machine gun opened up, easily cutting them down. He ordered the hay bales lit and pushed off. They rolled down the hill, increasing in speed and veering off to one side or the other, running men over. Everyone was under strict orders not to hit the supply wagon with any bombs or fire. He wanted that 105 ammo badly.

The remaining troops that weren't injured called a retreat and started running. Clint looked to a man on the hill and signaled him. The man started waving a red flag. From over the hill, 50 mounted cavalry charged down on the survivors. In the lead was the black flag.

One survivor would later tell the tale of the death riders. "It was like Death himself sat upon 50 horses. All dressed in black, with a pistol in each hand and the reins in their mouths, they charged forth. No army could face these fearless men. They feared not death itself and would charge the gates of hell." He would go on to say, "I swear their eyes were blazing red with fury. I prayed to God I would never have to see them in my life again, but they haunt me day and night. The sound of thundering hoof beats charging through our people as they cut them all down, shooting at point blank range, was chilling. Fleeing men had even tossed their rifles aside, but were still shot in the back. They cleared the end of the line and, using their knees to stop and turn the horses, reloaded and charged again to clean up the last of our men. There wasn't a man left alive after Death's second pass. The battle was over before it even began."

There were 10 men wounded that were kept alive, no others, just to get the layout of the operation in Green Bay. Any badly wounded were put down like rabid dogs, with a quick shot to the head.

They brought down wagons and stripped the troops of weapons and ammo; they saved anything useful. They cut down huge amounts of firewood, with logs 10 feet long, and started fires to burn all the bodies. One of the men came up to Clint and said, "Did you see that big blue dun that man was riding? That was Scott's horse. I checked the brand and it was his. Scott and Joe must be dead."

Clint signaled for John to come over and he told him the news.

John said, "I'll send a ten-man team to go look for them. They might still be alive, you never know, but, if they aren't, we'll bring their bodies back to their wives."

Clint replied, "I hope they are still alive. We need good men."

John said, "I'll go myself."

Clint said, "Let me know what you find in 2 days and then we're taking Green Bay and ending this nonsense once and for all. Now that we have the ammo for the 105, there's nothing stopping us. From what these prisoners are telling us, the "Governor" only has one 105 left and about 200 men. I want to end this now while we have the men and supplies."

"What are you going to do with the prisoners, once we have their base surrounded?"

"I'll send them back so they can give them our terms of surrender. If they refuse, the black flag will be flown."

Clint was happy they had lost only 12 men and 34 were wounded. He set up a field hospital and had the wounded treated.

Having missed the big surprise trap, Joe and Scott were trying to survive by going into the swamp. The men following them had a good tracker leading the way and they followed them in. The 2 men that were sent with orders for them to return had deserted and headed south. The last order these men were given was to capture these two snipers, dead or alive.

John knew where Joe and Scott had stashed their horses, so he checked the spot and followed the trail, finding the two dead Rainbow Warriors. He smiled. *They were still alive.*

One of his men called out that he found the .50 Cal and the bolt was missing. That could only mean they must be on the run.

John said, “By the looks of all this, quite a few men are chasing them.”

Chapter 31

The Battle of Green Bay

"Yesterday is history. Tomorrow is a mystery. Today is a gift. That's why we call it the present."
~Barbara DeAngelis

Joe and Scott had headed into the thick cedar swamp with the enemy still following them. They had 7 miles of hard traveling in front of them. Scott whispered, "You know what the nickname of this swamp is, don't you?"

Joe shrugged.

Scott grinned and said, "Dead Man Swamp."

Joe smiled. "You know all the cool places to hang out, don't you?"

"Hey, it wasn't my plan to head in here. We were kind of forced into it, if you remember. But there are people that have come up missing in here, about every other year. They say there is quicksand, an old cougar that hunts men and, of course, if you believe the Native American legends, an evil spirit that keeps all men from ever leaving here."

"Okay. Enough of the superstitious nonsense. How many people have really come up missing?"

"I think it's been right around 15, over the past 30 years. Two deer hunters, along with their truck and everything, came up missing back in '93. Searchers found their tent and a deer hanging at their camp, but no men or vehicle were ever was found."

Joe laughed. "They didn't show up in Las Vegas two years later, did they?"

"I am not joking around, just letting you know we have to be careful."

"Okay, I understand. What's the plan now?"

"We head directly north for 7 miles and we should be out on the road. Check your compass."

Joe pulled out his compass and watched the needle bounce all over the place. "What the heck is that all about?"

Scott smiled, "Well, part of the legend is that they think there is a large ore deposit under the swamp, so your compass is never going to work right. If you follow it, you will just end up going in a circle all day."

"Great. Okay, I'm following you."

They headed out and after 2 hours the swamp looked just like where they had started. The brush was thick and the deadfalls they had to climb over never seemed to end. It was like a bad nightmare. The marshy ground was spongy under their feet, but the good news was that they could hear their pursuers having just as bad a time.

Another hour went by and they came out into a clearing with a tiny stream and black mud all around it. Scott headed out towards it, thinking of making a trap where they could hide on the other side and then they could shoot a few down as they stepped out into the opening. He was about halfway across when the mud stopped supporting his weight and gave way and he sank clear to his chest.

Turning around, he tossed his rifle back to Joe and tried to use his elbows to pull himself out. This was a very bad idea because his elbows broke through and he sank up to his chin. Joe ran back, put the rifles against the brush and found a long, dead sapling. He raced back and carefully walked out, trying to stay on firm ground, and extended it to Scott. Scott, now up to his nose, grabbed a hold of it for dear life. He pulled himself about 2 feet up when the stick broke. At least he was up to his shoulders now. When the stick broke, Joe fell back on his butt, quickly getting back up. Scott was sinking again, right before his eyes. He stepped closer, afraid to rush in and have both of them stuck. Reaching out as far as he could, he said, "Listen to me. Slow down and try not to move so hard and fast."

In a panicked voice, Scott said, "Sure, that's easy for you to say. I'm the one in here sinking. Find some way to help me get out."

Joe handed him the stick again and they began the process over. Joe was coaching him. "Easy, slowly pull on that, hand over hand. Slow down. You are almost there. You've got it."

He reached out his hand and pulled Scott up on semi hard ground. Scott smiled. "Thanks. I would have been a dead man without your help."

Joe smiled and said, "Now we're even. You saved me from the wolves and I just returned the favor."

He continued, "Yes, this is a dangerous swamp. Now I can see how people come up missing, never to be found."

Retrieving the rifles, Joe said, "Wipe your hands off first. Scott was trying to fling the mud off his body. He even tried shaking like a dog to get it off. He finally wiped his hands on some ferns. They could hear their pursuers about 100 yards behind them. They took off at a steady trot, going around the clearing to avoid the quicksand. Scott wished they had the time to circle around the quicksand and lure the men into the trap, but there wasn't. They were easy to track now because, for the next half mile, Scott was leaving pieces of mud all along the trail.

Even though it was an Indian summer and a warm day for September, being in the 60s, Scott was cold and started shivering. They could see the land starting to rise up as the terrain was changing in elevation. They must be close to the road.

Finally they found the road and ran to it. Ten men on horses were waiting there, with guns drawn. *Damn*, Joe thought, *After all of that, only to be caught because of an amateur mistake*.

They both put their hands up and then heard a familiar voice. "Scott, Joe, is that you?"

He looked into John's eyes and burst out laughing.

John said. "What in the hell happened to you two?"

Scott said, "Let's talk about it later. We still have a ton of men chasing us. We better get out of here."

Two of the men came up and offered a hand, lifting them onto the back of their horses, and they took off down the road. They were about half a mile away when they stopped and, looking back, they saw the men coming out of the swamp and onto the road.

John said, "You two must have really pissed them off to have so many chase so few for so long."

Joe said, "Yes, they have no sense of humor. What is going on with the trap?"

John smiled and said, "We won. It's all over. We can go collect more men and then clean up these last 50."

He assigned 2 men to recon and watch where these remaining troops went. They would be on foot, so Joe and Scott used their horses and rode back to join the others.

They were going to spend the night and then head off to Green Bay in the morning. Clint had already sent a team of men to grab the 105 and bring it to a meeting location on the way.

Clint said, "I want to thank you and your partner for the suggestion of taking the 105 away from the enemy. It has evened up the odds and put us in a much better position to fight them."

Joe said, "It just seemed like the logical thing to do. That 105 would have cut us all to ribbons, so the only move we really had was to either disable it, or take it away from them. I just didn't really think they would attempt something like that without us. We missed all the action and a lot of good men died getting it."

Clint said, "Yes, good men did die. That's the problem with war. Good men die right along with the bad men."

Joe nodded his head in agreement. They looked searchingly at each other, each one taking the measure of the man standing in front of him.

Clint turned to Joe and said, "I don't want to lose any more men fighting those last 50 guys. Do you have any suggestions?"

Joe jumped in, "Sure. Tell them it's over. They lost and all of their army is dead. Tell them to drop their weapons and leave. Make them head south and tell them to never return."

Clint looked at him. "What if they think you are lying?"

"Simple. We take the Lieutenant's body and leave it in the road."

Looking at Scott and Joe, Clint nodded and said, "John will take care of it. You two go get cleaned up and get some rest because tomorrow we head to Green Bay and end this."

John took 100 men on horseback and caught up to the 2 men doing recon. They positioned themselves in front of the 50 men and would let them walk right into them. They broke up into small groups, setting up quick ambush spots. They dragged a log onto the road and propped the dead Lieutenant up on it. The 50 men marched right in and, upon seeing their dead officer, stopped cold. John called out, "You are surrounded. Just give up. Your entire army is dead. There has been enough killing, so surrender now."

They answered with hot lead and the fight started. They thought they were only facing a small band of snipers. Then, without warning, 50 men on horses, with a man waving a black flag, charged down through the middle of them, killing every one of them to the last man. They lost 5 more men in the battle and had 13 wounded, but all of their enemies were dead.

Later the next day that crazy junkyard guy, Bob, showed up driving a semi-truck. He had Doc, Amy and Jane with him. Everyone stopped what they had been doing and stared. It was the first running vehicle they had seen since the EMP.

"Where in God's name did you find fuel to get that thing running?" Clint asked.

Bob laughed. "Remember that TV show, Doomsday Prepper?"

Clint looked at him like he was nuts. "No. Not really. Was it one of those reality shows?"

Bob nodded. "Something like that. Anyway, it showed a guy collecting mineral oil out of an electrical transformer. Each one holds like 12 gallons and a diesel engine can run on that. I hit five transformers and collected the oil. I figure I have enough fuel to take the wounded back with me."

"That's great, but where did you steal the diesel semi from?"

He laughed and said, "eHH"That's another long story. We got one of the 4x4s going with a gasifier and, when we were out on a salvage run, we came across a semi that was out of fuel, meaning it had still been working. We jump-started it and bled the fuel lines and here we are. By the way the 4x4 is towing the cannon, so they'll be waiting for you when you get to the meeting spot."

Clint said, "When this is over, I think we should have a meeting and share information."

Everyone agreed that it would be a great idea. Bob went on to tell the story about Joe's partner, Preston, and how this all started and came about from his idea of making the gasifier.

They loaded all the wounded into the truck with them, with Doc, Jane and Amy tending to the men on the way home.

They were 2 days from Green Bay and they knew from interrogating the prisoners that the Army had taken over a pier where the food was kept as their base. It was easy to guard as they were surrounded by water, with the only access being the pier. They used empty shipping containers, three high, all of the way around the property, as a barrier fence and the remaining 105 was facing the main gate. They had one M-60 machine gun nest located in a watchtower and everything else was small arms.

Clint's plan was simple: use the 105 to take theirs out and then pound the front gate open. They would fire on them until they ran out of ammo, hopefully for 2 hours straight. He didn't want to waste any more of his men's lives.

Joe was given the .50 Cal rifle back and his job was to take out the machine gun nest.

After getting the cannon to within 5 miles of the base, they stopped and spent the night. At first light, the recon and sniper teams headed out. Joe picked a building that was across the street from the machine gun nest and Scott led the way up the stairs to the roof. It was a 10-story building and they walked out onto the roof. They could see the fires and smoke all around the base.

Scott said, to no one in particular, "What the hell is going on?" Using binoculars, Scott was scanning for life. Joe set up the .50 Cal and zeroed in on the tower. It was empty, not a soul in sight and no machine gun in sight. Had they gotten bad information from the prisoners?

Scott said, "There is a large freighter leaving the bay right now and it's sitting low in the water."

"Damn. They're making a run for it. I bet they burned the food to deprive us of it," Joe said in disgust.

They called down to a recon team to pass the word that it looked like they flew the coop, burning all of the food, and that there was no one in sight.

Clint sent four of the least wounded prisoners to enter and find out what was going on. The gate was wide open. They entered cautiously, expecting possible booby traps, but there were none. The area had been cleaned out. The freighter was only a tiny speck on the horizon now. They walked into the warehouse, which had been converted into a barracks, and everything was gone. They walked outside again and, in the bright morning sun, they looked at the smoke from 50 tons of grain floating across the bay.

Clint's men entered, seeing the same thing. It was a hollow victory. No epic battle. A victory stolen from them. But the good news was that he doubted they would ever be able to raise an Army to threaten their homeland again. A shipyard worker came up to some of the men at the gate and asked to talk to the person in charge. He was patted down, checked for weapons, and then taken to Clint and John.

John asked what was so important the man had to say. He told them, "We loaded up that freighter with all the food it could hold. The leftover grain is on fire, as you saw, but what you don't know is that there are some storage units that have food in them. We ask that you not take it, but leave it for the people here."

"How many people are still alive in Green Bay?" Clint asked.

The man said, "I don't rightly know. Maybe 3,500 or 4,000 would be my guess."

"Do you have troops to protect and distribute the food without causing a riot?"

"We are unarmed, but there are forty of us that have worked the docks our whole lives. We can set things up and make sure the food is handed out fairly."

"Why didn't you go with them?" Clint pointed out into the bay.

"Because this is my home. I only worked for them to get food. Once they took control of the city, it was the only choice any of us had."

He called out, "Sergeant, take a detail of men and have this man show you the food storage."

After the man walked out he asked John, "Do you think he is on the level?"

John said, "I would guess so. I mean, we took the base without a shot being fired."

Clint smiled. "It has been my experience in life that nothing comes free, or too easy. I say we leave the food, just in case it was poisoned and this man is a liar that is setting us up. I say we leave and go home. Let's call it all over. But just to be safe, pick the top men you have for recon scout to stay and watch the area for a week. Spread them out across the city, with strict orders to not interfere. Do not engage unless fired upon and, at the first sign of troops, they are to hightail it back to let us know."

"Are you sure? We could use the food?"

Clint had a serious look on his face when he said, "If there are 4,000 people here and we are talking 800 of us, do you really want to give them a reason to come find us for food in six months, or next fall?"

"Good point, but what about the so-called Governor?"

"Militarily speaking, he is down to 200 men. They must have had scouts out and saw what happened to their main Army. I would guess he's going to sail a couple of hundred miles south and take over a small city with a port. He may even sail across to Michigan. Either way, he doesn't have the manpower to threaten us again and we can't chase him down. Who knows, maybe he is going to try and sail out to the ocean. Either way, I don't think he is a threat to us anymore."

He added, "The other thing is that there were no booby traps. That tells me he isn't planning on coming back."

All of the locals that came out told the same story—they had spent 2 days packing the freighter up and left when they saw the rebels moving up to take their base.

Chapter 32

Back At Home

"In three words, I can sum up everything I've learned about life: it goes on."

~Robert Frost

Leaving Green Bay was a relief to the troops, as it was a depressing city. Nothing but death and destruction was left and everything lay in ruins. The riots, the looting and the aftermath of the survival-of-the-fittest was seen everywhere in the dreary, dirty town, with streets of burned out buildings. The one good thing that the Rainbow Warriors had done was clear out the traffic jams and stalled cars blocking the roads. The people they did see looked weary, tired and worn out. They were thankful for everything they now had.

The men that Clint had sent to locate the food lockers had returned and the dockworker asked what he was supposed to do now.

"That's up to you," Clint said. "Elect a leader and get to work rebuilding your city."

"What about protection?" he asked, "Are you our Militia, to call on the next time we are invaded?"

"It's up to you to rebuild your community. You have more manpower than we do. Build up your own militia. You have smart people here, so get everyone together and find your leaders, the people with skills to help you rebuild. You have plenty of cleared ground along the highways, so turn it into food production. You have seeds for replanting, but make sure you save some for next spring. It's all up to you. We are heading North to rebuild what we have and, when you have established your community, maybe we can come together."

Clint and all of the men left Green Bay and headed back to their families. Joe and Scott returned home on horseback, with a third horse carrying the .50 Cal rifle.

Joe said, "It was honor to fight next to you, Scott."

Scott replied, "Same here, Joe. Now what do we do?"

"First we survive this winter and then we have to come up with a plan for rebuilding. My thinking is that tribes were originally set up so that everything was shared equally. They made sure everyone ate, or everyone starved. The entire tribe had mutual protection, with everyone doing their part. Children were taught their roles earlier in life. The tribe ran like a machine, if you will. We are sort of like a tribe in a way; we come together for planting and harvesting, with mutually shared work in the fields. Food dictates everything else. Once food is covered, the next thing is sex and babies, to ensure that the tribe lives on. You have your warrior class, which are the hunters and protectors, and they make sure the tribe can function."

"Okay, but we both know that is not going to do it for us. We must come up with a money system. An honest money system," Scott stressed.

Joe said, "What we need are gold and silver standards that have a set value, with true weights and sizes, and that is going to take some time. Then we need to set up schools, but we must do a lot of rebuilding before that. The one thing I can't figure out is how to rebuild those transformers. I think Brett can figure out how to get the big windmills going, but that isn't enough, unless we can step the voltage to what we need for each house."

Scott asked, "Okay, where do we get the gold and silver to even start making coins? Are we supposed to find and use pre-existing coins, like the silver dollars?"

"I don't have an answer to that, but I think we need to take care of our need for food and make sure we have that well-organized. One bad crop year and we are all starving. We also need to set up some hunting regulations too. We can't allow people killing off all of the deer in the spring, when the fawns are born to replenish the herd. That is why we need to get the whole state up and working as a team, but this is going to take some time. We have to talk to Clint about expanding our community. Maybe even setting up trade routes, or something like that."

Meanwhile, back at the cabin, Preston finally heard the good news that his leg was almost healed. Amy's pregnancy was going well and the Doc said she was in good health.

Amy and Jane were still working at the hospital and Amy was being trained to be a nurse. They had too many wounded for Jane and the Doc to handle on their own.

Preston and Michael were back at work getting the winter firewood in and Michael was bugging the heck out of him about going bear hunting. He had made the rounds of the closest neighbors and asked everyone to save their grease, bones and table scraps for bear bait.

When Joe returned, he spent a day cleaning the .50 Cal sniper rifle. Gun cleaning solution was becoming a thing of the past, so he headed to the junkyard and talked it over with Bob. Bob remembered a homemade formula, so they began experimenting and came up with a mixture of kerosene and automatic transmission fluid to clean the bore. The kerosene provided a good lubricant coating to protect the weapon from rust, taking the place of gun oil.

Joe returned the rifle to Philip and thanked him. Philip was most interested in how the battle went and Joe gave him all of the details.

The daily events were turning into an enjoyable routine and life was good. Now they just had to deal with the struggle to survive.

During the first week of November, the first snow began to fall. Preston and Amy were standing in the living room in quiet reflection, lost in thought as they looked out and watched the snowfall. The snow danced along the porch in little swirls as the snowflakes slowly fell to earth. They felt at peace as Preston stood behind her, with his hands around her waist. He reached up and rubbed her growing stomach.

"I think we are going to make it. Our son is going to be a part of rebuilding America, with freedom first."

Amy smiled and said, "And what if it's a girl?"

Preston laughed. "Well, her boyfriends are going to hate me."

"Why's that? Are you going to be cleaning your guns when they pick her up?"

"Yep and she is going to be just as tough as any boy, out hunting, fishing, trapping and kicking ass."

She turned around and kissed him. "Thank you. I love you."

He said, "I love you too and, no matter what, we are going to survive and thrive."

Michael came in from the garage with greasy hands from scraping the fat off his very first bear hide.

Jane was in the kitchen cooking and said, “Don’t you dare touch anything before you’ve washed your hands.”

He frowned and said, “Yes, Mom. Jeez. It’s like having two mothers. When is dinner going to be done? I’m starved.”

Joe said, “Tell us something new.”

References

Author web site-
Professional grade self-locking snares
www.prosts.com

Kel-Tec KSG 15-Round shotgun
http://www.keltecweapons.com/our-guns/shotguns/ksg/

McMillan Tac-50 Tactical Rifle
http://www.mcmfamily.com/mcmillan-rifles-tactical-tac-50.php

Ram water pump
http://www.google.com/search?client=safari&rls=en&q=ram+water+pump&ie=UTF-8&oe=UTF-8

http://www.greenandcarter.com/main/img/ram_diagram.gif

Berkey Water Filter systems
http://www.bigberkeywaterfilters.com/

Corn harvest and making cornmeal
http://www.food-skills-for-self-sufficiency.com/making-cornmeal.html

Types of corn:
http://www2.kenyon.edu/projects/farmschool/food/corntyp.htm

Doomsday Preppers Show
View full episodes
http://channel.nationalgeographic.com/channel/doomsday-preppers/

Homemade Gun Cleaner
http://home.comcast.net/~dsmjd/tux/dsmjd/tech/eds_red.htm
http://home.comcast.net/~dsmjd/tux/dsmjd/tech/cap_ball.htm
http://home.comcast.net/~dsmjd/tux/dsmjd/tech/clean_lube.htm

Using charcoal lighter fluid
http://www.zombiehunters.org/forum/viewtopic.php?f=107&t=85441

Reusable Canning Lids
http://www.reusablecanninglids.com/

Wound Care
http://www.woundcaresolutions-telemedicine.co.uk/wounddressings.php#CarbonCharcoal

In the Crimean War, soldiers who suffered a gunshot wound would extract gunpowder from bullets and pack the residue into the wound to prevent infection.

Read more: How to Treat a Wound With Gunpowder | eHow.com http://www.ehow.com/how_7429632_treat-wound-gunpowder.html#ixzz2IL4r2bIh

Smoke Grenades
http://www.onlinefireworks.com/pullstringhandgrenades.aspx

Approx. 60 seconds of thick white smoke screen

Slow Burning Fuses
http://www.onlinefireworks.com/20footrollfuse-2-1-4-1-1-2-2-3.aspx

65 foot roll 1/8 inch Diameter Falling Fish Green Fuse. Burn rate 54 seconds per foot.

FEMA Wood Gasification
http://www.soilandhealth.org/03sov/0302hsted/fema.woodgas.pdf

CPSIA information can be obtained at www.ICGtesting.com
Printed in the USA
LVOW05s0028071014

407562LV00001B/44/P

9 781481 856683